Louise Allen loves immersing herself in history. She finds landscapes and places evoke the past powerfully. Venice, Burgundy and the Greek islands are favourite destinations. Louise lives on the Norfolk coast and spends her spare time gardening, researching family history and travelling in search of inspiration.

Also by Louise Allen

Marrying His Cinderella Countess
The Earl's Practical Marriage
A Lady in Need of an Heir
Convenient Christmas Brides
Least Likely to Marry a Duke

Lords of Disgrace miniseries

His Housekeeper's Christmas Wish
His Christmas Countess
The Many Sins of Cris de Feaux
The Unexpected Marriage of Gabriel Stone

Discover more at millsandboon.co.uk.

CONTRACTED AS HIS COUNTESS

Louise Allen

MILLS & BOON

First published in Great Britain 2019
by Mills & Boon, an imprint of HarperCollins*Publishers*
1 London Bridge Street, London, SE1 9GF

Large Print edition 2020

© 2019 Melanie Hilton

ISBN: 978-0-263-08619-5

MIX
Paper from
responsible sources
FSC
www.fsc.org
FSC™ C007454

This book is produced from independently certified FSC™ paper to ensure responsible forest management. For more information visit www.harpercollins.co.uk/green.

Printed and bound in Great Britain
by CPI Group (UK) Ltd, Croydon, CR0 4YY

3478050-5

For AJH for being a rock.

Author Note

An interest in a revived Gothic style, harking back to the pointed arches and rich ornamentation of the Middle Ages, developed in the later eighteenth century as an element of the Romantic movement and as a reaction to the cool perfection of the Classical style.

Horace Walpole's Gothic revival Strawberry Hill House in Twickenham was begun in 1749. William Thomas Beckford, the wildly eccentric art collector and author of Gothic novels, built his Fonthill Abbey—an enormous mansion in the style of a medieval abbey—between 1796 and 1813, and landowners began to litter their grounds with follies resembling ruined castles or monasteries.

I have based Madelyn's father, Peregrine Aylmer, on some of the more eccentric Gothic enthusiasts of the time, although he would probably have had most in common with the Thirteenth Earl of Eglinton, whose wildly ambitious Eglinton Tournament cost him between thirty and forty thousand pounds in 1839. Despite the contestants training with lances for up to a year beforehand, the tournament was widely mocked and suffered from dreadful weather.

More soberly, the Gothic style flourished in the Victorian age as the most 'suitable' style for churches, and was the chosen architecture for both the rebuilt Houses of Parliament—completed 1870—and Tower Bridge—1894.

Peregrine Aylmer would have approved of both, I am certain.

Chapter One

*Castle Beaupierre, the Kent countryside
—10th July, 1816*

Jack Ransome reined in his horse on the crest of the rise and looked down at a vision of the fourteenth century transported to the age of the Hanoverians. England was still littered with castles, large and small. Some were ruins, some were converted long ago into more or less comfortable houses, but none still fulfilled the function for which they had been built. Except, apparently, this one.

It helped, of course, if you were wealthy and more than slightly eccentric as the late Peregrine Aylmer had been. Then you could pour thousands of pounds and a lifetime of scholarship into creating your fantasy world.

Castle Beaupierre seemed to bask as it lay in

the sunshine that reflected off the polished slate of the roofs, the walls of creamy, perfect stone. Jack tried to estimate the cost and time involved in cleaning and repairing those walls and roofs and failed utterly.

From the centre tower a great black flag stirred and lighter pennants fluttered, red and blue and gold, around it. The encircling moat, full of water, was home to perhaps a dozen swans gliding in pristine white formation past the drawbridge. Which was raised.

'She invited me, Altair,' Jack observed. The big black gelding flicked one ear and then cocked a hoof comfortably, settling down to wait. 'The least she could do is lower the drawbridge. Perhaps I am supposed to send a page over in a rowing boat or have a herald trumpet my arrival. What is the etiquette for calling on people deluded enough to live in the Middle Ages?'

He gathered up the reins and sent the horse on at a walk down the slope towards the fairytale building. When they were halfway there the drawbridge began to creak slowly downwards until it reached his side of the moat with a dull thud. Someone was watching.

'Which leaves me faced with a portcullis,' Jack muttered. 'What is the matter with the woman? Her father was the lunatic who wanted to play knights in armour and he's been dead for almost a year.' Hence, he supposed, the black flag. As he spoke there was a rattle of chains from inside the walls and the wood and iron grid creaked upwards.

Now, faced with vast double oak doors studded with sufficient metal knobs to repel a charging elephant, Jack felt both amusement and patience slide away. 'I should have brought siege engines, obviously. If Mistress—*Mistress*, if you please!—Madelyn Aylmer wants me then she can open her confounded gates because I am not going to knock. I did not drag down to Kent in the middle of the Newmarket July race meeting to play games.' He clicked his tongue at Altair, who stepped on to the bridge, pecked at the sudden hollow note under his hooves, then walked on. Finally, the great doors opened.

The shadows were deep as Jack rode through the high archway, the sunlight blinding in the courtyard beyond a second opening. Here he was in the killing ground, where attackers could be penned in and assaulted on all sides from above, and he felt a prickle of awareness run down his spine as he rode towards the light. Someone was watching him. Jack circled the horse and looked up and back to a window high in the wall, making no attempt to disguise his scrutiny. A flicker of white, the pale oval of a face, the flash of spun gold and the watcher was gone.

Serve her right if I keep going right back where I came from.

But this was a commission, which meant money, and at least Mistress Aylmer hadn't expected him to dress up in medieval clothes for this meeting. Pride was all very well, but it was a hollow coin that bought neither bread nor horseshoes. Jack turned Altair back and rode into the courtyard where, finally, someone had come out to meet him.

It was a surprise that the servants were not dressed in tights and tabards, although the leather jerkin and breeches of the groom who took Altair's reins and led him away had a timeless look to them and the black-coated individual who came forward could have come from any period in the past hundred years.

'My—'

'*Mr* Jack Ransome to see Miss Aylmer, by appointment.'

'*Mistress* Madelyn will receive you in the Great Hall,' the man responded with the same emphasis Jack had used and without a flicker of either amusement or annoyance. 'This way, sir.'

Jack followed up stone steps, along passages hung with tapestries that glowed as bright, surely, as the day they had been made. Which was probably within the last twenty years, he reminded himself with a flash of cynicism. He suspected that appearances were all in this fantasy world.

The butler, if that was who he was, threw open double doors—more studded oak, of course— and stood aside for Jack to enter. They closed behind him with a dull thud.

The Great Hall was well named. Walter Scott would love it, Jack reflected. All it needed was a bearded bard in one corner reciting *The Lay of the Last Minstrel.* He preferred something with fewer draughts and more soft furnishings himself. The roof was a hammer-beam construction and he counted two, no, three fireplaces of the ox-roasting variety, sighed at the sight of a number of suits of armour and walked on past more tapestries.

At least there are no harps and minstrels...

At the far end was a long oak table that looked as though it had been built to support the ox once it had been roasted. On it was a carved wooden coffer. And there, standing behind the coffer, was a tall, slender figure in blue. The light from a high window caught golden sparks from her hair—the watcher at the gate, he guessed.

Jack walked towards his new client, boot heels striking on stone flags, the rushes that were strewn over the floor rustling as he went. The place must be an ice house in the winter, even with all the fires alight—and most of the heat would go straight up the chimneys. The local coal merchants must be rubbing their hands with joy.

Presumably Miss Aylmer thought to put him at a disadvantage by making him walk towards her for this distance. Jack kept a straight face and an easy pace and only produced a social smile when he was within six feet of the table. Strangely, now he was inside and had sight of his client, he felt his irritation increase.

Not that the woman in front of him was unpleasing to the eye, even if her appearance was decidedly unusual. She was wearing a gown of deep blue in some fine draped fabric, caught in under the bust with tightly intricate pleating at the front. The long sleeves belled out over her hands to the knuckles where the hems were embroidered with delicate floral work that matched the band beneath her breasts.

Gowns might be worn with a high waistline now, but this was quite definitely not a modern style. Nor would any woman over the age of fifteen wear her hair loose around her shoulders, and Miss Aylmer must be in her early twenties. The straight fall of pale gold was caught back with combs but otherwise unconfined, signalling, he assumed, her virginity. Some men might see that as a challenge, others as an affectation. Jack told himself to withhold judgement. The woman in front of him was, after all, about to offer him employment and mildly exasperated incomprehension was no reason to turn it down. He could always do with money.

'Miss Aylmer.'

'Lord Dersington.' She did not smile or offer her hand. Her eyes were the blue-grey of a winter river in her pale face.

Jack found himself oddly short of breath. She was not pretty, or beautiful, but she had something…something he could not put a name to. An ethereal quality, a cool serenity as though she was looking through glass into another world. He thought of stone carvings of female saints he had seen in cathedrals. She had the same rather long nose and oval face and those eyes that looked tranquilly on the horrors of the world of sinners. Plain by modern standards, yet somehow lovely and utterly remote.

'Will you not take a seat?'

He did not call himself by his title, Madelyn knew that, but it was important to see how he took aggravation. Well, it seemed, on the surface at least. She folded her hands demurely in front of her and willed them not to shake. 'My lord—'

'Jack Ransome,' said the Fifth Earl of Dersington, perfectly pleasantly, as he pulled out a chair and waited for her to sit before he took it, three feet away across the board. 'Simply Mr Ransome.' He put his hat and gloves on the table and ran one hand through ruffled hair the colour of the ancient oak panelling in the castle's dining room.

'Why do you not use your title, sir?'

'Because, as I am sure you are aware—unless you made no enquiries about me at all, which I cannot believe—I have neither lands, nor seat. What is an earl without land?' He asked the question as though they were debating an academic point, not something so personal to him. But the blue eyes were unamused.

'A landless earl is still an earl.' It felt like pushing a chess piece forward. How would he respond?

'The entire *raison d'être* of earls, and of all the rest of the aristocracy, was to support the Crown, to maintain retainers so they could put men in the field to fight. Of recent years the role has been one of governance and of economics. Men of title sit in the House of Lords to assist in the government and they contribute to the wealth of the country by the stewardship of its lands. I have no lands and therefore no retainers and no wealth. Therefore no power and, logically, no function as an aristocrat.'

'You could still sit in the House of Lords,' Madelyn pointed out, even more curious now she had heard the explanation from his own lips. They were firm lips, framing a mouth that did not seem designed for hesitation.

'I choose not to waste my time in a place where I can only pretend to have a function. You may consider it pride, Miss Aylmer, and you may be right. My peers call me John Lackland, which conveys the measure of their lack of respect for my position, would you not say? I prefer to spend my time and energies on what I can achieve.'

'King John lost all the English lands in France to earn the title *Lackland*. As far as I am aware you did nothing to deserve losing your birthright.' She was used to dealing with difficult men and she had steeled herself to confront this one. He was not going to make her stop probing until she understood who she was dealing with—there was too much at stake.

'No,' he agreed. 'But that does not make me any less inclined to carry on as though I command rolling acres. I prefer reality and I dislike fantasy.' Madelyn noticed that he did not glance around as he said it: clearly he expected her to be able to take his point. It seemed he despised her father's creation.

'I chose to make my own place in the world by my own efforts,' Jack Ransome continued. 'And I assume that is why you have summoned me, rather than to hold a discussion about my landholdings. Or lack of them.'

Best to stop probing before he got up and walked out on her, Madelyn concluded. *Or loses his temper.* She smoothed out a crease in the fabric across her knee until her fingers were steady and made herself continue. 'You are an enquiry agent.' She knew that, of course, but she was interested in how this man described himself.

'I act on behalf of others, for payment. I cause things to happen, or I prevent them happening. Often that involves making enquiries,' he said. The level, dark blue gaze held neither resentment nor impatience, but neither did he show pleasure at the invitation to talk about himself. *A novelty in itself...* He was intriguing and that helped steady her nerves.

'If sons find themselves entangled with unsuitable women or being bear-led by some sharp, I disentangle them. If the suitor for a daughter's hand seems just too good to be true, I establish his *bona fides.* If sensitive correspondence goes missing, or anonymous letters arrive, I'll get to the bottom of it for you. If you want a safe escort somewhere, I will provide it. If you wish to disappear, I can arrange that. Or perhaps you are being blackmailed. I remove blackmailers.'

She wondered if she was supposed to ask *how* he removed them. Or where to. Madelyn resisted the temptation. She needed none of those services.

Mr Ransome leaned back in the chair, crossed one booted leg over the other and raised an interrogative dark brow. 'And what do you want me to do for you, Miss Aylmer?'

Madelyn found she was not ready to tell him yet. She needed to find the courage first. Or perhaps she needed to bury her doubts about her father's will even deeper. Her conscience was troubling her. 'You know who I am, who my father was, why I live in a castle?' she asked.

She sensed rather than saw that she now had his full attention: he had studied his brief, it appeared. 'Your father, Mr Peregrine Aylmer, was obsessed with two things, the Middle Ages and his lineage, not necessarily in that order. He inherited a large fortune and used it to restore this castle in order to create and immerse himself in a fantasy world which, I gather, he could well afford to do, given the size of his inheritance and, no doubt, his successful investments. He has recently died and you are his sole heir.'

'Yes, that is all correct. There are no men of our name left. It derives from the Anglo-Saxon *aethelmaer*, which means *famous noble*. Our lineage stretches back beyond any recorded English kings, beyond any title of nobility surviving today.'

'All families, even the humblest, could be traced to the beginning of time if only the records existed,' said the man whose rejected title was a Tudor creation. She suspected that she knew the details of his family tree far better than he did. He shrugged. 'We all go back to Adam. Some know more about their history—or the fantasies about it—than others, that is all.'

'Our lineage is documented. All my father wanted was a son to hand the name down to, to continue the line, to continue his work. My mother died along with my infant brother six years ago. I have proved to be the only survivor of seven infants from two wives. He lost heart at that death.'

'Is that when the obsession with this castle became intense?' Ransome enquired coolly.

'He was not *obsessed*,' she protested. Father had been right, she had to believe that. Everyone was prejudiced against him. *Even me, sometimes*, she thought guiltily.

She had meant to rattle Jack Ransome's composure, but it seemed he had turned the tables on her. Madelyn lowered her voice, forced herself into her habitual calm. 'Castle Beaupierre is a work of great scholarship, an artistic creation, bringing a lost world back. My father's entire life was dedicated to that.' Surely anyone could see it? Even she, knowing the cost, had no doubts about the results, and Jack Ransome was an educated man: he would understand what it had cost in time and money and devotion.

'And were you a work of scholarship, a piece of art, to your father, Miss Aylmer?'

I was a disappointment. A girl. Of course I was not a piece of art. I was... I am...a failure.

'I naturally supported my father. He chose to live in an age of chivalry and beauty. A world set in the countryside of England, a world of craftsmanship. Not in a modern world of steam and speed and cities, of poverty and ugliness.' She knew all the arguments by rote.

'I see.'

It was clearly a polite lie. The face of the man opposite her was set in a severe expression that probably hid either a sneer or a desire to laugh. The fine lines in the corners of his eyes made her think that laughter was a possibility. She had no desire to be a source of amusement to him—in fact, she dreaded it, although not as much as she feared his anger. There was so much to be frightened of, but she was not going to give way now.

Madelyn controlled her breathing and made herself look steadily at Jack Ransome. Every report of him praised his intelligence, none spoke of irrational temper or violence, of ill-treatment of servants—not that he had many—or of either drunkenness or debauchery. He was in good health, a sportsman, which no doubt accounted for the breadth of his shoulders and the muscles revealed by tight breeches. He had turned his back on society, and in return society mocked him as Lackland or disapproved vehemently of his rejection of his title. But many of its members turned to him when they needed his help. He had friends, some unconventional by all reports, some very shady indeed.

He was dangerous, reports said, but they were

hazy about who he was a danger to, other than the aforementioned blackmailers, presumably. The judgement was that he was ruthless, but honest. Stubborn, difficult and self-contained.

No one had reported on Jack Ransome's looks, on that straight nose, on that firm, rather pointed jaw that gave him a slightly feline look. Certainly there had been no mention of a mouth that held the only hint of sensuous indulgence in that entire severe countenance. Other than those faint laughter lines…

So far, so…acceptable.

'You show no curiosity about why I have engaged your services, Lord… Mr Ransome.'

'No doubt you will inform me in your own good time. Whether you decide to employ me or not, I will present your man of business with my fee for today and for the time I will spend travelling to and from Newmarket and for my expenses incurred en route. If you wish to expend that money on chit-chat, that is your prerogative, Miss Aylmer.'

Very cool. Very professional, I suppose.

Madelyn had no experience of dealing with professional men beyond Mr Lansing, her father's steward and man of business, and he could hardly bring himself to communicate with her, he was so shocked to find himself answering to a woman. She had expected this man to show disapproval of her having no chaperon, but perhaps that was simply her lack of experience of the world beyond the castle walls, the place that held all her fears, her lost hopes.

She stood, glad of the table edge to steady herself, and he rose, too, a good head taller than she, despite her height. 'Please. Sit.' The lid of the coffer creaked open until it was stopped by a retaining chain, standing as a screen between Mr Ransome and its contents. Madelyn lifted out the rolls and bundles of paper and parchment that it contained and placed them on the table in a pile at her left hand, except for one which she partly opened out. She kept her right hand on that as she sat again.

'What I require, Mr Ransome, is a husband.' She had rehearsed this and now her voice hardly shook at all. In some strange way this situation went beyond shocking and frightening into a nightmare, and nightmares were not real. Father had left careful and exact instructions and she had always obeyed him, as she did now. Even so, she kept her gaze on the parchment that crackled under her palm.

'Then I fear you have approached the wrong man. I do not act as a marriage broker.' When she looked up, Mr Ransome shifted on the carved wooden chair as though to stand again.

'You do not understand, of course. I have not made myself plain. I do not require you to find me a husband. I wish you to marry me. Yourself,' she added, just in case that was not clear enough.

Chapter Two

Jack Ransome did get up then. He stood looking down at her while her heart thudded, *one, two, three, four.* Then he sat again, slowly.

Madelyn made herself focus on him and not on her own churning stomach. So, he was capable of being taken by surprise, of an unguarded reaction, however good he was at getting himself under control again.

'Why?'

'I have no desire to die a spinster, which means I must wed. And my father wished most particularly that I marry a man with bloodlines that can be traced back to before the Conquest, a man of impeccable breeding. He had intended approaching you with his proposition. And then he died.'

'My title, for what it is worth, was granted by Henry the Eighth. The Ransome of the time had his favour for reasons I have never understood, but it was probably something thoroughly disreputable. His father had awarded us with a barony because my ancestor chose the right side at the Battle of Bosworth, but Henry the Eighth created the earldom.'

At least he hasn't laughed in my face or walked out.

'There are no titles of nobility left at that date from before the sixteenth century,' she said. If he was interested she could lecture him on the subject all morning, but somehow she did not think he was. 'The Tudors saw to that, because the aristocracy was too closely tied by blood to the Plantagenets and so many had as good a claim to the throne as theirs. But Father traced your lineage to Sieur Edmund fitzRanulf, who fought at Hastings, and the intermarriages since then were very satisfactory to him.'

'They were very satisfactory to *me*, considering that I am the result of them,' Ransome said drily. 'Virtually all aristocrats have an ancestry that can be traced in this way, not to say hundreds, if not thousands, of gentry. The College of Heralds spends its time doing just that.' He was humouring her, she could tell.

Earning his fee. We will see about that, she thought, stiffening her spine. She had begun now, how much worse could it get?

'My father wished for an aristocratic connection. There are very few noblemen of ancient lineage who might be prevailed upon to wed me who are unmarried, of marriageable age, of good character and who are interested in women.' He looked a question and she managed not to blush. 'I do understand about that. There are, in fact, just seven of you at present who meet the criteria and who hold titles or are the heirs.'

'Thank you for the most flattering offer, Miss Aylmer, but I am not available for stud purposes.' Jack Ransome reached for his gloves.

He had kept his voice level, but the crude words were used as a weapon, the first betraying sign of an emotion besides surprise. He might well talk about pride—she had apparently pricked his painfully. The lines between his nose and the corners of his mouth were suddenly apparent, as though his whole face had stiffened.

Somehow Madelyn fought the urge to flee the room and shut herself in a turret for ten years, or however long it would take for them both to forget this conversation. But he was not the only one with verbal weapons at his disposal. 'No? Not even if my marriage portion includes the entirety of your family's lost lands and properties?'

Jack Ransome stared at her, his eyes unblinking, and she knew she had his full attention now as his pupils widened until the blue eyes darkened. 'My father, grandfather and elder brother between them broke the entail ten years ago. Over the course of eight years—the time it took all three of them to die one way or another—my father and brother managed to sell or gamble away virtually everything. I sold the last few remaining acres to pay the debts. How do you propose to restore all of that to me?'

'When my mother and brother died my father sought out the men who best fitted his criteria for me. He then made it his business to discover what was most likely to make the match acceptable to them. In most cases there was nothing that he could—' she almost said *use as a lever*, but managed to bite her tongue in time '—identify.'

The other candidates came from families that seemed, as far as Peregrine Aylmer could discover, quite secure and likely to be wary of an alliance with Castle-Mad Aylmer's daughter.

But Jack Ransome had inherited an empty title and so her father had become relentless in his pursuit of the scattered lands and properties. Relentless and ruthless, she feared, not above exerting pressure on whatever weaknesses he could find to secure a purchase. Antiquarian research had given him the skills to dig deep into family cupboards to discover the skeletons they held.

Madelyn pushed away the unsettling memories and made herself meet the dark gaze that seemed fixed on her face. 'Father searched out every scrap of land, every building, of the lost Dersington estates and acquired them. He identified your brother first, but did not add him to the list because of his way of life. But then Lord Roderick died almost as soon as he had inherited the title and you inherited.'

She could remember her father returning home, crowing with delight, ordering all the banners to be flown from turrets and battlements in celebration. He had found the ideal candidate and one he could exert a hold over.

Under her left hand the stack of deeds felt as substantial as a pile of bricks. Under her right, the unfolded parchment crackled betrayingly and she forced her fingers to stillness. 'Be grateful,' he had told her. 'I have found you a man free from his family's vices and I have the shackles to bind him to you.' She had known better than to protest that she did not want a husband who had to be coerced and shackled.

'Your mother and brother died six years ago,' Jack Ransome said blankly. 'Six—I was twenty-one when he started looking, twenty-three when Roderick died. How did he know I would not marry someone else?'

'Then your lost lands would remain in here.' She gestured towards the chest. 'They would be an incentive for whomever I did eventually marry. Collected together the Dersington properties make an impressive dower.'

It was an effort to keep her voice level and dispassionate, but Madelyn thought she was managing well enough. It was what she was required to do as a dutiful daughter, she reminded herself, yet again. As Jack Ransome was keeping his temper, she found her courage rising a little. 'Look.' She opened out the stiff folds and slid forward the large parchment under her right hand, her fingers spread, pinning it down at the centre. 'The deeds to Dersington Mote and its estates.'

The document was more than five hundred years old, made from the skin of an entire young sheep. Battered seals hung from faded ribbons at the bottom, thick black writing covered it with legal Latin. The Ransomes had held the manor of Dersington since the time of the Conqueror, but their right to castellate—to build a defensible castle—had been granted by Edward II with this document. It gave them no title, not then, but it set out the boundaries and the extent of the land they held, their rights and obligations as lords of the seven manors that it comprised. It was the heart of Jack Ransome's lost estates.

He stared down at it, his face unreadable. Then he put out his own right hand, laid it palm down on the parchment and drew it towards him.

Madelyn flattened her hand as she resisted the pull and his fingers slid between hers until they meshed. 'It is quite genuine,' she said.

'I know. I can see the seals.'

She had studied them, translated the motto embossed on them. *Quid enim meus fidelis.* Faithful to what is mine.

There was a long pause. She had time to register that his hands were warm, to feel the very faintest tremor and the tension as he tried to control it, to hear the deep even breaths he took and guessed at the control he was having to exert not to tear it from her grasp.

'Sell it to me.'

'No. You could not afford it.' Madelyn's voice was almost steady. 'Besides, I would sell all the lands and properties together, not just this one estate.'

His hands were shaking, try as he might to control it, and he suspected she could feel that also. Jack lifted his fingers from the parchment, away from contact with her cold touch, even though it felt as though the document would rip as he moved them. Just an illusion, of course. This was shock, he realised. A total, complete, unexpected shock, as though the massive stones beneath his feet had shifted.

'So, you want to buy a husband, Miss Aylmer?' he said, wanting to shake her poise, wanting to hit back in response to the thunderbolt she had just thrown at him.

'Are not all marriages between people of breeding a matter of exchange?' Madelyn

Aylmer asked, so coolly that it was an effort to keep the masking smile on his lips. 'They always have been, right down the ages. Titles for wealth, alliances for land, property for position. If this was the fourteenth century I would have been married off as a child for just those reasons. I cannot believe that the motives for aristocratic marriages are so different today. Or are you so resigned to your lost lands and status that you are hoping to make a love match?'

She was not used to fighting, Jack realised, pulling himself together with what felt like a physical effort. Under all that careful control, those pricking questions, Madelyn Aylmer was nervous and that was probably the only thing stopping him from losing his temper. Perhaps she was not even used to talking to men who were not her father or her own staff. If that was the case, then she had guts dealing with this alone, he had to admire her for that. She could have had no idea how he would react to her revelations. Somewhere at the back of his mind was a feeling of surprise that he was not shouting, was not overturning this great slab of a table in sheer shock and frustration.

He put his hands on the old oak, not touching

the document, and let what had just happened sink in. He had been offered the chance to regain everything his father and brother Roderick had squandered, everything his sick, confused grandfather had allowed them to snatch. *Everything.* Land, property, status. The title. Pride.

No, that was wrong, he told himself as the words buzzed and rang through his brain. His pride, his self-esteem, did not rest on what he owned, but on what he did. He had fought that battle with himself in the months following his brother's death in a drunken fall down the front steps of his club as he celebrated inheriting the title. It had taken almost a week to come to terms with what he had inherited: an empty title and a mountain of debts.

At the end of that painful struggle with reality he knew he had made the right decision— he was not going to be Lord Dersington, pitied for his vanished inheritance, sneered at for pretending to a standing he could no longer support. He would be his own man, a new man. It had not stopped the sneers, of course, it had only increased them. If there was one thing his class hated, it was someone turning their back on inherited status. It devalued the entire concept.

Now he was being offered his birthright back and he could feel the weight of the generations it represented pressing down on him. As he stared at the parchment, something stirred deep in his soul, the flick of a dragon's tail of possessiveness, of desire. *This is mine by right.*

Jack looked at the woman opposite him. He could say *Yes*, pick up those papers, live a new life. The life he had been destined to live. All that was required of him was to sacrifice his pride and to accept being a bought man. But there were two people in this equation.

What if Madelyn Aylmer was as eccentric as her father? She seemed to have lived cloistered in this place for years. What if she could not cope with the outside world that she had called *a world of steam and speed and cities, of poverty and ugliness*? But it was an exciting world, *his* world, full of scientific and technical advances, full of discoveries and possibilities. He was not going to turn his back on that to pander to the bizarre fancies of this woman. If she married him, then she was marrying a man of the nineteenth century and she was going to have to change and conform to *his* world, *his* time, not drag him back into her fantasies.

Every instinct screamed at him to snatch at what was being offered, but even so... He could not take advantage of a woman who, not to put too fine a point upon it, might not be in her right mind. 'You are doing this because it is what your father wanted,' Jack said, before common sense and self-interest could assert themselves. 'Is it what you truly desire, to marry a man you do not know? You must forgive my frankness, Miss Aylmer, but I want children, an heir, and that involves, shall we say, intimacy.'

'I want that, too.' She was blushing now for the first time and with her pale skin he thought the effect was like a winter sunrise staining the snow pink. 'I mean, I want children and I am quite well aware what that entails. I am not ignorant.'

'All you know of me is my ancestry,' Jack said in a last-ditch attempt to do the right thing.

The right thing for her, and perhaps for me, might well be to walk away from this. Do I really want to regain my pride in my heritage at the price of my pride as a man? Can I live with this woman?

She was not beautiful, she was probably almost as much of an eccentric antiquarian as her father and she appeared to have no society manners whatsoever.

A fine wife for an earl, he thought savagely. He was angry—he knew that in the same way that some part of his brain was aware he was drunk when he had overindulged with the brandy. Anger was no basis for making a decision of this importance.

To his surprise Madelyn Aylmer laughed. 'Of course your ancestry is not all I know of you. Do you think I sit here like a maiden in a tower waiting for my prince to come and hack his way through the brambles that surround me and meanwhile I have no contact with the outside world? I am perfectly capable of employing my own enquiry agents. I know a great deal about you, Jack Ransome.'

'You employed—who?'

'On the advice of my man of business I used a Mr Burroughs of Great Queen Street and the Dawkins brothers of Tower Hill. And my legal advisers also made enquiries.' The little smile that had seemed so tentative was suddenly sharp. 'What is the matter, Mr Enquiry Agent Ransome? Do you not like it when the boot is on the other foot?'

'Not so much,' he admitted. She did not appear to be either feeble-minded or delusional. It seemed Miss Aylmer had a quick wit and perhaps a sense of humour. He tried to see that as a good thing and found his own sense of humour had utterly deserted him. 'You were well advised. They know their business.' Anyone who knew him could have told that tone signified danger—but then, she did not know him. Not at all, whatever information she had been given.

So, what had his competitors told her? That he was ruthless, although he kept within the law—mostly? That he had recently ended a very pleasant liaison with a wealthy widow two years older than himself? That he had no debts to worry about and gambled within his means, but that he could be reckless when it came to a sporting challenge? That he had a short fuse when it came to attacks on his honour and had met two men on Hampstead Heath at dawn as a result? He was damned if he was going to ask, because the infuriating female would probably hand him the reports to read. Whatever was in them, it had not been bad enough to turn her from this course.

Time to shift the balance of this interview—

time to see whether he could tolerate this woman as his wife and to try to make a rational decision. Everything had its price and some costs were just too high to pay.

'Have you made your come-out? Been presented at Court? What do you know of the world beyond that moat?'

Madelyn made a small, betraying movement, the smile quite gone as she rose to her feet. 'Come into the garden,' she said and walked away towards a small door in one corner before he could reply. 'I think better outside. In the summer the Great Hall can feel rather like a vault.'

Jack strode after her and caught up in time to reach the door first and open it. 'Is it better in the winter?' he hazarded. 'With fires and hounds and good food?'

'Hounds? I agree, that would be authentic,' she said, glancing back as though to reassure herself that he was following along the passageway. 'We do have them, of course. But they are never allowed inside because of the tapestries. Do you like dogs?'

'Yes, although I do not have any at the moment. You do not own one? I thought medieval maidens always had small white lapdogs or miniature greyhounds.'

'I have an Italian greyhound called Mist. Father allowed that because she is very well behaved. She is shut up in case you did not tolerate dogs.'

'And if I do not?'

'I suppose I would have had to leave her here.' For the first time he heard real uncertainty in her voice.

We are not following her careful script, Jack thought, wondering if she saw everything as a stage setting with each piece in its place, every character performing their preordained actions, reading from their script. If that was the case, then life outside these walls was going to come as a severe shock to Mistress Madelyn.

'There would be no need,' he said. 'If we wed, that is. I like dogs. You were about to tell me...' And then Madelyn opened the door at the end and he lost the thread of whatever he had been about to say and stood silent, staring.

'Come in.' Madelyn held out her hand, and he stepped out into paradise. He must have said the word aloud because she smiled. 'Yes, that is what the Islamic gardens were called. A paradise. Technically this is a *hortus conclusus*. But you do not want a lecture. Wander, relax, think: that is what this place is for. I will send for refreshment before we talk further.'

By the time Jack had pulled himself together in the haze of perfume and colour and warmth, she had gone and the door was closed. He began to explore, still faintly bemused, strolling along grass paths between knee-high hazel hurdles that held back over-spilling colour. There were roses, ladies' mantle, banks of herbs that were smothered in bees, banks of lavender where the buzzing was almost deafening.

He looked around and realised that this was the interior of the castle, walled on all sides, a sheltered suntrap. In the centre a circular pool held a fountain and he passed intricate knot gardens as he made his way towards it. A wave of lemon scent assaulted him as he brushed past a bushy green plant, then his feet were crushing thyme underfoot.

The fountain was surrounded by low grass banks, and he sat down, wondering if he was drunk on scent or whether he had been transported back five hundred years. He had to make a decision about the woman who dwelt in the middle of this fantasy and he was beginning to think that she had put a spell on him and that he was in no fit state to decide anything. Or perhaps it was simply shock.

The ends of the turf seats were marked by tall wooden posts painted in spiralling red and blue and white, each topped by some heraldic beast. He leaned back against the unicorn post, closed his eyes on the sun dazzle from the fountain and tried to think.

What do I want? What do I need? What would be the right thing to do?

Chapter Three

Jack Ransome was asleep in the midst of her garden when Madelyn returned, and she indulged herself for a moment, watching him relaxed in the sunlight. Long dark lashes lay on those high cheekbones, the deep blue eyes were shuttered, that expressive mouth relaxed. He appeared about as safe as a sleeping cat must look to a sparrow, she thought, gesturing to the maid to put down the tray on the turf seat a few feet away from him.

When she put one finger to her lips the girl flashed a smile in response and tiptoed away. Madelyn sat on the fountain rim and looked, not at Jack Ransome, but at her own reflection in the edge of the pool. Occasional water drops broke the image into fragments, but she knew what she was looking at well enough.

She was not attractive by the fashionable standards of the day—she understood that perfectly from the journals and newspapers and books she'd had brought to her in the months since her father's death. She was too tall, far too blonde— brunettes were most admired, she gathered— and far, far, too pale. Pale skin was a sign of breeding, of course, but pink cheeks and rosebud mouths were admired. Her hair was straight, her bosom too lush, she had realised as she studied the portraits of fashionable beauties and scanned the fashion plates. She had no idea how to dress, what to do with her hair, how to behave. She had no conversation. The very thought of a crowd of people made her feel a little ill.

Fish began to rise at the sight of her, but she had brought nothing for them, so she trailed her fingers through the water, breaking up her reflection, sending them flickering away with a flash of sunlight on fin and scale.

'Are you sure about this?' Jack Ransome said from behind her. He had woken silently and picked up the conversation almost where they had left off.

Madelyn nodded without looking round. What else was she going to do? She was fitted for nothing but to live in a time long past and she knew she was not going to fall in love—that chance had gone two years ago. She might as well marry this handsome man who, by all accounts, was intelligent enough to keep her interested and who looked virile enough to give her children. He seemed chivalrous and thoughtful. At any rate he had not snatched at what she was offering without probing her own feelings first. And he appeared able to control his temper. She could cope with many things simply by enduring them, but blazing male anger terrified her.

Not that she was prepared to reveal her thoughts to him. It had not occurred to her before this meeting that an emotionless match might be easier than one where real passions were engaged, but now it seemed so much safer.

'Yes, I am sure. I would not have sent for you otherwise.' She turned and found him right beside her.

A poor choice of words, perhaps. His eyes narrowed. 'If you marry me, you enter my world, you start living entirely in the year 1816. Do you understand? Clothes, style, home, manners.'

'But this—' Madelyn gestured around her '—I must tell you, it has been left in trust to my children. My husband would not be able to sell it, or to use the income for any other purpose than its maintenance or to control its management.'

Jack Ransome shrugged. 'It is the Dersington lands that I want. All that I want. This would be maintained, of course, according to the provisions of the trust. But if it is to be one of our homes, then it must function as such and not as some medieval fantasy. I will not live in a museum. If I marry you and reclaim all my estates, then they will have priority for my time and attention until I am certain they are restored as I would wish. Do you understand?'

It was hard to control her reaction to that harsh demand, to the flat statement. But what mattered was fulfilling her father's wish, of continuing the line. She had failed him by being a girl, she understood that. She looked at the man surrounded by her flowers, thought of the children they would have and nodded. 'Yes, I understand.'

Some of the tension left the lean body so close to hers. Jack Ransome held out his hands, and she put hers, cool and wet, into his grasp and let herself be drawn to her feet.

'A kiss to seal our bargain?' he asked as her gaze locked with his.

He is still angry, she thought, momentarily daunted. *He is not showing it, not shouting, but he hates the position I have put him in, he loathes being indebted to someone.* The fact that he could control those feelings, still behave in a civilised manner, was almost more frightening than a display of temper would have been. *Will he hate me also?*

When Madelyn closed her eyes and leaned in towards him, he gathered her closer and then his lips brushed over hers, pressed, and she gave a little gasp as his tongue licked across, tasting. Then he lifted his head and she opened her eyes and found herself lost in the darkness and a heat that was more than anger.

Desire? For me? And then whatever it was had gone and he was smiling and stepping back, releasing her hands. It was her imagination, obviously. Imagination and inexperience. Or wishful thinking. Wishing for something she had not realised that she wanted any more.

'I imagine the next step is for my lawyers to talk to yours. And you have trustees, I assume?'

'Trustees, three of them. But they are bound closely by the conditions of my father's will and cannot oppose this marriage. I will give you their various addresses before you leave, Mr Ransome.'

'Thank you.' He made no move to go. 'Did your mother create this garden?'

'Yes. When my brother died and she was… When she knew she would not get better, she asked me to continue looking after it. There are three gardeners. It takes a lot of maintenance.'

He glanced around. 'I have seen very few servants.'

'My father preferred them to stay out of sight as much as possible. One needs a large number to manage a castle and it proved impossible to keep them if he insisted on the correct period costume. He felt it spoiled the appearance of the castle to have them walking around in modern clothing.'

Jack Ransome did not try to hide his reaction to that. 'Your father was obsessed, was he not?'

It was hard to deny it. 'Perhaps. It was everything to him and he was a perfectionist. I suppose all true artists are.'

'That must have been difficult for you if he expected the same standards from you at all times. Or are you as devoted to this as he was?'

'This was how I was raised. I love this place

and I would like to see it become a home, even if it has to change for that to happen.' As soon as she said it she realised how revealing that choice of words was. *Home. A house, an ordinary house, imperfect, comfortable.* She loved this place, it was all she knew, but it was not a home, it was a statement. Jack Ransome gave her a fleeting look that might have held sympathy or perhaps pity. Or even exasperation at her sentimentality. Madelyn tipped up her chin and stared back.

'How long ago did your mother die?'

'A month after the baby.' Yes, he was definitely feeling sorry for her. 'I imagine you will want to be on your way, Mr Ransome. If you come with me, I will find you the addresses you will need.'

'Will you not call me Jack now? We are betrothed, after all.' He sounded more amused than seductive, although his voice was low and the tone intimate. He had suppressed his anger, it seemed, and now he was bent on humouring her, she supposed. That was better than she had feared: a man who simply snatched at what she was offering, took it—and her—and then disregarded her.

'Very well. And you may call me Madelyn.' Not that he would wait for permission.

It seemed to take a long time to find the addresses, to have his horse brought round, and she found herself without any conversation. Jack filled her awkward silences with polite remarks about the castle and its furnishings, questions about the armour, apparent interest in the problems of having tapestries woven when the Continent and its skilled craftsmen had been out of bounds until the last year. It was perhaps her imagination that he was tense with barely controlled impatience to be gone.

Madelyn supposed she answered sensibly enough, but she had no experience of making small talk. As he was drawing on his gloves Jack looked around again at the empty Great Hall. 'You have a companion living with you, I suppose? An older relative, perhaps?'

'No. I have no close relatives at all. I have my maids.'

'Friends, then? I realise that you are still in mourning—' he glanced, frowning, at her coloured gown '—but when you come up to London to buy your trousseau and so forth, you will need someone to show you how to go on. The year since your father's death will be up very soon, will it not? I imagine by the time we have matters settled there can be no objection to you appearing in society before the wedding. London is very quiet at this time of year, of course.'

'No. I mean, yes, I will be out of mourning shortly. I only wore black for a few days.' There was no one to be shocked, after all, so why worry past the funeral? Draping herself in black to symbolise the emotions she felt was hypocritical, she had decided. Besides, white was the correct mourning colour for a lady of the upper classes in the Middle Ages, and she looked so frightful in white. 'I have no… Father did not socialise in the area.' He had fallen out with virtually all of their neighbours over one thing or another and those he had not upset regarded him as peculiar at best and a lunatic at worst.

'That must have been lonely.' He was feeling pity for her again.

Madelyn set her teeth and managed a smile. 'One becomes used to it. And Father had numerous guests to stay.' All male, of course, virtually all middle aged or elderly and equally obsessed with the Middle Ages. Probably society ladies in London would consider her eccentric, too, and would not care to be friends, but at least she would not be tied to these walls, however much she loved them. *And one day there will be children*, she told herself. She clung to that hope even as butterflies swarmed in her stomach at the thought of venturing into the world outside or to trusting herself to this stranger with the intelligent eyes and the lips that touched hers with the promise of intimacies that frightened her.

At last the groom led his horse into the courtyard and she had something safe to talk about. 'What a lovely animal.'

'Thank you. His name is Altair. He is Irish and has great stamina. Do you ride?'

'Yes. I have a palfrey.' He looked surprised by her choice of word. 'She has an ambling gait, if you understand the term. They are rare nowadays, of course.'

'I would be interested to see it. But does that mean you do not ride with a modern lady's saddle?'

She nodded. 'I suppose that is something else I must learn.'

'Or you would attract a great deal of interest

in Hyde Park. I believe the medieval side saddle involves sitting with your feet on a board?'

He surprised a laugh from her. 'In the Middle Ages most women rode pillion or they rode as I do, astride.'

'Not in Hyde Park you do not!' The groom looked over and Jack dropped his voice. 'Or anywhere else you might be seen. I will teach you to ride side saddle after we are married.'

'Thank you.' She suspected that would be far more limiting than she was used to and riding, along with her garden, was her great freedom, her escape. 'But Catherine the Great of Russia rode astride, I believe.'

'Catherine the Great did a number of things I would be alarmed to see my wife doing,' he said. There was something in his voice that made her think that most of those things were thoroughly shocking and he had no intention of telling her about them. She would find a book and discover for herself.

'I must be gone.' Jack Ransome took her hand and raised it to his lips with a courtly gesture that took her aback. 'Today has been a day of surprises, Madelyn.'

'Pleasant ones?' she asked, knowing what the true answer would be.

His eyes narrowed and she wondered if he thought she was trying to flirt. 'Some of them. Cultivate your garden, my lady. I will write to you.'

Madelyn climbed to the top of the gatehouse tower and watched Jack ride away on his big horse. He took the far slope at an easy canter, sitting relaxed and very much at home in the saddle. She stood there, thinking for a long while after he had vanished from sight. That man was going to be her husband. She would lie with him, know that long, hard body. She would share the trivial day-to-day incidents of domestic life with him. She might grow old with him. She would come to know the real man behind that carefully controlled exterior.

The breeze strengthened, snapping the banners over her head, sending her hair whipping across her face. Madelyn shivered and went to find Mr Lansing, who had been her father's employee and who was now, with quite clearly gritted teeth, working for her.

Her father had told her nothing of his affairs because, as he said, women's brains were not made for such matters. She suspected that it was a question more of education and expectation than mental capacity and at first she had no expectation that Mr Lansing would think any differently.

She had been resigned to a state of ignorance, then, months after her father's death, she heard the groom and the coachman discussing someone who had died in the village. His heir, it seemed, had been disgruntled to find the will left the dead man's money and possessions to him, but only after the payment of his mortgages, debts and loans.

'Which is a fair old amount,' Tom, the coachman, had said. 'Still, I don't know why he was grumbling, it is how it is always worded.'

But there had been nothing about debts, loans or mortgages in her father's will. She wondered about it for a few days and the wondering had turned to worry. What if there were debts? Loans and mortgages, she assumed, would be paid at their due time by Mr Lansing. But debts? It would be very like her father to neglect to pay local people until he absolutely had to.

Now she realised that she had to make certain. Lansing was at his desk, surrounded by ledgers.

He put down his pen and stood up when she entered, very correct and polite, but she could tell he was repressing a sigh at the interruption.

'Mr Lansing, did my father leave debts, loans and mortgages?'

'Well, yes, Mistress Aylmer.' He did not meet her gaze, but began to fiddle with his pen. 'That is normal for any gentleman. Loans and mortgages assist with the flow of money...'

'Yes, yes. But debts?'

'There were some, yes,' he said cautiously.

'And they are still outstanding?'

'Yes. It was the Master's instructions that they were to be paid only on the threat of... I mean, not immediately.'

'I see.' And she could, only too well. No wonder her father was a rich man if he never paid those he owed until the point of legal action. He had used loans and mortgages to make his money work all the harder, she supposed, but she was hazy about how that would function.

'Well, Mr Lansing, my instructions are that all outstanding debts will be paid in full immediately. All future bills will be met within the month and all loans and mortgages will be repaid.' The man's jaw dropped. 'I am getting married, Mr Lansing, and I wish to start married life with an absolutely clear slate.'

'I… But, Mistress Aylmer, I would have to make some sales to meet those obligations at short notice. The debts are one thing, but the other obligations… It is very complex, you understand.'

'No, I do not. There is this estate and there are the Dersington lands. It appears simple.'

'Well…er…yes. Although there is also the… I mean, it will be necessary to sell out of funds, sell some property.'

'I thought my father was a rich man.' She turned to stare at him. Had Lansing been dipping into the money chests?

'He was, he was, Mistress. But finance is a complex matter. Having cash sitting around is bad policy—it needs to be out there, working and earning.' He was gabbling now. 'This sort of demand at short notice—'

'Do it, Mr Lansing. You will not sell any of the Dersington properties, you understand. It is Lord Dersington that I am to marry.'

'I am certain His Lordship will not wish for

anything hasty to be done. You do not quite understand—'

'It seems quite clear to me. And I assume you are perfectly aware of the trust relating to this property. Are you telling me that what I am asking is impossible for some reason?'

'No, Mistress Aylmer. But—'

'Do you wish to retain your position, Mr Lansing? Because it seems to me that you are very reluctant to carry out my instructions. And I am your employer.' Inwardly, she was quaking. What had come over her? In one day she had proposed to a complete stranger and now she was threatening someone who had been in her father's employment for years. She never threatened anyone, not even the most careless kitchen maid.

'Of course, Mistress Aylmer. It will be exactly as you order.'

The poor man has gone quite pale. I am as bad a bully as my father, it seems.

'Thank you, Mr Lansing. That is very satisfactory,' Madelyn said with a smile.

She left him mopping his brow with a vast spotted handkerchief. Now he was probably even more convinced that women were not capable of dealing with financial matters, but she did not care. She would not have unpaid debts to hardworking people on her conscience.

Chapter Four

15th August

The settlements having been agreed and signed, and given that your period of mourning has passed, I suggest that now would be the best time for you to come to London to acquire your trousseau and for us to make arrangements for the wedding.

Madelyn tapped one finger on the page as she looked out of the carriage window and tried to decide whether what she was feeling—besides plain panic, of course—was irritation or apprehension.

I have engaged the services of a companion for you.

Louisa, Lady Fairfield, is a widow in her thirties with admirable connections. I am sure you will find her of the greatest use as you accustom yourself to London life.

Of course what Lord Dersington really meant was *as you are dragged kicking and screaming into the nineteenth century.* That and, *as you are remodelled so as not to embarrass me.*

It was definitely panic churning inside her, she decided. And irritation with the bland euphemisms her betrothed was using and the way he was making decisions without consulting her.

If you would be so good as to inform me of a convenient date I will send a coach with outriders and the abigail that Lady Fairfield has found for you.

It was amazing how temper calmed nerves. Perhaps it was the novelty—she had never been allowed, or allowed herself, to lose her temper. Madelyn inhaled a long, calming breath, then let it go as she read on, even though she could probably have recited the letter by heart now.

Naturally, if the woman does not suit, then changes can be made when you reach here.
I am assuming that you will wish to reside at the Dersington town house in St James's

Square. Your man of business informs me that it has been maintained in good order, although it has not been occupied for some months. He assures me that the building will be prepared for your arrival and a full complement of staff engaged.

Trusting that this finds you in good health, Yours,
J.R.

There really was nothing to take exception to, she told herself for perhaps the fiftieth time as the carriage rolled into Sittingbourne. She had agreed to marry the man and she had to learn how to go on in fashionable society. Everything he had done was correct, scrupulously so. That was probably what was so annoying, Madelyn concluded. That and her own naivety. Jack Ransome was not her lover, or her friend. He was not even an acquaintance and it was foolish to think of him as any of those things. This was an arranged marriage between strangers, organised by her father from beyond the grave. She should be grateful that her betrothed did not insult her with protestations of emotions he did not feel, or expect her to pretend reciprocal affection.

'Miss Aylmer? Do you wish to go into the inn to take refreshment?'

That was another thing. Maud Harper, the abigail who had arrived with the carriage and its two outriders, two grooms and coachman, was perfect. *Of course she was.* Competent, tactful and highly skilled. Chosen to perform a transformation.

'Thank you, Harper, no.' Then she thought again. She did not want to use the facilities, but the maid perhaps did and would be too well trained to leave her mistress alone while she did so. 'On the other hand, it would be sensible to take a cup of coffee and, er, so forth.'

They trooped into the George Inn, footman in front to open doors, Harper one step behind. Her new gown, sent down by the unknown Lady Fairfield, seemed insubstantial and far too flimsy; the unaccustomed stays were uncomfortable; the weight of her hair, plaited, crimped and caught up by some alchemy of Harper's, was entirely wrong, leaving the nape of her neck cold and exposed. The image staring back at her from the mirror had seemed totally unfamiliar—nose too long, lashes too pale, bone structure lost against curls and frills.

The landlord remembered her esteemed father so there was much bowing and scraping even though the carriage was a hired vehicle, as were its horses, driver and grooms. She had wondered that the Earl had not sent his own carriage, then realised that he probably did not own one. It was interesting, she thought fleetingly, that he had not been spending her money in anticipation.

I am going to have to get used to this, too, Madelyn thought, sipping a cup of coffee she disliked but knew she was must learn to drink and pretend to enjoy. *Is this what prisoners feel like when the gates swing open after years of captivity and their longed-for freedom proves to be a frightening new world? I want my garden. My moat. My walls. My safety.*

It was not until the carriage had rolled over the drawbridge, sending echoes rumbling round the old walls, that she realised that over the past few months she had been free. Free of the fear of her father's tempers, emancipated to do as she wished, to think as she wished. And she had not taken the opportunity to change anything, she realised with a pang of something close to anger with herself. She had been set at liberty and now she was closing the door of the cage again, of her own will.

Before, she had no control over any aspect of herself or life except for the thoughts in her head, but at least she knew her father, could predict his moods, his actions. Very soon she would be entirely at the mercy of a man who was alien to her. Jack Ransome might be an apparently considerate alien, but he could as well be from distant Japan for all she understood about his world. She doubted he was feeling kindly disposed towards the woman who would restore his lands at the price of his pride.

Lord Dersington had sent a punctilious letter every week enquiring after her health while telling her absolutely nothing about himself or what he was doing.

Other than constructing my new world, my new identity, of course.

Madelyn gave herself a mental shake, something that she was finding herself doing almost hourly. Either she could stay walled up in her castle or she could come out and learn to live in the real world, and it was wrong to fight the process to make her fit for that world. *Ungrateful.*

'Shall I pour you another cup, Miss Aylmer?'

'No, thank you, Harper.' The cup rattled in the saucer as she put it down and there was a rushing sound in her ears.

What is the matter with me?

The room steadied after a moment and Madelyn stood up, managing a smile for the maid who was looking at her anxiously. 'It is so stuffy in here. Shall we go?'

London appalled her. It was like an overturned ant heap with human-sized ants. Noisy, dirty, feral ants that seemed furiously busy, scurrying in all directions amid smoke and smells and crowded chaos. Harper seemed to be proud of what they were seeing out of the windows and kept up a running commentary. Madelyn forced herself to pay attention and to learn.

'This is Blackfriars Bridge, ma'am. And there's St Paul's—you get ever such a good view of the dome from here. And now this is Fleet Street and here comes Temple Bar and we're out of the City now, ma'am.'

The Strand, Northumberland House, Charing Cross… 'There's Whitehall, ma'am, with Westminster Abbey right down at the end of it and all the government offices and Parliament.

Now we are in Pall Mall. Look, ma'am, here's Carlton House where the Prince Regent lives. They say it's ever so splendid inside, all gold. I expect you'll be going to receptions there soon enough.'

Madelyn had a glimpse of white stone and a screen of pillared railings with a courtyard behind and a crowd peering in and then the carriage swung sharply to the right.

'We're almost there, ma'am. This is St James's Square.'

There were fine tall houses, although so tight together it must surely be impossible to be ignorant of one's neighbours' business. In the centre was a railed, circular enclosure with some water inside that and a statue in the middle. There was no grass and it seemed very bleak. The throng of vehicles and pedestrians made it seem worse, somehow.

'No gardens? I thought London squares had gardens.'

'Not all of them, ma'am. But the house does, a fine big one at the back.'

The carriage came to a halt outside a house with a flight of steps up to a wide glossy black door that was opened so perfectly in time with their stopping that someone must have been watching out for them, Madelyn realised. Two footmen came down the steps, the carriage door was opened, she was handed out and bowed into the house by a rotund little man, all in black, with a striped waistcoat.

'Partridge?' That was the name of her new butler, according to Mr Lansing who had written to the best London agency to secure the staff. Given the cosy shape of this man his name seemed all too appropriate.

'Miss Aylmer. Welcome home.'

Home? I suppose it must become that. This is the beginning of my new life.

She blinked at the amount of gilding in the hall, the highly polished furniture, the torchères at the foot of the staircase. 'It seems very... shiny.' She had ordered the changes, of course, researched them meticulously as she had been taught by her father, but she had not expected how very bright everything would look.

'Yes, Miss Aylmer. Your steward—Mr Lansing, is it not?—he told me that you wished the house renovated to the highest standard. He has directed a firm of decorators and upholsterers according to your instructions, and of course items have been arriving from Gillow's and Heal's, but I fear only the main rooms on the ground floor have been completed so far. The drawing room is here, ma'am. Tea will be served immediately.'

'Thank—' *Crocodiles?* Madelyn stopped dead on the threshold. 'Oh, yes, of course. The Egyptian fashion.' They seemed to be life-sized and somehow she had not imagined that. The totality of the objects she had studied in catalogues and from drawings were overwhelming when she saw them all assembled. She gazed round at more gilt, couches with scaly crocodile legs, lamp holders in the shape of turbaned figures and an array of what appeared to be miniature pagodas on the mantelpiece.

'I understand that your orders were for the house to be redecorated in the latest style, Miss Aylmer.' Partridge stared around him as though seeing the room for the first time, his feathers decidedly ruffled by her reaction. 'Mr Lansing assures me that everything ordered is in the current mode.'

'Oh, yes. It is. This is what I decided upon,' she agreed faintly. It was hideous, she hated it and the light flooding in from the large windows made it all worse. Madelyn reminded herself that immersion in the Middle Ages was not going to be a fit preparation for appreciating contemporary style. 'This is following the Prince Regent's taste, I understand.' She knew a little of that. Her father—who would be turning in his grave if he had any idea of what she had perpetrated here—had ranted about it for what had seemed like weeks after attending a reception at Carlton House. That had been followed by a letter from a fellow medievalist who was in shock after an ill-advised visit to the Pavilion at Brighton.

'A hideous cacophony of styles, no research, gimcrack fakery' had been the mildest of her father's opinions.

But if this was the mode then she would have to accustom herself to it and at least Jack could not fault her for allowing the house to be neglected, or for skimping on her research and on the quality of the objects ordered. Not that the house had been allowed to fall into any kind of disrepair. There had been a succession of highly respectable tenants, Mr Lansing had assured her, just as there were with all of the Dersington properties her father had acquired that were fit to be rented out.

All the tenancies were on short leases, but this house had been let furnished and would have seemed hopelessly outdated now, she was sure. There were still the other floors to be dealt with, of course, but perhaps Jack would tolerate that if the public rooms were acceptable.

The tea tray arrived, shortly followed by Harper to announce that hot water could be taken up the moment Miss Aylmer expressed a wish to bathe. The maid had been tight-lipped over the facilities at the castle, although Madelyn was not sure what the woman expected. Her mother had, after all, made one of her rare protests when her husband had wanted to use the medieval *garderobes*—draughty little turrets with an alcove equipped with a plank seat with a hole and a long drop to the moat below. Mama had insisted on an earth closet in the inner court, although baths had to be taken in large wooden vats that were lined with linen sheets before the water was poured in.

'I will take a bath in half an hour,' she told Harper. 'First I will finish my tea and write a note to...' How would Jack want to be addressed now? Was he using his title yet? 'To Lady Fairfield to let her know I have arrived. Do you have her direction?'

'A footman went as soon as you arrived, Miss Aylmer. Mr Ransome's orders.'

That answered her question as far as the staff were concerned, although she had no idea when he would make a general announcement that he was accepting the title.

Madelyn pushed down the feeling of resentment at being managed and told herself it was a thoughtful gesture and showed her betrothed's concern. She put down her cup, jumped at the sound of the door knocker and winced as the spindly table rocked on its faux bamboo legs.

'What the *hell*?' demanded a voice from the hall.

'Sir.' Partridge's fluting tones carried clearly through the half-open door. 'Miss Aylmer—'

'Miss Aylmer had better be at home, because I want to talk to her. Now.' Jack's voice was unmistakable, even through the anger.

As the cab rattled along Piccadilly towards St James's Street, Jack decided that he had reason to be pleased with himself. He had managed to secure the assistance of an excellent companion and social tutor for Madelyn and the staff for the London house had been appointed through Madelyn's man of business, Lansing.

With the wedding he would begin to use the title and he saw no problem with that, other than the inevitable gossip. His claim had been ratified by both the House of Lords and the College of Heralds on the death of his brother and he could expect nothing but approval now that he was finally accepting it.

None of the arrangements had been problematic—the difficult thing was not demanding the keys and taking possession of the house in St James's Square the moment he arrived back in London. It was not his yet, he had reminded himself more than once over the past weeks as the temptation built like a dull ache.

The family seat, Dersington Mote, was in Suffolk. It was ancient and should have been the place he yearned for, he supposed. But he'd had a miserable childhood there, one he was in no hurry to remember. As his grandfather became older and more confused the old man was happier in the London house, which was smaller, warmer, a little faded and old fashioned, but a home where he was less disorientated by the world. With his mother dead, his grandparents had taken their younger grandson to live with them, and Jack had loved the house. The Earl might be vague about who he was most of the time, but he was invariably kind and Jack's grandmother was indulgent to a boy who would sit and listen for hours to her read out loud or tell stories.

Now it would be his again. He could almost feel the worn leather of the desktop in the study under his fingers, smell the familiar scent of lemon and beeswax polish, pipe smoke and his grandmother's lavender soap.

Soon he would set foot in that room for the first time in more than six years. When his grandparents died his father made the house his London base and Jack had removed himself before he was thrown out. First he wanted to drop into Brooks's where his post was directed when he was out of town. He had been accepted as a member years ago, before his father died and, despite the fact that most of his fellow members considered that he was letting them all down by refusing to use the title, he ignored the dark looks and mutterings for the sake of convenience. The wives of the members were concerned only that he, landless, did not flirt with their impressionable daughters who should be making good matches, or lure their sons into the kind of dissipation his brother and father had been infamous for. They generally ignored him, omitted him from their guest lists and pretended the aristocratic black sheep did not exist.

It was ironic, he had thought in the early days when the snubs and whispers had hurt. His father and brother had been frivolous, spendthrift, indolent wastrels, but they were accepted. Jack had neither the taste, nor the time and money, for indiscriminate wenching, reckless gambling or drinking himself into a stupor, but he was the one looked down on.

His fellow aristocrats might despise him, but they did not shun his talents for solving problems on their behalf. He had spent the past week in Lincolnshire, concluding the last commission he intended taking, and wondered if he would miss the work. Not the tedium, of which there was plenty, but the puzzle of solving a problem and the occasional excitement, even danger. This last case had involved the plausible gentleman who had insinuated his way into the life of a certain young viscount, much to the alarm of his trustees The man had put up a satisfactory fight when confronted by Jack and the officers of the law armed with a warrant for his arrest on forgery charges and it had been a pleasure to let off some of his tight-wound emotions.

Jack was absently rubbing his bruised knuckles as the carriage turned down St James's Street and pulled up outside the club. Yes, some things he'd miss. Earls were supposed to be respectable these days, on the surface at least.

'Mr Ransome.' The hall porter opened the door for him. 'There is post awaiting you in the office, sir. Would you like it now, sir, or when you leave?'

'Now, thank you.' Jack tipped the man, then carried the correspondence through to the library. With a twinge of amusement he recognised the need to clear away everything to give himself a fresh start.

An hour later a plump little butler flung the door open with a flourish as Jack made himself walk slowly up the steps. 'Sir. Welcome. I am Partridge.'

Jack stepped inside, took a deep breath, looked around. 'What the *hell*?'

Chapter Five

'Sir? Miss Aylmer—'

Jack looked around the hall and almost turned right around again. It was the wrong house, surely? But there was the famous twisted ironwork of the staircase, the foliage and hidden birds he had searched for and delighted in as a child.

'Miss Aylmer had better be at home because I want to talk to her. Now. What the devil *is* this? It looks like a damned bordello designed for Prinny and his cronies.'

Partridge took a step back and then, bravely, held his ground. 'The redecoration of this floor has just been completed, Mr Ransome. The house had been let furnished for some time—it required modernising so Miss Aylmer gave instructions. No expense or effort has been spared, I assure you.'

Jack strode past him to the end of the hall and stopped, one hand on the study door, his stomach churning. This was the heart of the house for him, the place where his grandfather had sat behind the battered old desk that had been his own father's, reading and rereading his familiar books, shutting out the reality of the baffling world outside. Jack would sit in the armchair in the corner, his feet not reaching the floor, and listen to the old man's rambling stories while his grandmother sat sewing, watching the two loves of her life.

The door opened at a push. He took one look and spun round to the butler. 'Where is the furniture? The books? Where is the damn desk?'

'Mr Ransome—' The butler was positively wringing his hands.

'Is something wrong?' enquired a voice behind him.

The author of all this. He turned so sharply that Madelyn took a step back. Then she stopped, met his furious gaze, chin up, blue-grey eyes steady. There was the smallest furrow between her brows, but otherwise her face was expressionless. He saw her swallow, hard.

'This.' Jack swept his hand round in a gesture

to encompass the entire hideous gilded mess. 'This abomination.'

'I instructed Mr Lansing to refurnish in the most modern taste. Is this not correct in some way? I carried out the most extensive research on what was fashionable.'

'It is hideous. Appalling.'

'I know nothing about fashionable interiors, but—'

'That much, Miss Aylmer, is evident. You ordered this? Have you no taste whatsoever?' She opened her mouth, but he swept on. 'Where are the original contents?'

'Partridge?' She said it calmly enough, but her eyes were wide now and her cheeks white.

'Everything was moved to the upper floors, Miss Aylmer. As I said, only this floor has been completed and there were sufficient rooms to store everything until we had orders about its disposal.'

'Nothing will be disposed of except for this… this tawdry rubbish. Get whoever was responsible for the decoration and the furnishings back here, have it all reinstated as it was. Starting with the study.'

'Mr Ransome, if I might have a word?'

And a knife in my back by the sound of it.

A faint tremor underneath the taut words made him stop, breathe. Jack had his anger under control by the time he turned back to her. 'Of course, Miss Aylmer.' He followed her into the drawing room, winced at the crocodile couch and closed the door.

Madelyn sank down on to a hard, upright chair, her back perfectly straight, her head up. Her hair had been curled, crimped and piled up, leaving her neck naked and vulnerable.

She looks like a plucked bird, he thought.

Lady Fairfield was presumably responsible for the eau-de-Nil travelling dress she was wearing. Neither the hair style or the gown suited her and she seemed unlike herself, as though she was dressing up. For some reason that only increased his bad humour. He had not realised his wife-to-be was quite so plain, quite so awkward.

'Where am I to reside while this work is carried out?' she asked. Somehow, she was keeping her voice steady, but the hem of her gown moved. He assumed she was controlling anger with an effort, trembling with indignation. He did not care. Let her have a shouting match if that was what she wanted.

'They can do it room by room. I imagine that will not discommode you too much. There are enough apartments on this floor to provide alternative dining and drawing rooms and I assume you can manage without the use of the study.' He sat down on something that appeared to have been looted from a pharaoh's tomb. At least sitting on it he did not have to look at the thing.

'Certainly I can. I regret that my assumption that you would wish your London house to be in the latest mode was so far misplaced.'

Anger at the shock at finding everything so changed was subsiding into a roiling stomach and a strong desire to down half a bottle of brandy. He hadn't felt this bad since his grandfather died, he realised. It was like losing him all over again.

Jack looked across at his betrothed and felt a pang of guilt. This was still Madelyn's house and she was trying to do the right thing. Probably, at this moment, she was wondering what she had done to promise herself to such an angry man.

'I apologise for swearing. You meant it for the best, no doubt.' He was a gentleman, he reminded himself. He should not take out his disappointment and temper on a lady, even if she was the cause of that disappointment.

She turned that wide blue-grey gaze on him, and he found he could manage to get the scowl off his face if he really tried. 'This was my home, but why I should imagine it would stay unchanged for so many years I do not know.' It was an explanation and, he supposed, a poor sort of apology.

'Your home? But I had assumed that Dersington Mote would be the house that was of chief importance to you.'

'That was where my father and brother lived. My mother died when I was ten and my grandparents did not think it was the right place for a child.' That had been on the day when his grandmother had arrived to find he had a black eye and bruised cheek as a result of disturbing his father by crying at night over the loss of his mother. He tipped his head back against the hard, uncomfortable upholstery, closed his eyes and wondered why he felt so weary.

'Your father's parents?' When he nodded she said, 'But did they not live at the country house?'

'My grandfather became confused with age. This smaller house was easier for him and, in

London, my grandmother was closer to her friends who supported her.'

'Oh, I understand now.' There was a rustle of fabric, and he blinked. Madelyn was sitting on the footstool by his knees, hands clasped in her lap, ruffled skirts pooling around her. 'I will speak to the workmen myself, make certain everything is just as you want it again.' The faint scent of old roses and warm female drifted up.

'You have a great deal of experience making certain that the men in your life have exactly the surroundings they desire, haven't you?' He found he was irrationally irritated by that. That was what ladies did, after all. The household was their kingdom but they were managing it for their husbands, fathers and, sometimes, brothers.

'Yes.' She tipped her head to one side, clearly puzzled at this sudden change of mood. Those ugly curls bobbed, but the movement sent up another disturbing waft of fragrance, a memory of her secret garden behind the massive stone walls. 'But not *men*. There has only ever been my father to please.'

'And what do you want? Where do *you* want to live? How do you want to live?'

'Me?' The suggestion that she might express a preference made her rock back on the stool as though to get him into better focus. 'What is the point of wondering that? If I want children, a family, then I have no choice in the matter.'

'Take this house, for example. We both agree we hate this.' He rapped his knuckles on the gilded scales of the arm chair.

'Yes,' Madelyn agreed warily.

'I want the study back how I remember it, I want this Egyptian nonsense gone. But there is no reason why we cannot decide on the rest of the house together.'

'Truly? But if this is not the mode, then I have no idea about other possibilities. And what if we disagree?' She hesitated, bit her lip. 'Then it would be your decision, of course.'

'No. Then we discuss it. Compromise, perhaps.'

It was as though he had handed any other woman of his acquaintance a very large diamond. 'Oh, yes.' Her face lit up with an unguarded smile that had him smiling back.

Jack caught her by the shoulders and bent his head until he could feel the warmth of her breath on his lips. 'Oh, yes?'

* * *

Madelyn nodded, felt the warmth of the blush rising, although she kept her gaze locked with Jack's, only closing her eyes as he came close. Jack tasted of something that she remembered from the castle garden—something indefinably spicy—and perhaps of his recent anger as well, and her lips parted immediately as he stroked his tongue over them.

Had he pulled her up or had she risen into his arms? She wasn't sure, but she was there now, on his lap, arms twined around his neck, his body warm and hard and exciting under her hands.

And then the door opened and shut again with a click that sent her toppling off, bouncing onto the stool, then the carpet, in an ungainly tangle of limbs. Jack reached for her, she felt his hand curl around one silk-stockinged ankle, then he let go and ended up sprawled on the floor next to her.

Madelyn struggled to sit up, impeded by the unfamiliar stays that jabbed in her ribs. Jack flopped back on the thick gold and black carpet and laughed. 'I think we have scandalised our new butler.' He rolled over onto one elbow and looked at her, apparently more than happy to continue where they had just left off.

Scandalised, Madelyn scrambled to her feet. 'I will open the door.' She knew she was pink-faced with embarrassment. How she was going to face Partridge...

'Leave it.' Jack spoke so sharply that she stopped dead, turned and sat in the nearest straight-backed chair, chin up, struggling to get her breath under control. She knew she was shaking, then it dawned on her that it was not only fear that he was losing his temper and would shout at her. There was this alarming urge to give free rein to all the things inside her that were fighting to be expressed. She had no practice in showing her feelings, let alone in losing her temper, but it seemed she was going to begin learning now.

Jack stayed where he was, quite at ease cross-legged on the floor. 'Really, Madelyn, there is no need to be so bourgeois about it. This is our house, or rather, yours and—'

'Yes,' she said steadily, ignoring the distracting sight of tight breeches straining over his muscles. 'It *is* mine, just at the moment. And they are *my* servants. And whatever else I may be,

I am not a *bourgeois*.' It was amazing that she could speak so clearly, she thought, as though watching herself from afar. *Any moment now he will stand up and he will shout—or worse—and I will dissolve...*

'I did not say you were, but the servants should conform to your standards, not you to theirs. It is not their place to be shocked.' He was not shouting. Yet.

Emboldened, Madelyn shot back, 'I see that you have adapted again quickly to the behaviour of the *ton*, Lord Dersington.' She was shaking and she was appalled to realise that part of that was because of unsatisfied desire. She *wanted* to be rolling about on the floor with this man, which was appalling. What was he doing to her? She had never felt like this before, not even with Richard, the man she had dreamed of marrying...

'I have never been out of society. The *ton* might have been shocked by my refusal to use my title, I might be disapproved of, snubbed and gossiped about, but I have hardly been existing in some back slum. And I am not going to bicker over this. You are about to become the Countess of Dersington. *You* will set standards and if you choose to make love to your husband on the drawing-room carpet, then you will do so and the staff will have to learn to be discreet about it.'

'Very well. I will set some standards now.' Madelyn stood up and Jack rose, too. Clearly, whatever she thought of him, he was not going to sprawl on the floor when a lady was on her feet. 'I do not *choose* to have my husband tumble me like a milkmaid in a haystack.' She had the door open before he could reach it. 'I will have these rooms restored to their former state. I doubt I will be receiving anyone at all until that is done.'

She swept out and found herself face-to-face with Partridge in the hall. 'Show Mr Ransome out, Partridge. I am not at home to anyone except Lady Fairfield.'

Goodness, so *this* was what losing one's temper felt like. How very invigorating—and apparently it was not necessary to shout or lose one's dignity to do it. This was power, Madelyn thought as she climbed the stairs, almost tripping over her feet as the unfamiliar flimsy skirts failed to give her the stability she was used to.

She gave them an irritable shake with one hand and lifted the other to her lips. A chaste kiss, yes, that was perfectly acceptable between a betrothed couple, surely, but to romp on the carpet, to ignore the fact that the servants had observed them, was too much.

And the problem was, she admitted as she stalked along the corridor looking for her maid, she had enjoyed it, just for a moment. Enjoyed Jack's kisses, responded to the touch of his hand on her leg, responded to the laughter in his eyes when the two of them tumbled on to that wretched rug.

'Oh, Miss Aylmer. I did not hear you ring.' Harper looked out from a door just ahead of her. 'I am very sorry, ma'am.'

'I did not ring. Mr Ransome has left. I came to see what state the rooms up here are in.'

'They're full of furniture and I don't know what else, Miss Aylmer. All excepting your chamber and dressing room. Like one giant lumber room it is.'

'Most of that is going back downstairs,' Madelyn said grimly. 'I will have my bath and change and then I have a great deal to organise before dinner.'

* * *

And the most important thing I must organise is my own mind, she thought as she sank into the bath.

But when she closed her eyes, the better to think, all she could see was the image of Jack's face, the way the corners of his eyes had crinkled with amusement, the heat in his gaze, the anger…

It would be a hard woman to please who did not find Jack Ransome attractive, however sheltered she was.

But I am going to have to sleep with him and I do not know him in the slightest.

It was no use reminding herself about all the medieval heiresses who were married off as mere children, expected to bed with virtual strangers the moment they reached womanhood. However she had been brought up to behave, she did not live in the Middle Ages.

The invigorating anger drained away, leaving her feeling slightly sick, just as she always felt when her father had been in one of his rages. Perhaps letting her feelings out was not such a good idea after all.

'The soap, Miss Aylmer.'

'Thank you.' Madelyn opened her eyes and began to wash. She had seriously miscalculated, she saw that now. She had imagined her dealings with Jack Ransome would be a simple matter of commerce—his lands in return for her marriage—and she had not considered the human aspects of the bargain at all.

He had yielded as far as accepting the arrangement—and that was all. If she had thought that she could manage the man in any way, she had made a major error and she had gone from being under the control of one man, her father, to that of her husband. Those few months of freedom she had experienced when the castle had been all hers suddenly seemed very precious indeed.

But now she knew she did not have to meekly obey. She could argue back—she could even become angry and hold her own with him. If she had the courage. Now she was feeling queasy with reaction again. How could she have forgotten herself like that? What if he said he would not marry her after all? No, she decided after an inward struggle with her imagination. No, Jack Ransome wanted those lands, this house and all the rest of his lost inheritance too much to be put off by one flare of temper from her. And men found it so easy to deal with *difficult* women. They simply shouted them down or completely ignored them.

'Are you cold, Miss Aylmer? I have laid out the simplest of the evening gowns, ma'am, seeing as you'll be dining alone, but I saw you shiver. The Kashmir shawl would go well with it and it is very warm and light,' Harper said. 'Which jewels do you wish to wear?'

'What would be suitable?' Changing for dinner, when it was a meal she would be eating all alone, was a new concept. And jewels? Harper had guarded the dressing case containing her little hoard of gems fiercely on the journey, but she had been unable to hide her dismay at what it contained.

'I… I confess I am not certain, ma'am. They are all of such an old-fashioned design except that diamond set and most need cleaning.'

'Then I will wear none of them.' And if Partridge was scandalised by such lax standards, at least it was less shocking than being surprised kissing a man on the carpet.

Chapter Six

The drawing-room door closed firmly in his face. 'Well, I'll be damned.' Where had that gone so wrong, so fast? Jack resisted the temptation to storm after Madelyn—being caught by the butler kissing his intended was one thing; having a full-scale argument in front of the servants was quite another. He counted to ten, then let himself out into the hall. This needed thought and he was not going to brood under the eye of a collection of gilded crocodiles.

Partridge appeared, expression perfectly bland, and produced his hat, gloves and stick. 'Good day, sir.'

Jack strode down King Street, giving Almack's a glance as he passed by. Somehow he was going to have to get Madelyn through those hallowed doors despite the fact that he was not on terms with any of the notoriously difficult Patronesses.

He turned up St James's Street, dodged the traffic as he crossed it and exchanged nods with two acquaintances, all without stopping. He was in no mood for conversation, which meant only one place was safe—his club, where a gentleman could brood in isolation without any fear of interruption.

The porter at Brooks's expressed himself pleased to see Mr Ransome twice in one day, relieved him of his hat and confirmed that, yes, the small library was likely to be quite deserted at that time of day.

Jack settled himself in the deepest armchair, rang for a glass of brandy and a selection of the morning's newspapers and barricaded himself behind *The Times.*

Where had he gone wrong in his assessment of Miss Madelyn Aylmer? He would have thought his judgement of her character sound—he had, after all, spent some time in a career where assessing character was essential, but it seemed he had misjudged the woman he was committed to marry.

If he had been asked to describe her he would have said sheltered to the point of ignorance of the modern world, virtuous but with a natural sensuality that promised passion once she had overcome her shyness, intelligent if uneducated and determined to carry out her father's wishes for her marriage. She wanted children and she had appeared to wish to be married. She said that she had accepted that she must learn to live in the nineteenth century, not the fifteenth, and he recalled some uneasiness that her father had dominated her to the point where she was completely subservient to male will.

Jack did not want a wife who was a meek little shadow with no character, no opinions, and he had been wondering how to draw out some independent spirit from Madelyn. He turned over the page of foreign reports, which he had been staring at blankly for ten minutes, and failed to focus on the Court Circular. It seemed he need not have worried. Yes, she was still meek and pliant when it came to interior decoration, but displease her and she turned into an icy fury. And looking back, she had been quite remarkably determined on the subject of their marriage.

Clearly her experience with managing staff was different from his. As far as Jack was concerned your staff knew more about you than you did yourself, however discreet you were, and to expect anything else led to sad disillusionment. Or perhaps it was that she had imagined that all lovemaking would be confined to the bedroom with a locked door between them and the rest of the world. If that was the case, then she most definitely had no understanding of men in their twenties with healthy appetites and a new wife.

That was probably the problem. She was shy, she was inexperienced and he had shocked her when what had started as a simple kiss had turned into something that she thought must look like a disgraceful romp to Partridge.

Control was important to her—somehow he had overlooked that. Loss of control made her unsettled, nervous, and so she had hit out at him. Jack folded the newspaper and picked up the brandy, sipping it more for the aroma than any desire for alcohol at that time of day.

So… He would give Lady Fairfield time to school her pupil in the mysteries of London society and he would allow Madelyn space. He would control any inclination to kiss her, let alone make love to her and then, when they were married, she would have found her feet, be more confident and all would be well.

Patience, Jack told himself. He had not asked

for this marriage, but it would deliver him something he had not understood that he had fiercely desired, and common decency alone must make him treat Madelyn with consideration. Common decency—and the fact that he was aware of a definite, surprising desire for her.

She was not at all in the usual style of women who attracted him, he brooded. The ladies who he admired tended to be small, dark and vivacious with a sense of fun and, importantly, a certain sophistication. Madelyn was too tall, too blonde, too serious and utterly without any social experience. She was not pretty, she moved with none of the grace that he thought he had remembered from the castle. And he could not make up his mind whether she was intolerably managing, worryingly pliable or a potential termagant. None of which added up to a woman to stir his blood. And yet…

'*Confound* it.'

Across the room another member who had entered unnoticed jumped perceptibly and returned a cool nod when Jack made a gesture of apology. Someone else who disapproved of him, apparently.

He was an earl and it was about time he started

behaving like one and forced society to accept him. His Countess would conduct herself in a manner befitting her rank or she could retire to her fairy-tale castle. His houses would reflect his taste and if he wanted to make love to his wife on his drawing-room carpet—or the billiard table for that matter—he would do so. With the lady's consent, naturally. He was not a barbarian.

Jack failed to suppress a sudden snort of laughter at the thought of dressing up in one of Castle Beaupierre's numerous suits of armour and ordering his maiden to submit in a manner that would doubtless have won the approval of their assorted medieval ancestors. No, a modern gentleman was bound by different rules of conduct altogether.

Across the room its other occupant cleared his throat ominously and Jack got to his feet. He had work to do and there were the family lawyers, the College of Heralds, his bankers and the numerous other sombre gentlemen waiting on his pleasure for decisions and signatures.

Lady Fairfield called at eleven the next morning. 'My dear Miss Aylmer, such a pleasure to meet you at last. I apologise for calling so early in the day, but I felt it best to establish your requirements as soon as possible.'

Early? Madelyn had been up since dawn making lists and exploring the stored furniture. Restoring the downstairs rooms to their former state was the absolute priority although, now she had managed to inspect the old curtains and other fabrics, she was beginning to have qualms about how possible that was going to be.

'Thank you. I am very glad you agreed to help me.' She offered her new mentor a seat and waved a hand to the footman to pour the tea, a beverage her father had banned on the grounds that it was anachronistic. A faint gasp from Lady Fairfield was enough to alert her that she had already committed some error.

'My dear, a lady always pours tea for her guests,' she said as soon as the door closed behind the man.

'I have never done so.' Madelyn took a sip and tried not to grimace. 'It is something else I must learn.'

'Oh, really? I thought perhaps Mr Ransome— Lord Dersington, I mean—was exaggerating about your previous way of life, but perhaps not.

You have truly been living a medieval existence in that castle?'

'I have been living in the fifteenth century, Lady Fairfield. I think if you assume that I have just arrived from the Moon it would be best.' She smiled, hoping to make light of the matter.

'I see.' Lady Fairfield looked daunted, then rallied. 'Good heavens. In that case perhaps my first question is answered. I had wondered whether you had brought a chaperon with you, but I can see it would be best if I take up residence here, if you find that acceptable. I think my advice is going to be required from morning to night.'

'Thank you,' Madelyn said with real feeling. 'That would be very helpful because I have so many questions and there is so much to learn.' She had no idea whether she was going to take to Lady Fairfield, but one did not have to like the rope thrown to you when you were drowning, only to clutch it firmly. 'I will have a suite prepared for you, which should be ready tomorrow, if you have no objection to it not being freshly decorated.' It would mean moving some of the stored furniture, but they would manage. 'I think we should start with advice about my jewels and some thoughts on where I can match as exactly as possible some old curtain fabrics.'

'And we must consider your wardrobe as a matter of urgency. Those few gowns I sent you are only the beginning.'

'Something warmer, perhaps?' Madelyn suggested hopefully. 'I find these cotton and silk gowns feel as flimsy as a shift—not that the undergarments are any more substantial—and they are so short. And pale,' she added, looking down at the white muslin. 'And low.'

'But my dear Miss Aylmer, you are an unmarried lady and only pale colours and white will do. The cut of the neckline and the length of the skirts are precisely in the mode. And it is the height of the summer, so cottons and muslins and fine silks are most suitable. It would not do to become overheated and flushed.'

'Yes. I mean, no,' Madelyn agreed dubiously. Pale colours did not suit her and although she had to agree that a modern house in London was much warmer than the castle, she still felt as though she was walking around in her night shift. 'But I will be married soon,' she consoled herself aloud. 'I may wear stronger colours then, can I not?'

'Certainly, but you can hardly go into hiding until then,' Lady Fairfield said briskly. 'Now, I would like another cup of tea. Shall we practise the rituals of the tea tray?'

'Yes, of course. It can hardly be more difficult than learning to spin, after all,' Madelyn said, hoping to lighten the mood.

'Spinning? Oh, my goodness, I do hope you will not mention doing anything so eccentric in company!'

'But I do a great deal of embroidery and I need the yarn.'

'Embroidery is quite unexceptional,' Lady Fairfield approved. 'But you will *purchase* your wools and silks. There is no shortage of excellent shops for that kind of thing.'

It seemed frivolous not to be carding and dyeing and spinning the wool herself, but it would certainly save a great deal of time and that, Madelyn suspected, was going to be in short supply.

'Now, let us pretend that I have just arrived to make a morning call. Morning calls take place in the afternoon, of course…'

'Of course,' Madelyn echoed faintly, taking the empty teacup.

* * *

'Rundell, Bridge & Rundell are goldsmiths and jewellers to the Crown,' Lady Fairfield explained as the carriage made its slow way past Temple Bar and down Fleet Street the next morning. 'They are the very best. The shop is in the City, of course, which is not somewhere a lady would go unaccompanied, naturally—'

'Why not, Louisa?' They had progressed rapidly to first names over the intricacies of the tea table the day before.

'It is the business area. Your legal advisers, your bank and so forth are located there, I have no doubt, but their representatives come to you, not the other way around. It is the haunt of merchants and traders, not a place for the *ton* to live.'

Madelyn made herself pay attention. Modern life seemed to be full of snares and pitfalls and she was floundering as she tried to assess what would be considered merely eccentric behaviour, what would be embarrassing and what would constitute a major *faux pas.*

At Louisa's suggestion she had brought along every item of jewellery she possessed, packed securely in the dressing case that Harper held on her knee. The doors of the carriage were locked and there were two footmen holding on behind as well as the groom up beside the driver. London thieves were brazen enough to snatch jewellery from the necks of ladies whose carriages were held up in traffic, Louisa warned her, so no risks were to be taken.

The carriage went steeply downhill, then up again. 'Ludgate Hill. We are here.'

The door was unlocked, the footmen flanked the steps as the three women descended and a doorman ushered them into the shop where they were shown through into a private room by a man who Madelyn had thought at first glance must be a customer. But apparently this was Mr Sedgwyck, the manager, condescending to inspect Miss Aylmer's jewels personally in response to a note from Lady Fairfield.

He spread them out on black velvet. 'A very nice diamond parure. Not perhaps in the very latest style and in need of cleaning and a repair to the loose clasps. We could reset the stones if you wish.'

'The set was my mother's. She never wore them in recent years.' Not, in fact, since Father had become determined on total historical accuracy in dress as well as manner of living. 'Cleaning and repairs will be all that is required.'

'Certainly. And these pearls are very fine. They never go out of style, of course. The earrings are freshwater pearls of some age, I imagine. I would advise restringing the necklace. And these... Good gracious, are they original?' He was lifting out the first of the old pieces her father had bought for her mother.

'Most of them are early sixteenth century. That one and that are, I believe, earlier. And these are recent settings of old stones.'

'Magnificent and most interesting.' Mr Sedgwyck was poring over the gems with a magnifying glass. 'Quite unwearable these days, of course—' He broke off at a knock on the door.

One of the assistants looked round the edge. 'Mr Ransome is here, sir. He saw the carriage and is enquiring if he might join Miss Aylmer.'

'Yes, of course.' He had hired the carriage for her, so she supposed he had recognised it. Or more likely the team of matched bays harnessed to it.

Jack came in, making the office seem even smaller, was greeted by Mr Sedgwyck who clearly knew him well and shook hands with the ladies. 'I should tell you, in strictest confidence, Sedgwyck, that Miss Aylmer and I are betrothed.' He turned to Madelyn. 'Do you mind if I join your discussion? You have brought your jewellery to be overhauled, I see.'

'Yes. We have agreed that the diamond set is to be cleaned and checked over and the pearls restrung.'

'I was admiring the antique pieces,' the jeweller remarked. 'Museum quality, most of them. Unless of course Miss Aylmer wishes to have any of the stones recut?'

'Certainly not.' Madelyn put her hand down protectively, fingers spread over the richly coloured, rounded stones and the heavy gold links and mounts.

'When these were made faceted cutting was not technically possible,' Jack began.

'I am perfectly aware of that.' She bit the inside of her cheek before she could say anything more. She certainly did not need a lecture on antique jewellery.

'The colours will show to more advantage and the stones will sparkle if they are recut,' he persisted.

'That would be vandalism—virtually all these

stones have a recorded history. Besides, I prefer to wear them as they are.'

'They would be quite unsuitable for anything but a masquerade,' Jack said flatly. 'Sedgwyck, they had best be stored here, I believe.'

'I was about to suggest that.' The two men nodded, quite in agreement, Madelyn saw, smarting at their assumption that they had resolved the situation.

'No.'

'Ma'am, Her Majesty the Queen has her jewels in our keeping. I assure you they would be quite safe.'

'No. Thank you. I am sure they would be in good hands, but, no.' She would be civil if it killed her. 'Please have them cleaned and the clasps and links checked and then they will all be returned to me, if you please.'

'Er…yes, Miss Aylmer.' Sedgwyck shot an uncertain glance to Jack, sitting beside her.

'I am not married yet, Mr Sedgwyck.' She smiled as she said it, and he tittered nervously, uncertain whether she had been speaking in jest.

Beside her, Jack made a low sound suspiciously like a growl, but when he spoke he sounded perfectly pleasant. The man was a good actor, which was something she should be wary of. 'And in the meantime you will need some jewellery to wear, my dear.' He turned and smiled and she saw that he was quite deliberately calling her to order, expecting her to behave herself in front of the jeweller and not display any of those worrying eccentricities, such as a liking for ancient gems or a refusal to do as two men told her.

She returned the smile sweetly, finding an unexpected pleasure in this duel. It had never been any use protesting to Father. He would not notice any dissent unless it was a full-blown tantrum or a flat refusal to do something—and either of those reactions met with swift retaliation—but Jack Ransome was very aware of her and her reactions and that was strangely stimulating.

'If you say so, *dearest*.' She returned his smile with one just as false and saw his eyes narrow. 'What do you suggest?'

'Something suitable for afternoon wear and less dressy occasions. Your diamonds and pearls will be with you again before you need formal evening wear, I imagine. Some citrines, perhaps. Or what do you have with aquamarines and pearls, Sedgwyck?'

Trays of necklaces and earrings were brought and displayed. They were pretty, clearly of the highest quality, but to Madelyn they seemed too fine, too delicate, for her. She was tall, she preferred strong colours and bold shapes and these dainty pieces felt wrong, bloodless even. They had no life, no past, no romance.

She tried necklaces, slipped on bracelets, held up earrings and pretended delight with everything Jack chose for her. They were going to disagree, if she could find the courage to argue, but she was not going to fight her battles in front of shopkeepers and over a few trinkets. For a moment she wished she did not have to fight at all, that she could just give in. Jack was persuasive, attractive and reassuringly certain about everything. It would be so easy…

Chapter Seven

'We will take them,' Jack said, apparently making the decision for both of them. Sedgwyck bustled out to have them boxed and wrapped and Madelyn made a sudden resolution not to take the easy path, not to lose herself and what she needed.

Lady Fairfield roused herself from her silent contemplation of a display of tiaras. 'Lady Dalesford is holding a soirée tomorrow evening. I thought it would be a suitable occasion to make your acquaintance aware of your impending marriage and the fact that you will be using the title, Lord Dersington. A word in a few ears and it will be all around town within twenty-four hours without unnecessary fuss, don't you agree?'

'I believe not. Better for Madelyn to become

known and to feel easier in society before we complicate matters, in my opinion.'

No, I do not agree.

For a moment Madelyn thought she'd had the courage to say it out loud, but, of course she had not. She wanted to get her debut over with and, surely, the status of being betrothed would help her reception?

And all the attention will be on Jack if he announces he is assuming the title, a small voice whispered. *They won't be looking at me...*

Surely Louisa would counter his argument, stand up for her proposal? But, no.

'If you think it best, of course. Now, the gown with the white silk gauze over the ice-blue under-slip and the floss trim will be just the thing. I do not think you have tried it on yet, Madelyn—it is one of those I ordered when I selected the day dresses I sent down to Kent for you.'

Madelyn knew exactly how she would look in it and repressed a grimace. Her protests about how little pale colours and flimsy fabrics suited her had been firmly set aside the second time she raised the subject—young ladies, especially those not yet presented at Court, wore only the palest colours and, as for fabrics, what she liked was apparently so far removed from the mode that she would be a laughing stock.

'Fatal, my dear, quite fatal,' Louisa had assured her. 'Especially in your situation.'

'Which is?'

'One in which you must avoid all suspicion of being an eccentric. What is allowable in a scholarly gentleman is quite impossible for a young lady and, given your intended's own somewhat irregular career up to now, it would be most unfortunate. You must not stand out in any way.'

So Madelyn had bitten her tongue, yet again, and had applied herself to reading the latest editions of the journals Lady Fairfield ordered, the most fashionable novels from the circulating library and the Court and Society columns in all the newspapers. Dancing lessons would begin tomorrow and those, she was assured, would help with her deportment.

'You are so very tall,' Louisa had lamented. 'And you have...' she had waved her hands vaguely at Madelyn's shoulders and bust '...presence. You walk like a duchess—you command the room. And that will not do for an unmarried girl, especially one who is, if you will forgive me, not yet in the current...er... fashionable style.'

Tiny steps, chin down, modestly lowered eyes, absolute observance of every rule and she would pass muster until she was married and by then she would know how to go on, Louisa had assured her.

Now she followed behind as Jack, very correctly, escorted the older woman out of the shop to the waiting carriage. She smiled sweetly at everyone and sat looking blankly out of the window at the thronged pavements as Harper settled herself with the purchases on the rear-facing seat. The feeling of dizziness that had come over her in the inn on their way to London was threatening again, along with a strange sense of being quite dissociated from everything around her.

I want to go home, I want to pull up the drawbridge and tend my garden and ride my mare in the water meadows. I want Mist with me to talk to.

A flicker of colour jerked her back to the City: a woman in a bright red spencer over a blue gown was making her way up the hill, a fat white pug at her heels. Heads turned as she passed and

Madelyn's mood lifted. She had given her word, agreed to marry, agreed to live in this strange new world. If she wanted children, wanted a future that was not a dream, then she had to do this, had to make it work. And somehow had to hang on to this temper that she had not known she possessed.

'Now,' Louisa said brightly, 'you wanted to match some curtain fabric, I think, Madelyn. St James's Square, then Harding, Howell in Schomberg House,' she said to the footman who was holding the carriage door and waiting for orders.

'That is in Pall Mall,' she explained as they set off. 'Just around the corner from the town house. We will drop off Harper with the jewellery first. Do you have your fabric sample?' Her eyebrows rose at the sight of the square of heavy silk that Madelyn unfolded. 'But that is very faded.'

'I want to find something that looks as this did thirty years ago, but not brand new,' Madelyn explained. If nothing else, she was used to recreating the past. The real question was whether she could create herself a present.

* * *

The half-dress evening gown was every bit as unflattering as Madelyn had expected. The fit was perfect once Harper had worked her magic, but inside the dainty pale perfection Madelyn knew she looked clumsy, awkward and plain. Jack's choice of refined jewellery did not help. She simply could not manage the baffling requirements of being an acceptable young lady—modest yet responsive, shy yet poised, pretty but not seductive. The creature she was attempting to ape seemed a mass of contradictions. She knew herself to be reticent and unused to company, yet Louisa criticised her confident deportment, lamenting that she seemed more like a young matron than the blushing debutante she was supposed to be.

'No, no, do not round your shoulders and stoop!' she cried as Madelyn made another attempt to walk towards her and curtsy.

'But you say I am too tall and clumsy. I was trying to look smaller.'

'I know. Oh, dear, I do not know what it is, but you have *presence.*'

'I have a bust,' Madelyn corrected, peering down at the effect that tight lacing had on the area exposed by the low neckline of the gown. 'And I think it is rather more...*generous* than is ideal for this style of gown. Could I not leave off the stays?' she asked hopefully.

'*No.* Oh, whatever will you say next? Harper, bring the curling tongs, Miss Aylmer's ringlets are drooping and, yes, Madelyn, you must have ringlets unless you want to appear quite out of the mode. Perhaps some rouge... No, too obvious on that white complexion.'

I look like a perfectly blanched stick of celery with the leaves still on top, Madelyn thought as she stared resentfully at the long glass in the corner of her bedchamber. *If someone had pondered for a year on how to create a gown and a hairstyle to suit me as badly as possible they could not have done better than this.*

The sight of the other guests at the soirée did nothing to lift her mood. She could see exactly what Louisa meant as she looked at the throng of unmarried girls, all fluttering like fragile butterflies in their pale gauzes and muslins. Their cheeks were pink, their lips were rosy, their hair glossy and curled and all without any evidence of the slightest artifice. They took small steps, they kept their eyes modestly lowered and yet somehow managed to cast winsome, innocently flirtatious glances at passing gentlemen as though they had spent two hours a day practising. *Perhaps they do.*

Madelyn caught a glimpse of herself in one of the mirrored panels on the landing as they approached the receiving line for her to make her first curtsy to polite society. She repressed a shudder. She was not vain, but she was used to the way she usually appeared and fancied that it suited her height, her figure and her looks. This, on the other hand...

'My dear Hortensia, what a charming party, exactly what we need to enliven a London summer.' Louisa Fairfield was exchanging kisses in the air with a handsome middle-aged woman whose diamonds made Madelyn blink. 'So good of you to invite my young friend, Miss Aylmer—this will be her first party in town, you know. Lady Dalesford, Miss Aylmer from Kent. Madelyn, my dear friend Lady Dalesford.'

Madelyn curtsied, smiled, did her best to sound grateful for the treat in store and pretended not to notice the older woman's sharp scrutiny.

'Charming,' Lady Dalesford murmured, almost managing to sound convincing. 'So pleased to meet you, Miss Aylmer. Are you related to the Aylmers who have that castle?'

'Castle Beaupierre? Yes, ma'am. It was my late father's life's work.'

'How...*interesting.* I expect you are very glad of the opportunity to come to London.'

Madelyn was still smiling through gritted teeth when they entered the first of what looked like a series of large reception rooms.

'The ballroom has a partition which has been brought across,' Louisa explained, pausing for an instant on the threshold to survey the throng of guests. 'With the anteroom it makes three more intimate chambers.'

Intimate was not the word Madelyn would have chosen, but she kept the smile in place as she followed Lady Fairfield, concentrating on taking small steps, on not stooping, not staring, not worrying about the amount of ankle and bosom that she was displaying. Perhaps if she bent at the knees a little... No, she felt she was walking like a duck when she did that.

Louisa seemed to have a destination in mind, even as she worked her way from group to group, introducing Madelyn as she went. She was picking out matrons of her own age, but no men, Madelyn noticed, and the group sitting in a far corner seemed to be her target.

'That is Lady Macclesbourne. She has three delightful daughters,' she murmured in an aside. 'Such lovely girls, *such* a success, two have made the most eligible connections last Season and the youngest cannot be far behind her sisters. You could do worse than to model yourself on them.'

Lady Macclesbourne—*Dearest Eliza* to Louisa—professed herself delighted to make Miss Aylmer's acquaintance and introduced Dorothea, a lively blonde, Daphne, a pert blonde and Caroline, a graceful blonde. They all managed to look enchanting in cream, ivory and shades of pale blue and not in the slightest washed out, despite their hair colour.

No wonder their mama seemed pleased to see me and asked me to join them, Madelyn thought. *I must show them up to perfection.*

The sisters turned periwinkle-blue eyes on Madelyn and proceeded to interrogate her thoroughly. She lived in a castle? How romantic and Gothic! But perhaps there were draughts or ghosts? And a moat with swans? So pretty!

And had she any brothers? No? What a pity, they would love to meet a knight in shining armour, just like a hero of Walter Scott's poems. Did she not just *adore* Mr Scott? Did her father wear armour? Or perhaps she had one of those pointed hats which must be so difficult to keep in place. Miss Daphne had worn one to a fancy dress ball and had been forced to abandon it after half an hour.

'Oh, see by the door.' Miss Caroline, the only unengaged one and therefore the only one supposed to show any interest in eligible gentlemen, nodded towards the entrance. 'It is that mysterious Mr Ransome just come in. Do give us your opinion—do you not think him good looking, Miss Aylmer?'

Madelyn looked. 'Very,' she said, attempting a slightly patronising, light tone and failing dismally. Jack was a good-looking man when he was dressed for riding or for paying calls about town, but in evening dress he was… 'Er, yes. Quite distinguished. Very…um, acceptable.'

Acceptable? You have certainly accepted him, you ninny. Will this be another trial of being married to him, that he will be ogled and pursued by other women?

Severe black and white suited Jack and showed off an athletic figure to full advantage. As he strolled in their direction, showing no sign that he had seen her, she saw that the gaze of the ladies followed and that some of the gentlemen watched with speculation clear in their expressions.

'Acceptable?' Lady Macclesbourne said sharply. 'His breeding is excellent, but he has no lands. The man does not even use his title. Such eccentricity is beyond what is pleasing. I am very surprised to see him here. He tends not to be invited, you know. One can hardly cut an earl to his face, even under the circumstances, but he is not good *ton*.'

'Possibly he has other attributes,' Madelyn remarked, earning herself a very pointed look from the older woman.

'He is a fortune hunter, I have no doubt. I would take care, Miss Aylmer.'

Too late. 'But the proverb tells us that fair exchange is no robbery,' she said, marvelling at her own courage in the face of the Lady Macclesbourne's disapproval.

Beside her Miss Caroline tittered and Madelyn felt herself blush at her unintended suggestion that one would be buying the Earl's undoubted physical attributes. Or was it unintended? She would certainly be in possession of them… The heat in her cheeks burned.

Jack entered the noisy, brightly lit salon in no very good temper. It was beginning to dawn on him that this business of marrying to secure his lands and then beginning to use his title was not going to be the straightforward process he had thought it. His reception here had been a case in point. He'd had to ask a favour of a friend to secure an invitation and it was clear that Lady Dalesford was doubting her own judgement in sending one.

He could feel the curious stares like fingers poking him between the shoulder blades, hear the whispers. Some people looked away when he caught their gaze, a few matrons glowered at him. He knew what they all thought—he'd heard it enough, after all. He was a traitor to his class—he was as good as saying that a title did not matter. He was probably being blamed for the actions of every radical writer of seditious literature, every mill owner in Manchester who wanted the vote and said so at the top of his vulgarly accented voice, every beggar who spat when a crested carriage passed, splattering him with mud.

It was a while since he'd deliberately put himself in a position where he had to deal with this. Now he was going to have to come to terms with these people if he wanted to use his title, return to society, bring up a family who would be accepted in this world.

He was not going to grovel and apologise, that was certain, but somehow he was going to have to negotiate his return to the fold and keep his temper at the same time. And how, exactly, did he let it be known that he would answer to *Dersington*? It was hardly something that one announced in the press or stood up and shared at a social gathering. He could tell his closest friends and tell them to spread it about, he supposed, grudgingly aware of just how much talk that would cause. There would be less if he let it be known before his marriage, but that went against the stubborn principle that had kept him from using it in the first place. No lands, no title.

So, wed first and start a whole new life as the married Earl of Dersington? There was still time to decide, but now where was his intended?

Slightly behind him, he heard someone murmur, 'It's Lackland', and felt the social smile harden on his lips. It seemed he was no longer able to shrug off that particular slur so easily. He turned, identified the young Viscount who must be the one who had spoken, then turned away when the man dropped his gaze from the challenge in Jack's eyes.

And there was Madelyn, sitting beside Lady Macclesbourne and her three pretty daughters. Tall, clearly ill at ease and managing to look dowdy even in what was clearly a very expensive gown. And she had been foolish enough to attempt to counter her natural pallor with lavish amounts of rouge. With those limply dangling ringlets it made her look like a wooden Dutch doll, he thought irritably as he got closer.

Surely he had found her more attractive when they first met? He distinctly recalled a feeling of attraction, a desire to kiss her. He had been too angry over the changes to the house to really notice her appearance the other day, now his mood darkened further at the thought of tying himself permanently to this eccentric, stubborn woman. He had thought Madelyn had style, a certain strange elegance, but he must have been in a state of shock at the revelation that she held all his lands and so he had seen what he wanted to see. Perhaps that garden had drugged his senses. Or maybe he had fallen into a fairy story and been bewitched.

Bewitched or not, he had agreed to marry her, he had given his word and, however little was left to him of his inheritance, he was still a gentleman. Jack rescued a smile as he arrived in front of the seated ladies. 'Lady Macclesbourne, Miss Macclesbourne, Miss Daphne, Miss Caroline. Miss Aylmer.'

'Mr Ransome, good evening.' Lady Macclesbourne looked as though she had bitten a lemon, unflattering little lines appearing all around her lips. 'You know Miss Aylmer?'

'We met in Kent,' Jack said, deriving some enjoyment from Lady Macclesbourne's uneasiness at his presence. In the past he had flirted a little with Miss Caroline and knew the last thing her mother wanted was her fixing her interest on a landless man who did some kind of unspecified but doubtlessly dubious work for a living. Teasing her by paying attention to her daughter would repay a number of slighting remarks in the past, but he could not be so careless of Madelyn's feelings.

'Would you care to take a turn around the room, Miss Aylmer?'

She looked so taken aback by the suggestion that for a moment he thought she would refuse, but she rose from her chair and took his proffered hand. 'Thank you, Mr Ransome. Excuse me, Lady Macclesbourne.'

'How are you enjoying London society?' Jack enquired, attempting to ignore the fact that quite the tallest lady in the room was stiff and unspeaking by his side and that they were the subject of some interest, very little of it kindly. Any other young woman would be flirting by now, sending him intimate glances, smiling. Not Madelyn Aylmer, chin up, lips pressed together, holding herself as though he was leading her to the stake. A glance told him that the high colour in her cheeks was natural and wondered what she was blushing about. Perhaps she was one of those unfortunate girls who turned bright red when too warm. At least that long nose had not gone pink.

'*Enjoying* myself?' she echoed. 'Why, not at all. But then I did not expect to.'

Chapter Eight

'Why do you dislike this so much?' Jack was conscious of a shock that was not so much disapproval as interest that Madelyn should feel no need to pretend, even if it was only to him.

'I feel awkward, uncomfortable, out of place and I dislike the clothes,' she said with devastating honesty.

'Why?' Jack asked, equally blunt as he steered her towards the nearest footman. He nodded to the man who came forward with a tray of glasses. 'Champagne?'

'Thank you.' She took the glass, still frowning over his question, sipped, sneezed. 'This is remarkably peculiar wine.'

'Persist, you may come to enjoy it,' Jack suggested. Perhaps alcohol would help Madelyn relax. 'You were telling me what is wrong with the clothes.'

'They are indecent. My ankles show, the fabric is as flimsy as cobwebs, the bodice—such as it is—is about to slide off my shoulders and the stays pinch.'

Stays? Jack took an incautious sip of champagne and choked. 'Pinch?'

'And poke apart and push up. How one is supposed to breathe I have no idea. Are you laughing at me? Because you can have no idea of the discomfort of the beastly things.'

'I am glad to say I have not.' Jack managed to get his amusement under control. Madelyn might not flirt, but she certainly knew how to take the wind out of a man's sails. 'I should point out that men wear them, too. No, not me!' he protested as she cast him a dubious glance. 'Those inclined to corpulence, like Walgrave over there. See? In the navy-blue waistcoat and the ridiculously long tails.'

'I imagine that he creaks,' Madelyn observed dispassionately. 'He is fat. I am not.'

'I would suggest that the garment you are wearing would feel even more indecent without them,' he suggested. It would certainly look it. He got a firm hold on his imagination and discovered, to his surprise, that he was in a much better mood. Although what Lady Dalesford would say if she knew he was carrying on a conversation about ladies' underwear in the middle of her salon he shuddered to think.

Beside him Madelyn sighed, then stopped dead. 'I hate this gown.' They were facing one of the long mirrors that hung on the rear wall of the room to echo back the windows opposite. Their reflections faced them, a man in fashionable clothes and a tall woman, awkward and uncomfortable.

'Do you want to go back on our agreement?' Jack asked. 'Because I can promise you that styles are not going to revert to the Middle Ages and corsets are not going to vanish.'

He felt Madelyn's reaction as her fingers tightened on his arm. 'You think I am not happy simply because of the clothes? How shallow you must think me. But I gave my word and I will abide by it.' There was a pause and Jack could hear her take a long breath. 'I would be obliged if you would introduce me to some more people. I find my acquaintance somewhat limited at present.'

'Where is Lady Fairfield?' he asked, annoyed. 'She should be making more effort. Ah, there she is with the Macclesbournes, looking for you, I imagine. Much better if she makes the introductions—we do not want to start any speculation.'

'Do we not?' Madelyn enquired tartly as they crossed the crowded room. 'When, exactly, are you intending to announce our coming marriage? Or will you simply produce me along with your title and hope no one actually notices?' She gave a little start as though she had alarmed herself with that abrupt question, then took her hand off his arm and walked away, back to where the two friends had their heads together, deep in gossip.

Hell and damnation. She is quite right. I have to face up to this even though I cannot decide what is the best way to go about it. Or the least bad way.

It was no good putting things off, even though he was beginning to realise that he was committing himself to a woman who was going to make an exceedingly prickly wife. On the other hand, life was not going to be dull...

'Taking pity on the maypole, Lackland?' Lord Ivor Handley, younger son of the Duke of Evesham, drawled as he strolled up, clearly bent on mischief. 'Probably as eccentric as her father—but rolling in money unless the old lunatic spent it all on his fantasy castle. Thinking of trying your luck? Be all right if you keep your eyes shut, I suppose.'

Finally, a legitimate target for his ill humour. 'You are speaking of a lady of my acquaintance, Handley. I'll thank you to keep your opinions to yourself.'

'Oh, come on, Lackland, you are not serious—'

'My name is Ransome and I am finding you increasingly boring, Handley. My tolerance for bores is never very high. Or perhaps you would care to continue this conversation outside?'

Handley was handsome, rich, indulged and rarely thwarted, let alone told he was a bore. He turned an unlovely shade of red and began to bluster. Jack flexed his fingers and toyed with the idea of planting the man a facer right where he stood. *No, bad tactics. Best to get him outside first...*

'I say, Ransome, just the man I need. Tell me, is it true that Fakenham's selling his greys?' Charlie Truscott, one of Jack's closest friends, blundered cheerfully between them. 'Evening, Handley. You all right, old chap? You look a bit

feverish. I'd cut down on the curried lobster pat-
ties if I were you. Now, Ransome, what about
those greys?'

Handley turned on his heel and cut through
the crowd towards the door. Truscott looked
after him, shrugged and quirked an eyebrow at
Jack. 'Hitting someone in the middle of a soirée's not the thing, you know. What's the fool
done now?'

'Insulted a lady and bored me.'

'Fair enough, but hit him later, not here is my
advice. Now, do you know about Fakenham?
There are all kinds of rumours going about that
he's in difficulties.'

Jack watched Handley's disappearing back in
case he decided to go and be unpleasant to Madelyn in retaliation, but he answered his friend.
'He is selling his greys and his high-perch curricle, that's true. But it is nothing to do with his
finances. After that last accident his wife put her
foot down. Stop racing or lose his—how shall
we put it?—*privileges.*'

'Phew! That's a lady with spirit.'

'She said they had two children already and
she did not want to be left with any more father-
less infants when their father broke his neck.'

Truscott's hoot of laughter had heads turning, including Madelyn's. She was being introduced to a small group of young matrons, Jack saw with approval. He knew of them all and they were lively, fashionable and likely, he hoped, to be kind enough to an unconventional newcomer.

'Who was that I saw you with just now? Not a female I recognised—a proper long Meg, if ever I saw one. Not your style at all.'

'Miss Aylmer.'

'What, not Castle-Mad Aylmer's daughter? How come you know her? Rich, of course.' He shot Jack a swift glance and cleared his throat. 'Er…interesting lady, I imagine.'

'She considered using my services at one time,' Jack said repressively.

He should have known better, Truscott immediately picked up the edge to his voice. 'Oho. Saw she got value for her fee, did you?'

'I was on the verge of calling Handley out for insulting her just now,' Jack said mildly. 'The lady is still in the nature of a client.'

'Peace, peace.' Charlie held up both hands, palms out in the fencer's gesture of surrender. 'Of course she is.'

'Actually, there is more to it. I could do with

your advice,' Jack said, suddenly determined to get this thing out in the open.

'I was just thinking this is becoming an intolerable squeeze. Fancy coming back to my place and trying the new brandy I've just discovered? We can put our feet up, discuss horses or whatever else takes your fancy.'

'I will, thank you.' Jack looked over to Madelyn, who had Lady Fairfield at her side, decided she could well do without him to aggravate her and turned for the door. 'And where did this brandy come from, might I ask?'

'The Rector of my parish sent me a cask up. The stuff keeps landing on his doorstep. Most mysterious and, of course, he has to get rid of it.'

'Nothing to do with leaving the keys of the crypt in the lock on moonless nights, I suppose?'

She was as aware of him and the people he came into contact with as she would be a pebble in her shoe, Madelyn thought resentfully as she struggled to find something harmless to talk about. Jack Ransome always seemed to be at the edge of her vision, even as she concentrated on memorising the names of the pleasant group Louisa had introduced her to.

There was that attractive brunette who had brushed against him and then pressed close when he turned to apologise, the pair of giggling debutantes—he had dodged neatly behind a large woman in a turban to escape them— and then that good-looking young man with the sneer. She had thought for a moment that something was wrong there, Jack had seemed suddenly formidable somehow and the other man was clearly annoyed. Then that stocky man who looked as though he'd be happier on a horse than in a ballroom had intervened and now he and Jack were laughing—had she ever heard him laugh before?—and leaving. *Leaving?*

She should be pleased—it was not pleasant trying to conform to his expectations while under that deceptively lazy scrutiny. But she felt safe when he was there, as though he was a link to the Castle, to where she could be herself and not this out-of-place awkward creature that people pretended not to stare at.

'Madelyn, dear?'

That was Louisa, indicating yet another new acquaintance. She had Louisa, of course, she reminded herself as she went through the ritual of smiles and handshakes and polite responses to the same questions yet again. Yes, *that* castle in Kent. No, she was nothing like the scholar her father had been, unless it was of garden history. She received an unobtrusive nudge from Louisa for that—young ladies were not supposed to be scholars of *anything,* even something as feminine as flowers.

Madelyn had expected to feel afraid of this new world and had thought that lifelong habits of obedience would somehow get her through. She had followed her father's wishes and proposed to a man, after all, and that had been terrifying enough. Now there were still those moments of panic and dizziness, although she was learning to disguise those. But what she had not expected to feel was anger. Anger with these so-polite people who could barely disguise the fact that they thought her an oddity. Anger with Jack for expecting her to adapt and conform and lose her real self so entirely. Anger with herself for not fighting back.

That at least she could control and she did not care how dizzy with panic it made her feel. Madelyn smiled at Lady Brondesbury, who had observed that she must find so many aspects of

modern life vastly superior to existing in the
Middle Ages. 'Only one, ma'am.'

'And what might that be?'

'The modern privies are so much less draughty,
I find.'

Beside her Lady Fairfield made a sound that
might have been a gasp of laughter or, more likely,
horror. Lady Brondesbury said, 'Draughty?'

'Yes. You know those little projections from
castle turrets, like tiny lean-to buildings? Well,
they overhang the moat, you see. Those are garderobes, or privies. They are called garderobes
because the fumes keep the moths away,' she
added helpfully, ignoring sounds of real anguish
from Louisa.

'And you observed antique modes of living so
accurately? I had no idea.'

'Naturally I followed my father's wishes,'
Madelyn said, attempting to look demure. It was
amusing to tease her ladyship and not reveal her
mother's insistence on modern closets.

'Most dutiful,' Lady Brondesbury said faintly.
She seemed uncertain whether to be appalled or
approving as she left them.

'Madelyn, you really should not talk of such
matters,' Louisa whispered. 'Privies! Fumes!'

'I do not care, they think me odd anyway. Have we stayed long enough, do you think? I want to review the work the decorators have done before they start again tomorrow.'

'Yes, I think so. It will be assumed we are going on to another reception.' Louisa looked as though she was glad to be able to escape, Madelyn thought, feeling more cheerful than she had in days.

'Your post, my lord.' Eight days after the Dalesford soirée, Tanfield, his manservant, placed a small salver beside Jack's breakfast plate. 'More coffee, my lord?'

'No, thank you.' Jack reached out and flicked over the letters. Most were addressed to Mr Jack Ransome but a few had *Lord Dersington* above the address. It felt very strange. Lord Dersington had been his grandfather, then his father. Not his brother, though: Roderick had held the title for such a short time that it had never seemed to be his.

But now it *was* Jack's and, after a long discussion with Charlie Truscott, and the best part of a bottle of brandy between them, he was using it and the word was spreading, along with the news that he was to marry Miss Aylmer.

In the past week Tanfield had mentioned it to all the tradesmen and told his fellow valets and menservants in the club-like public house they patronised in the back streets of Mayfair. That would reach their masters by the first cup of coffee the next morning. Charlie had promised to gossip in all his clubs and at Tatt's, and it had not taken long for the less stodgy newspapers to pick it up.

Jack glanced at the *Morning Post*, which always ran a hotchpotch of gossip beneath its formal Court and Society items.

A collision occurred on St James's Street at midnight on Wednesday, when two young gentlemen of title, in a condition of elevated spirits owing to intoxication, attempted to roll in barrels down the hill towards the Palace. It is understood that three broken limbs ensued and that the casualties were removed to the nearest Watch House.

It appears that the Earl of D—n has finally resolved to pick up the burden of the coronet that fell from the hands of his late brother after so tragically short a time and has resumed the title amid much speculation.

Large sums were wagered and lost on Mr Percival Bromidge in a hotly contested foot race against Maurice 'The Footpad' Jennings over ten miles in Newmarket yesterday. The favourite...

So, he rated more highly than a foot race, but was apparently of less interest than drunken antics in St James's Street. After that, however, the news would most definitely be all over town.

The post included two pages of moralising on the *Duties Owed to Your Position*, from his Great-Aunt Hermione, who expressed herself thankful that he had come to his senses at last, and several invitations from hostesses who had in the past either taken little interest in him, or had cut him comprehensively. Apparently his lack of lands and wealth was slightly mitigated by the title. He found their hypocrisy did little for his dark mood.

The last letter addressed with his title was from Madelyn. It was short and to the point.

Miss Aylmer presents her compliments to Lord Dersington and wishes to inform him that the ground floor of the St James's Square house has been restored to its former decorative state, should His Lordship wish to view it.

As Miss Aylmer notes that Lord Dersington is now using his title she would appreciate some intimation of His Lordship's intentions in regard to his projected marriage and his immediate plans for the weeks following, in order to ensure that she is adequately equipped for all eventualities.

Jack re-read the note with a grudging amusement. *If His Lordship had any clear idea of what he wants to do about this wedding, let alone the weeks after it, he would be glad to inform you, Miss Aylmer.*

His immediate instinct was a special licence and a wedding in the drawing room of the town house. But deeper thought told him that the only way to deal with the interest this was going to arouse was to brazen it out with a lavish, full-scale society wedding. *If anyone accepts the invitations.*

Quite what Madelyn would say to that, he could only guess, but he supposed the time had come to discuss it with her.

He finished his coffee and strolled into the room he used as a study. He rented the first floor of a house in Ryder Street off St James's Street and it gave him a living room, a bedchamber and dressing room, the study and a room for Tanfield. The retired valet who ran the house with his wife provided cleaning, coals and breakfast and, with notice, other meals as required. It suited Jack very well and he suspected that living in the space of the town house, let alone any of his other properties, was going to feel very strange.

He trimmed the nib of a quill with his penknife while he thought, then dipped it in the inkwell and wrote rapidly.

Lord Dersington presents his respectful regards to Miss Aylmer and proposes calling on her this afternoon at three of the clock to discuss those matters to which she referred in her obliging communication.

He dusted it over with silver sand and reached for the sealing wax. He could be just as pompous as she, if provoked.

Chapter Nine

Madelyn sat alone in the drawing room with one eye on the clock and fought with the now-familiar flock of butterflies that seemed to have taken up permanent residence in her stomach. Would Jack approve of the restoration of these rooms? Was he going to have made plans that she would hate for the wedding? Would he kiss her again?

'Do I want him to?' she said out loud as the clock struck three and there was a brisk knock on the front door. Yes, she did want Jack to kiss her. She also wanted to run away back to Kent because none of this was becoming any easier. The noise of London, the crowds, the constant need to be what she was not, to watch every word and action, rubbed on her nerves until she could scream. She was still treated as though she was some exotic and faintly dubious sideshow, a subject for curiosity rather than approval even though she was received and no one was actually unkind.

Learning to be what her father had demanded had been so much easier. She had grown up with it, grown into it, and she loved the castle and her garden and her safe world out of time. As long as she did not displease her father all had been well and there was none of the cold disapproval or the sudden explosions of anger that she dreaded so.

But now she had to learn to please an entirely different man, one with whom she would be living on intimate terms. She had soon realised that Jack's position in the polite world was ambiguous at best and that whatever he did, let alone marrying her, was going to provide enormous entertainment and scandalised gossip for the *ton.* She was increasingly fearful that she could not face it. Yesterday she had felt so panicked when she woke that it had been a physical effort to get out of bed. Only the strange and unsettling discovery that she could become angry, that she could use that anger and direct it, stopped her packing her bags and fleeing back to Kent.

'Lord Dersington, Miss Aylmer.' Partridge opened the door with a flourish.

'Thank you, Partridge, send in the tea tray, if you would. Good afternoon, Lord Dersington.'

'Madelyn.' He took the hand she had held out for him to shake, but bent to kiss her cheek. It took her by surprise and she moved, their lips brushed and she jerked back, breathless.

'Jack. How good of you to call. Would you like to inspect the restoration of the rooms on this floor?' She was braced for him to find fault and, like a visit to the dentist, would rather have it over and done with as soon as possible.

He looked around. 'This seems much as I recall it from the old days. Shall we look at the study?'

He held the door for her and again when they reached the study. Madelyn held her breath and forced herself not to gabble nervously to break the silence.

'This looks familiar,' he said slowly as he walked to the desk and took the chair behind it. 'But there is something…'

'The curtains? I tried to match them as closely as possible because the old ones were badly faded in patches.'

Jack closed his eyes, placed his hands palm-down on the leather top of the desk. 'The curtains seem perfect. No, it is—'

'The books? I expect they are not exactly arranged as they were, I'm afraid.'

'No. Not that.' He opened his eyes and smiled and she let out the breath she had been holding. 'The smell.'

'What should it be?' Madelyn asked as she sat down in the old armchair, knees decidedly wobbly with relief and the impact of that smile.

'Lemon and beeswax polish,' Jack said, eyes closed again as though to conjure the memory better. 'Lavender. Pipe tobacco.' He opened a drawer and poked among the contents. 'Ah, yes.' The battered round brass tin he laid on the desk was difficult to open, but it yielded at last. 'This has been in here so long it has become dry and the scent has gone. Ah, well,' he said as he dropped it back into the drawer. 'Not everything lasts. Thank you for this. I apologise for my loss of temper over the changes.'

'It obviously means a lot to you,' Madelyn ventured, watching not his face, but the long fingers moving in a gentle caress over the battered desktop.

'Sentimentality. Foolishness.' Jack stood up abruptly. 'Shall we return to the drawing room? The tea will be getting cold.'

'Of course.' Men did not show their softer emotions and were embarrassed if they did let something slip. She had noticed that, even with her very limited experience of the sex. When Jack had said *foolishness* he had meant *weakness*, she was certain.

Madelyn was rather proud of her skill with the teapot and all the fiddling business of mote spoon and lemon slices. Presumably it was a tribute to her new-found ability that Jack did not even seem to notice. It began to dawn on her that acquiring all this new expertise was going to be a thankless task—no one would remark on it unless she made some ghastly error.

Like cleaning the house, she thought. *No one remarks upon it unless it is not done.*

'Is anything wrong?' Jack put his cup down on the little table beside the chair. 'You sighed.'

'Did I? No, nothing is amiss.' She made herself sit up straighter and tried to put aside the unsettling thought that she was erasing all traces of her former self and that she was the only person who would notice. Or care. 'We were to discuss the wedding.'

'I thought St George's, Hanover Square.'

'That is very fashionable, is it not? And quite large?' She had driven past it with Louisa one day after shopping in Bond Street.

'Yes, it is both. And I intend filling it with guests.'

Madelyn dropped a slice of lemon into her teacup, creating a small tidal wave. 'But I hardly know anyone. I mean, I have met dozens of people, but they are not friends.'

'If invited, they will come out of prurient curiosity if nothing else,' he said. The smile that twisted his lips now was hard and cynical. 'I will invite everybody who is anybody—I am related to most of them one way or another, after all. The last thing I want is to begin this marriage giving the impression that it is something we want to hide. We make a noise, a splash. We give them enough to talk about that they will cease to make snide comments about eccentric fathers and landless noblemen.'

Madelyn nodded. That sounded sensible, even though her instinct was simply to go to the nearest church, armed with a licence, and marry there with the sexton and the verger as witnesses. 'And a wedding breakfast here?'

'Yes, just a small affair. We can seat thirty in the dining room. How long will you need to organise your trousseau?'

'Two weeks?' Madelyn hazarded. The modistes that Louisa recommended had her measurements already and she had undergarments and accessories enough.

'Excellent. I will go and make the arrangements immediately and send out invitations.' Jack grinned so unexpectedly that she found herself smiling back at him. 'I must engage a secretary immediately. This sudden change to conventional life is making a great deal of work. Which reminds me, the wedding gown should be from the best dressmaker—the ladies' journals will send artists to make sketches outside the church and it will all help in our campaign to win you acceptance.'

'Yes,' Madelyn agreed. 'The very best, of course.' As she spoke she remembered the drawings she had made when she had dreamed of her wedding day, when she had dared to hope that she would marry a man because she loved him, not for the sake of a bloodline.

What had she done with those sketches, those swatches of fabric and pieces of lace? Her first instinct when her father had told her that under no circumstances was she going to marry some country squire's son—and one whose grandfather had been an iron master, just to make things worse—had been to throw them on the fire. But she had folded them away at the bottom of a chest in a small gesture of defiance.

She had met Richard Turner in the orchard, their special place, and told him what her father had said. They would elope, he declared. But the next day he was not there, only a servant with a note. His father had received a letter from hers. If they married, she would be cut off without a penny and Squire Turner, appalled that his only son, who was expected to make a prudent marriage, should have offended the most important man for miles around, had threatened the same thing.

Squire Turner decreed that Richard would one day marry Tabitha Arnold, whose father ran several hundred sheep on the marshes. It was a good match and a suitable one. He and his true love could go and find a cottage to starve in or they could obey their fathers.

Madelyn had been willing to risk the hovel, but Richard was not prepared to see the woman he loved pulled down by marriage to him, he said. They must obey.

Now she looked at her distorted reflection in the silver teapot and felt the hurt that had faded long ago flood back. Yes, she would obey the man who now controlled her future, obey in everything but this. She would have a wedding day on her own terms. She would behave as he wished, but she would look as she wanted.

The room swam in front of her eyes.

Nerves, she thought. *But I must to be strong or I am going to vanish altogether.*

'And what do we do after we are married? Do we stay in London?'

'I think it best to let the gossip we are about to stir up die down again. If we are away for a few weeks, then perhaps we can return as Lord and Lady Dersington, not John Lackland and Castle-Mad Aylmer's daughter.

'We will go down to Dersington Mote. I must pick up control of the estates. Your man Lansing tells me that the tenant at the Home Farm is on a short lease, so I must see about terminating or renewing that, depending on what I think of him. I understand that the house is under dust covers.'

'It proved rather difficult to let,' Madelyn admitted. 'When I decided that I should marry I told them to stop searching for a tenant.'

From the narrowing of Jack's eyes, she expected him to say something about her searching for a husband instead, but all he did remark was, 'The place is less than welcoming, as I recall. Possibly not the perfect place for a honeymoon, either, now I come to think of it. I am sorry.'

'Please, do not apologise. It is hardly as though this is a love match, is it? I cannot imagine that you wish to stroll through the gardens hand in hand while we gaze into each other's eyes.' It came out sounding harsher than she meant, but she did not know how to soften it.

I am going to spend the rest of my life with this man, she reminded herself. *Somehow I have to learn how to compromise without becoming completely lost.*

'No, indeed. In that case, I imagine it will be perfect,' Jack said pleasantly after the smallest of silences. 'I am sure we will find plenty to occupy ourselves from breakfast time until dinner.' He stood up and placed his cup on the tray. 'I must bid you farewell and get on with organising this wedding and increasing my staff. I will let you know as soon as I have a confirmed date.'

She stood up and he very properly kissed her cheek and smiled and let himself out into the hallway before she could ring for Partridge. All perfectly amiable, Madelyn thought as she heard the front door close.

So why do I feel as though everything is wrong?

No, I do not want to stroll through the gardens hand in hand, Jack thought savagely as he walked around the square towards Piccadilly. *No, I am not going to pretend we are in love and that we will spend a week or so billing and cooing and* making love *and telling each other the secrets of our hearts.*

Madelyn was refreshingly honest about this. Yes, that was definitely the right word—refreshing. As a bucket of ice-cold water over the head was refreshing. He had no need to pretend feelings that he did not have and he need not worry about wounding Madelyn's feelings, either. She had made it abundantly clear that this was all about giving her the family she desired while obeying her father's wishes.

So why did he feel as though he had been kicked in the teeth just now? Surely he was not such a coxcomb as to believe that she would have fallen for him after half-a-dozen business-like conversations and a few kisses, he thought, taking off his hat as he took the short cut from Jermyn Street through St James's churchyard.

He tossed a penny to a crossing sweeper and made his way across Piccadilly, turned left and was walking past the entrance to Albany before he stopped to wonder where he was going. What he should be doing was hailing a hackney to the Inns of Court to get a licence or calling on the vicar of St George's. Instead, he realised, he was making for Manton's. Jack shrugged. There was no reason why not—he had time to look at a new shotgun or culp a few wafers while trying out a pistol, he told himself. Have some fun before the shackles of matrimony closed around his wrists, and by the time the bill arrived he would be a wealthy married man.

Two of his acquaintances were lounging in front of the counters when he reached the gunsmith's shop in Dover Street. Viscount Carston greeted him absently while squinting along the sights of a duelling pistol the assistant was showing him. His companion, George Cary, grinned maliciously at the sight of Jack.

'What's this I hear—using the title and marrying an heiress? My dear chap, whatever has come over you?'

'Respectability and the onset of middle age,' Jack said. 'I swear I found a grey hair the other day.'

Carston snorted and handed the pistol back to the man behind the counter. 'I'll take them. Have them sent round, will you? You're younger than me, Ransome, and I don't feel the urge to hurl myself into parson's mousetrap, even for an heiress.'

'You've got three brothers,' Jack pointed out. He realised that no one knew Madelyn's dowry included his lost lands. Was that going to make matters better or worse? Better, he supposed—at least he would be seen to have a very personal and understandable reason other than her wealth for marrying the eccentric Peregrine Aylmer's daughter.

'Come and have a cup of coffee in Franklin's.' Cary nodded towards the coffeehouse opposite. That was unusually friendly for him, but then,

Jack reflected, Cary did like to be abreast of all news, the more scandalous the better. 'Tell us all about it—are we invited?'

'But of course.' It occurred to him that these two might be useful, because he had been wondering how to deal with the fact that Madelyn had approached him, had suggested the marriage. It was well known that she had been secluded in her castle, which meant it was highly unlikely they would have met. For her sake he wanted it to appear that he had proposed, not that Miss Aylmer was desperate for a husband.

They settled into a booth, ordered two pots of coffee and one of chocolate to satisfy Cary's sweet tooth. 'I'd been thinking about buying back some of the family land,' Jack said. No point being coy about it, they knew perfectly well that his father and brother had lost the lot. 'Turns out that Aylmer had bought everything up, so I went down to Kent, met Miss Aylmer and was decidedly intrigued.' That mangled the truth and the order of events somewhat, but it was close enough. 'She accepted my suit and here we are.'

'Interesting lady,' Carston said carefully, not

meeting Jack's gaze as he stirred sugar into his coffee. 'Met her at the view at that new gallery in Spring Gardens the other day. Finding London a novelty, I gather.' It wasn't quite a question.

'I believe so. Very loyal to her father, kept house for him, but the man was somewhat demanding and kept her close to home,' Jack said easily.

'So she is not an antiquarian like him, then?'

'Good lord, no. Can you imagine me marrying a bluestocking?'

'No,' Carston said drily. 'I can't.'

Jack returned the smile. It did not matter that everyone knew he was marrying Madelyn purely for her spectacular dowry, just as long as no one realised that she had proposed to him— that would complete the picture of the eccentric bluestocking he was trying so hard to avoid. And it would hurt her pride, he knew that. For all her calm, businesslike approach, she had not found it easy to do what she had, he was coming to realise.

It was confusing to discover that he cared as much as he did for her feelings—she had made it clear enough that, as far as she was concerned, emotions did not enter into their marriage. Jack gave a mental shrug—doubtless it was basic gentlemanly instincts, nothing more. He hoped not: the thought of finding himself developing a *tendre* for the prickly, awkward female was distinctly unnerving.

He shifted on the thinly padded bench and gave his smile more of an edge. 'I know I can rely on my friends to make Madelyn feel at home in London.' And if they made her feel unwelcome, the smile promised, no doubt they all, like Carston, owned serviceable duelling pistols.

But this encounter only served to emphasise the fact that everyone was going to be looking out for unconventional behaviour from Castle-Mad Aylmer's daughter and, for the sake of her future, and of the children, come to that, he needed to make certain that no one found anything peculiar about her. Vouchers for Almack's, presentation at Court, the hope of finding suitable female friends—all hung in the balance.

Then he had a nightmare premonition of whispers eighteen years in the future: *charming girls, but their mother is most singular...*

'You all right, dear boy? You've gone quite pale,' Cary said.

'Just the headache of all the wedding preparations,' Jack said. 'Do either of you know where I can find a reliable secretary?'

Chapter Ten

Jack called the next day to ask whether the fifth of September would suit and to take her walking in Green Park. Madelyn agreed that date would be most acceptable and went to put on a light spencer and the quite ridiculous little straw hat that Louisa assured her was just the thing to wear with it. She studied the effect in the mirror, decided that she looked like a sunflower with a rather large bee on top, and joined Jack in the hall, resigned to appearing ridiculous.

'Do you like my new hat?' she enquired, striving for the light and frivolous tone that Louisa assured her was correct for conversing with gentlemen.

'A delightful piece of nonsense. I imagine the price is in inverse relation to the size,' he observed as Partridge opened the door and handed him his own hat.

'How did you know that? I imagine the cost of men's headwear is not related in any way to that for ladies.'

'I have purchased the occasional piece of fripp— Do look, is that Byron over there? No, of course not—foolish of me. He left the country in the spring.'

As she had never read any of the poet's works, the attempt to distract her failed. 'You were about to say *frippery*, I think. For mistresses, I imagine.' It had not occurred to her until that moment, but of course Jack must have had them. He probably still did, which was a lowering thought. But why should she care? He did not pretend to love her, he would undoubtedly be discreet and not embarrass her by flaunting an irregular arrangement. *But I do care.* It was a matter of self-respect, nothing more.

'I can assure you,' Jack said stiffly, 'I am not involved with anyone at present and, naturally, would not be after our marriage.'

'Naturally? I thought most men kept mistresses if they could afford to, married or not. My father certainly did.' Mrs Milbanke, a most obliging widow in the next parish, to be exact.

'I would not.' It sounded as though his teeth

were gritted, although as they were negotiating the traffic in Pall Mall it was difficult to tell. 'And even if I did, a lady ignores the situation.'

They arrived safely on the other side of the road and turned towards St James's Palace.

'That must be difficult if she has any affection for her husband,' Madelyn said after a while.

That was received in silence. Jack nodded towards the red brick mass of the Palace. 'The Palace is where Drawing Rooms are held. I will take you to be presented to the Queen after we are married. It will be a debut for both of us, the first time I will appear at Court using my title.' Mistresses had clearly been dismissed as an unsuitable topic for conversation.

'Louisa showed me a picture of Court dress. I thought she was in jest, but apparently I am supposed to wear something like a vast bell and have ostrich plumes in my hair. Quite idiotic.'

'I suggest you do not make that observation to Her Majesty. Console yourself with the thought that you will not be alone in your discomfort. I have to carry a *chapeau bras*, trip myself up with a ridiculous little dress sword and try not to rip my best silk hose with it. Tradition, my dear. I would have thought you would approve of it.'

Interesting... The survival of the past into the present. Do the lords and ladies putting on their Court dress think of it like that? I wonder. And if it is acceptable to dress in a palace as though one was in 1750—

'Look out!'

Madelyn found herself lifted and swung to one side. She arrived back on the flagstones with a bump. 'What on earth?'

Jack pointed at the pavement. 'The milkmaids bring their cows to graze in the park this way and do not clear up after them. You need to take care where you put your feet. It might be best to take my arm if you are going to walk along with your head in the clouds.'

'Thank you.' Madelyn slid her hand under his proffered elbow. 'You are very strong to lift me like that.'

'That, I believe, is my cue to say that you are as light as thistledown.'

'And mine to reply that I do not believe such nonsense for a moment,' she retorted. 'But Louisa would tell me that I must behave as though I do not have a sensible idea in my head, so please imagine I have just simpered and said something like, *Oh, my lord, you flatter me and what wonderful muscles you have.*'

Jack made a sound that was suspiciously like a snort of laughter. They had reached the edge of the Park and he began to point out landmarks. 'This is Queen's Walk. The reservoir is up there next to Piccadilly, and you can see the Queen's House across the grass in the distance in that direction. Which way would you like to go?'

'It is very green. Oh, there are the cows you were talking about, over by the trees. But where is Rotten Row? Is that not the fashionable place to promenade?'

'That is in Hyde Park.' Jack pointed at a far corner. 'That way.'

'I see,' she said, suddenly realising why they were in this particular park. 'You do not think I am ready to be seen in such a place as Rotten Row?'

'It is always crowded, always confusing if you do not know everyone and I think you would find it easier to take in the scene and recognise people if you were in an open carriage,' Jack said easily. 'Besides, I want to drive you, not walk, and I am negotiating for the purchase of some horses at the moment. You would prefer to appear behind a good team drawing a high-perch phaeton to a pair of job horses and a hired carriage, would you not?'

It was perfectly reasonable, but why did she have the feeling that Jack was tactfully attempting to control her movements? *Probably because he is,* she thought. Louisa had let slip that it was not she, but Jack who was deciding which invitations they would accept, who Madelyn was to be introduced to. Now she was not to be allowed to wander at will in Hyde Park, it seemed.

'You do not trust me, do you?' Madelyn said, suddenly desperate. The dizziness was back, the feeling of panic, of being trapped. 'You do not trust me to learn my lessons, to behave as I should, to fit into this world. You think I am going to be an embarrassment to you because I am different.' She should stop, but she could not. The words seemed to be tumbling out, taking a shortcut between her feelings and her tongue without any intervention by her brain. 'Well, if that is how you feel there is an easy remedy. We call off the wedding.'

Jack stopped and turned to face her. She braced herself for his reaction, but he only sighed and said, quite calmly, 'You feel it is too soon, that we are rushing things? We could wait another month. Would that help?'

If he had been surprised, or confused or even angry, she might have thought again, but his patient tone made it clear he was managing her, being forbearing. Patronising her.

'What would *help* would not to be betrothed to you,' Madelyn said.

All around them there were the sounds of the Park and London going about its noisy everyday business. Children were screaming with delight as they played beside the reservoir, a cow lowed mournfully from the trees, the sound of wheels and hooves on the stones drifted over from the surrounding streets, but where they stood was only a bubble of appalled silence.

Then Jack drew in a deep breath through his nose, released it and said, 'You have signed documents, you have allowed the preparations to be made, you have said nothing as the news of our impending marriage spread through London. And now you want to go back on your word. If I did that, you could sue me for breach of promise and have an excellent case, but perhaps you have been so far removed from the real world that you have no more idea of honourable behaviour than you have of how to dance the quadrille.' He turned around.

'Where…? Where are you going?'

'Preparing to escort you back to St James's Square so you can write to your solicitors.'

'Are you going to sue me?' He had expected to receive all his lands, he had swallowed his pride and begun using his title again. Why wasn't he angry? Then she saw his eyes and took a step back.

'There is no need to flinch from me, Madelyn. I no more strike women than I sue them. Shall we go?'

'It is better than an unhappy marriage, surely?' she stammered, not moving.

'Why would it be unhappy? I have assured you that I would be faithful, that I am not violent. What has changed since you asked me to marry you? Perhaps you were misinformed about my character and you have found that I gamble or drink to excess or that I am cruel to animals, perhaps?'

'You know I have not. What has changed is that I now realise just how little you trust me, that you will supervise me and order my life and… I might just as well be shut up in my castle again. At least there I was my own mistress,' she finished saying desperately.

'I would really prefer not to be having this discussion in the middle of Green Park,' Jack said, still sounding perfectly calm, perfectly reasonable, exceedingly dangerous. 'Would you please go and sit on that bench over there for a minute, Madelyn? There is something I must do.'

Madelyn walked to the bench, sat down, decided that she was not going to faint, or be sick or burst into tears because even she knew that was unacceptable within screaming distance of the Palace. It would be nice to stop shaking, though...

She watched Jack walk up to a tree. He stood there looking at it, then kicked it. Hard. Then swore. She couldn't hear what he said, but that kick must have hurt.

Then he walked back, rather obviously trying not to limp. 'I appear to have two things you want: my bloodline and the ability to father children, although you will have to take that on trust because I have no offspring to demonstrate my capacity. You have two things I want: my lands and yourself.'

'You... You want *me?* I mean, you *want* me?'

Then she felt herself blush as she realised just what he meant by *want.*

'Yes. I am presumably out of my mind because I have never come across a more provoking and difficult female, but, yes, I find that I do.' He was frowning at her in a most unloverlike manner, but then, he was only talking about carnal matters, not pretending for a moment that he had fallen in love with her.

'You are certainly not trying to charm me,' she said with a pitiful attempt at a laugh.

'No, I know perfectly well that will not work. You are not an idiot and we are not in love. You say I am patronising and controlling, but let us be clear about this. My father and brother behaved in ways that shame me and I am considered dangerously radical, a traitor to my class, for not using my title. Your father was considered by most people to be wildly eccentric and by a significant minority to be not in his right mind. If we are going to marry and raise a family, then I am not going to begin it by encouraging anyone to think that you are as strange as your father or that I am truly a radical or as ramshackle as my family. We can relax once we are married, but if we start with a scandal—or, perhaps worse, being a laughing stock—then it will be hard to make up the ground.'

'I see,' Madelyn said. 'I understand. But I am not going to do anything scandalous. I find small talk very difficult, but I do not talk about history or the castle except to answer questions. I have been careful not to say anything to make people think I am trying to be an antiquarian. Most people seem kind, or at least, they tolerate me. I just want you to trust me to do my best, Jack.'

He says he wants me. Perhaps he is telling himself that to sugar-coat marrying me for the land. He might be pretending, of course, but when he kisses me he does seem to enjoy it. So do I, she admitted to herself. *But I do not look like the pretty girls and the elegant ladies he must encounter every day, so why should I believe he wants me? Perhaps, when he is kissing me, he does not have to look at me and, being a man, that is enough.*

'If I leave everything to Lady Fairfield's judgement so the two of you can make decisions about social events and what you still have to learn, will that make a difference to how you feel?'

'I…'

'Because I warn you, if you jilt me at the altar

steps, Madelyn, there will be hell to pay—for both of us. And let us be clear about something else as well, if we are to talk of trust. I give you my word of honour that I will be faithful, that I will look after you and protect you and any children we may have. I am my father's son, but I will not squander or risk my family's future. In return I expect fidelity and honesty. There will be plain dealing between us or there will be nothing. Is that clear?'

She had been on the verge of apologising. But not in the face of threats. 'Very clear,' Madelyn said as coolly as she could manage. It came out sounding icy. 'Yes, I will continue on that basis. You have my word that I will be faithful and I will deal honestly with you.'

All she got in return was a sharp nod of acknowledgment and a silent return to St James's Square, but as her anger cleared, she wondered if she had just glimpsed something very important about the man she was to marry. Trust and honesty mattered a great deal to him.

Lady Fairfield was more than happy to receive a note from Lord Dersington to say that he would leave his intended's social engagements entirely to her own judgement. She was less happy when Madelyn told her that she need not trouble herself to accompany her to the modiste to order her wedding dress and the other gowns for her trousseau. 'Harper will be adequate company, Louisa. I really do not want to drag you out to sit in shops for hours when you have a cold coming.'

Louisa sneezed daintily into a minute handkerchief, dabbed at her pink nose and sighed as she reached for a very much larger linen square. 'Harper does have very good taste, I will admit, and we have already prepared the list of what you need. Provided you have a footman in attendance, I suppose you can do without me.'

'Where do I purchase a domino?' Madelyn asked. 'That is the correct thing to wear for a masquerade if one is not going in fancy dress, is it not?'

'Why, yes. Harding, Howell or the Pantheon Bazaar would be best. It is not as though one need worry about fitting for size. But which masquerade is that, dear?'

'We had an invitation yesterday to accompany Lady Hitchin and her party, do you not recall? It is in two days' time.'

'No, no. Carola Hitchin is not at all the thing! Received everywhere, of course, but she is fast to a fault and those sisters of hers are as bad. Any masquerade that she thinks of attending will be a sad romp. I was about to reply and regret that we had another engagement.'

'Oh. I see. Never mind, I will write. You really ought to be resting, Louisa, not worrying about correspondence.'

And so Madelyn did write to Lady Hitchin. As she had not said what she would reply, accepting the invitation for herself alone was not exactly a falsehood, she told her conscience. Nor had she said that she would not buy a domino to wear. Her immediate thought on hearing about the fancy dress was that she should go in medieval costume, but that, she realised, was exactly the sort of thing that Jack had meant. People would be reminded about her father. But she was determined to go to the masquerade and use her own judgement about how to behave. Jack thought she could not navigate the shoals of London society: she would prove him wrong, show him that she could be trusted to behave appropriately.

* * *

Louisa's cold developed rapidly and she took to the couch in her bedchamber with a pile of handkerchiefs, peppermint lozenges and a stack of all the lightest and most frivolous novels the circulating library at Hatchard's could find for her.

And that, without any necessity for evasions or downright lies, gave Madelyn all the freedom she could wish for to interview a very bemused modiste and place a large order—free of Harper who was dispatched to purchase everything on a long list of trifles from handkerchiefs to silk stockings, including a wide range of soaps and lotions, veils and chemises. 'I'll not need you while I'm looking at patterns,' Madelyn said airily. 'And you'll know far better than I where to find all these small things. But leave anything we can obtain from the Pantheon Bazaar—I have heard so much about that I want to see it for myself.'

Harper had thought nothing strange about Madelyn buying a domino, 'Just to have handy in case of an invitation, you know,' she said airily.

'And you'll need a mask, Miss Aylmer. There

are some very pretty silk ones here. Velvet looks lovely, but it gets so hot and you don't want a shiny nose.'

'I assume masquerades are respectable entertainments,' Madelyn remarked as they waited to be served at a crowded counter.

'Some are, some aren't, Miss Aylmer. Those like the public ones where anyone who can afford it can buy a ticket—why, they are very unseemly, from what I've heard. You get women of a *certain profession,* if you know what I mean. And flash types and all sorts.'

'But the kind a society lady would go to?'

'Oh, those would be perfectly acceptable, I should think.' Harper finally reached the head of the queue. 'Here's a stool for you, Miss Aylmer.' She turned to the assistant. 'The tray of masks for the lady to try, if you please. The silk ones. And a selection of dominos.'

So that was all right, even if Louisa did not approve of Lady Hitchin. But, Madelyn rationalised, if she was received everywhere, she could not be that bad. And she had said she was making up a large party, so it was not as though Madelyn would be forced into her close company for the evening once she had paid her respects to her hostess. Presumably the masquerade itself was at the home of one of her friends.

The problem was to leave for the evening without alerting Louisa, but the doctor—summoned when none of the housekeeper's infallible home remedies made any impression on the sore throat and cough—ordered early nights and complete rest for a week. Louisa tottered from couch to bed and Madelyn went to her desk and penned a note that she sent off to Lady Hitchin with a footman.

The reply came by return. Lady Hitchin would be delighted if Miss Aylmer joined the party at her house before they set off and sent the afflicted chaperon her best wishes for an early recovery. Madelyn decided to keep that to herself, at least until tomorrow morning.

Now, all she had to do was to choose a gown, have Harper do something with her hair that would not be completely flattened by the hood of the domino and she would be ready. The thought of the mask gave her a really surprising amount of confidence. Or perhaps she was simply becoming used to London social events.

That was good. That would show Jack that she did not care for his opinion or need his patronising attempts to manage her life.

Chapter Eleven

'Kicking over the traces, are you?' Charlie Truscott lounged in the far corner of the carriage. Jack could not see his face in the darkness, but he could tell he was grinning. 'Never thought you'd agree to come to this with me.'

'I've been to masquerades before,' Jack tried not to snap.

'Not ones like this one, not when you've got a fiancée,' said the man who was supposed to be his best friend and who was about to end up on his backside in the streets of Chelsea if he kept on needling. 'Still, if you are going to become a respectable married man, then it is good to get these things out of your system.'

Jack growled.

'They say that Grover has arranged for an entire troupe of opera dancers to attend, just to liven things up,' Charlie persisted, then, failing to get a rise with that remark, added, 'Shouldn't you be squiring Miss Aylmer around somewhere this evening?'

'We do not live in each other's pockets.'

'That's plain enough. I've never seen a cooler lover than you. If you want my advice—'

'Which I do not.'

'—you'll write a poem or two, send flowers, show the lady off in the best box at the Opera House. Otherwise she will find a handsomer buck than you now she's loose in London and has had a chance to look at the field.'

'Madelyn is not *loose* in London, she is not assessing men like racehorses and the wedding date is all fixed, as you well know. If you think this is part of the duties of the best man, let me tell you, you are wide of the mark.' Charlie said nothing. Jack knew he was being drawn into filling the silence and found he could not resist the bait. 'You know perfectly well that this is not a love match. Miss Aylmer and I have agreed on a mutually beneficial marriage, which is something that happens every week of the year. Damn it, she'd wonder what I have on my conscience if I started playing the lovesick swain all of a sudden.'

'I'd have thought you wanted more.' Jack made an impatient sound and Charlie said, 'Look, perhaps it isn't my business, but I've known you since we were scrubby lads and you're my friend and you've had a pretty rough time of it with that family of yours.'

Rough time? Yes, that summed it up. A father to whom loyalty and honour meant nothing, who would exploit his own parents in their sickness and old age and whose idea of raising the son who was the unneeded spare was a mixture of neglect and brutality and a brother who was a selfish boor.

'Don't you want something…*more* for yourself than this?' When Jack still said nothing Charlie blurted out, 'Surely *she* wants more?'

'Miss Aylmer wants a family and someone who will allow her to fulfil her father's wishes for her future. She has made it quite clear that she does not want me fussing over her.' He would be faithful, he would protect her and their children as he had promised. He had given his word and it was important to him that he keep it, that his wife would be true to her promises, too.

'What if she falls in love with you, Jack?'

'There is no chance of that,' Jack said and

could have bitten his tongue. That had come out sounding far more bitter than he had intended. He had begun to wonder what it would be like if Madelyn did see something in him beyond a suitable pedigree and the unpleasant suspicion that he was becoming fond of her was keeping him awake at night. Love was the most dangerous investment in the world and the riskiest.

Fondness or not, a thoroughly inconvenient state of arousal was making him restless in those long, dark hours.

Damn it, she's not pretty, she's as prickly as a basket of cross cats and she's got some very peculiar ideas. You're all about in your head, you fool.

Charlie's silence convinced him that he had betrayed more than he had intended. 'Where did you say this confounded masquerade is? We've driven almost to Richmond.'

'Nowhere like that far. Can't be much longer now. Grover's hired a barn in the middle of a field and fitted it out, by all accounts, as a cross between a sultan's palace and fairyland. The man has just inherited all his great-uncle's money and the old man was as rich as Croesus, so he's set on celebrating in style.'

Charlie was right. They turned off the King's Road, lurched along what felt like a cart track and heard the noise ahead of them grow in volume. Music, laughter, the sound of coachmen shouting at each other as they tried to deliver their passengers and turn around, shrieks of excited laughter.

'This do, my lord?' The driver leaned down. 'Can't get any closer. Looks as though there's space over there to wait, if that's all right with you?'

Jack, still without his own town coach, had hired one for the week and was finding the driver amusingly casual. 'Yes, here, get yourself some refreshments, but I'll want you sober when we get back.'

'We're promised acrobats, fire eaters, stilt walkers and a special performance by the dancers,' Charlie said as the driver tipped his hat and drove off. They made their way towards the huge barn that was surrounded by canvas tents and covered carts. 'And there's the fire eater.' He pointed to where a man in a skin-tight crimson costume painted with yellow flames was causing a gaggle of cloaked figures to screech in horrified enjoyment as he plunged a burning brand down his throat.

'Let's get inside,' Jack said. 'I could do with a drink.' He wanted to drink too much, dance, flirt with completely disreputable women—preferably small, pert brunettes—and drink some more. If the evening ended with a brawl or a kiss, then that would be quite welcome, too.

Sir Horatio Grover, newly endowed with a baronetcy and a fortune, had ordered boxes to be constructed around the sides of the barn, dance floors to be laid inside and out and a podium set up for the band. Colourful boxes lined the inner dance floor and a stream of waiters were darting about the guests with laden trays of glasses and bottles.

'On your right,' Jack said and, as though they'd rehearsed it, Charlie snagged a bottle of wine as he swept up two glasses. 'There's an empty box over there. Let's take it and survey the scene.'

'Good idea.' Charlie handed him the bottle, vaulted over the front of the box without troubling with the rather rickety half-door, then took glasses and bottle while Jack followed him, neatly managing to catch up his domino before the long folds tripped him. 'Got a mask?' He produced one and tied it on, transforming himself from amiable man-about-town into something slightly sinister. 'Better wear it. You don't want reports getting back to the lady that you've been out ogling opera dancers.'

'Speaking of which—' Jack nodded towards the open doors of the barn where a flock of scantily clad young women were running in. He tied his mask, made himself comfortable on the bench and poured the wine as the band struck up. He settled back, lifted the glass and prepared to banish all thoughts of problematic fiancées for one night.

The dancers were…adequate, he supposed. Pretty enough, but then the magic of stagecraft meant that any of them would be transformed once they were on stage. Skilled enough, too, although not up to the standard of the big theatres and the Opera House. All around them men were cheering and staring and making lewd remarks and he felt a wave of distaste. They were not even becoming excited over reality, just masks that hid a number of young women, all of whom were different under that paint and glitter. Some plain, some pretty, some intelligent, some less so. Some kind and some, no doubt, spiteful or dishonest or sulky.

Why that should make him think of Madelyn he had no idea, unless it was because she was putting on a mask now she was in London, pretending to be something she was not in order to fit in. That was an uncomfortable thought and he splashed more of the thin red wine into his glass. These ordinary girls had been transformed into fairy-tale creatures. He was asking a woman from a fairy tale to become ordinary and conventional.

Which is necessary. Those dancers have to make a living to survive in the real world, and Madelyn has to exist in it, too.

The acrobats who followed the dancers were a welcome distraction and so were the masked figures who drifted past their box, many in fancy dress, others in dominos. Some—both male and female—stopped and leant against the low front wall and made eyes at the two men sitting inside. Charlie, safely masked, flirted back cheerfully with either sex, but refused all lures to step outside the box.

'Idiot,' Jack said mildly when yet another comely youth sauntered off, laughing at one of

Charlie's more outrageous sallies. 'You know you don't like blonds.'

The floor was being cleared for dancing. 'Shall we?' Charlie suggested.

'I am not dancing with *you,*' Jack said, ducking as his friend, whose real interest was very firmly with the opposite sex, feigned a playful punch. 'In fact, I am not dancing at all. I shall lounge here like a pasha surveying his court and watch you making a fool of yourself out there.'

'You do that. See that pretty little redhead by the band? Watch the master at work.' Charlie took a gulp of wine. 'I'll send a waiter over for a food order if I pass one before I persuade my mysterious beauty to dance with me.' He let the half-door close with a bang behind him and wandered off into the crowd.

It was, Jack considered, more entertaining to watch than to fight one's way amid the crush of sweating, over-perfumed bodies. Charlie was as good as his word and a harried waiter arrived with a tray of plates for Jack to choose from, then fought his way along to the next box.

Several King Henry the Eighths passed by the box along with some overheated knights in knitted chainmail, four daring Grecian maidens whose scanty costumes were at least keeping them cool and quite a flock of medieval damsels. Having had the opportunity to observe the nearest anyone was going to come these days to the real thing, Jack was unimpressed. They didn't know how to walk in those gowns any more than Madelyn did in modern dress.

The cheese tartlets were surprisingly good. Jack brushed crumbs off his domino and noted that more than half the guests were wearing the same thing, rather than indulge in the complexities of fancy dress.

Now there was someone who moved beautifully. He watched appreciatively as a tall masked figure glided past in a deep green hooded domino. She walked as Madelyn had done in her medieval gown, the heavy folds of the cloak brushing the ground around her.

Then she turned to listen to someone in the group she was with and Jack saw her face, half-hidden by a spangled green silk mask. He saw the pale skin, the pure oval of the face, the long nose and shot to his feet, the plate of pastries falling unheeded to the floor with a clatter.

Madelyn here?

What was Louisa Fairfield thinking of? This was no place for a respectable lady without the escort of a gentleman, let alone an unmarried one. Then the orchestra reached the end of a piece and he heard Carola Hitchin's unmistakable braying laugh.

Hell's teeth, Lady Fairfield's lost her mind.

He slammed back the door to the box just as a masked highwayman stopped in front of Madelyn, swept off his tricorne in a low bow and, quite clearly, asked her to dance.

A party of young bucks, already half-seas under, pushed past in front of Jack, but not before he saw Madelyn's reaction to the highwayman. She recoiled in shock or dismay, then his line of sight was lost as he barged his way through the drunks, ducking a swing one took at him and elbowing another in the ribs to make him give way.

At least she'd been properly shocked at being accosted. Besides, he comforted himself, her dancing lessons had hardly begun, she wouldn't want to risk making an exhibition of herself in public yet.

He reached the edge of the dance floor as the

band struck up a waltz and there, in the arms of the highwayman, was the tall lady in green, held close, her face tipped up to his. They were quite obviously talking. Jack took a step and a heavy hand came down on his shoulder, caught him off balance, spun him around, then a fist made contact with his chin and he went down among the feet of the dancers.

She should have listened to Louisa, Madelyn realised within minutes of arriving at Lady Hitchin's large town house. By medieval standards, or modern, the woman was brash, loud and outrageous and her party of friends was no better.

I should have said I felt faint the moment I arrived, Madelyn thought as she found herself caught up in the rush for the waiting carriages and then bundled into the third one with a jester, King Henry VIII and three giggling young women, two of whom were wearing Grecian costume. It was a tight squeeze.

'Come and sit on my lap,' Henry invited and two of the Grecian girls promptly obliged, which at least made more room and meant that the jester's thigh was no longer pressed so insistently against hers.

'Where are we going?' Madelyn asked when, after ten minutes, it was obvious that they were not about to arrive at some fashionable Mayfair venue. In fact, she was fairly certain they had passed through a toll gate, although it as difficult to see past the jester's strange belled headdress.

'Chelsea,' King Henry said, glancing up from his appreciative study of the neckline of the girl on his lap.

'Chelsea?'

That was miles out of town, surely? Two or three at least. She could walk that far, and often did, but not at night, through strange streets and in evening slippers. How much had she in her reticule? Not a lot, just a few coins for tipping the maid in the ladies' retiring room, that was all, but perhaps she could find a cab to take her home and send one of the footmen out to pay when she arrived.

The thought sustained her until she realised that they were not in a busy little village, but bumping along a cart track through a field.

Now she had no idea where she was, how to get back…

In other words, you are stuck with this party and let that be a lesson to you. At least Jack will know nothing about it and I will not repeat the mistake of ignoring Louisa's assessment of people in future.

It was not much comfort.

The barn, which is what the venue turned out to be rather than the ballroom she was expecting, was crowded, noisy and colourful. But Madelyn began to relax a little when she remembered that her mask shielded her identity. At least her reputation was safe. All she needed to do was to stick closely to Lady Hitchin until it was time to leave. That proved easier thought than done.

'Excellent, there is dancing,' Lady Hitchin said, urging her party towards the dance floor.

'I think I will just watch from over there,' Madelyn said, casting round for somewhere to sit.

A masked highwayman stopped in front of her, his skin swarthy beneath the mask. 'Fair beauty, I salute you. A dance or I demand the forfeit of a kiss.'

'Certainly not!' She gathered the folds of her domino around her as though they would be some kind of protection. 'Go away at once.'

He stared at her as she spoke. *'Madelyn?'*

'Richard? Richard Turner?' Her lost love from the past here, in front of her, in the middle of this appalling masquerade?

'Yes! By all that's wonderful, Madelyn— I never thought I would see you again. Dance with me.'

As if in a dream she let him draw her on to the dance floor, take her in his arms. 'What—?'

'It is a waltz. You waltz, don't you, Madelyn?'

He did not wait for her denial or seem to notice her gasp of shock at being taken in his arms, although at least that stopped her tripping over her feet as she was swept around. 'Richard, what are you doing here?'

'I am here with new friends, finding my feet in England again—and then there you were. I would know your voice anywhere. But how is it that you are in London?'

'You know that my father is dead?'

'Yes—' He broke off to navigate a path around a group of revellers. 'I heard eventually, but I was in India. I have only just got back and the

Company—I am with the East India Company, you see.' He pulled off his mask to reveal his familiar features, but transformed by a tan, still dark despite the sea voyage.

In India? Had he taken his wife with him?

'Is your wife here?'

'No. I'm not married,' he said, twirling her around so she almost fell against him.

'Richard, I really do not know how to do this dance!' He laughed and slowed down. 'I thought you were going to marry the daughter of that rich grazier.'

'Tabitha Arnold? We found we could not suit and her father died before the contract was signed, so we were able to agree not to go through with it. I found it very hard to think of another woman after you and I think she realised it.' The expression in his dark eyes made her catch her breath at the sudden unhappiness there. 'I joined the Company to defy my father, but I soon realised that it suited me and that I couldn't go on living in the past.'

'You are happy with the life?' He had an air of confidence and competence she had not seen in him before.

'I love it. And I have an aptitude for trade and

money that I had never suspected before. I specialise in taking failing concerns and turning them around, rooting out the discrepancies in the books, dealing with incompetence and corruption. Fascinating—or at least I find it so.'

It was so good to see him happy.

I should tell him I am betrothed.

Madelyn lost the train of thought as her hood slipped off. She grabbed at it, but failed to catch the slippery silk as Richard jolted to a halt. 'What the devil?' Most of the dancers had stopped abruptly as a fight spilt out on to the dance floor.

A tall man slid across the boards on his back, then stood up, wrenched off his domino, lunged back into the fray, grabbed another man by the shirt front and felled him with a blow that left his nose streaming blood.

Women shrieked, applause broke out among some of the male onlookers and Richard said, 'What a right hook!'

The bleeding man scrabbled backwards across the floor, ending up virtually at Madelyn's feet, and the tall man strode after him, fists clenched, then stopped abruptly, his gaze locked with hers.

She was suddenly aware that not only had her hood had slipped back, but that her hair was coming down. Which would not have been so dreadful if it was not for the fact that the masked man facing her was unmistakably Jack Ransome.

Chapter Twelve

Jack stepped over his prone opponent as though the man had been a fallen branch on the ground. 'What the devil are you doing here?'

'The lady is dancing with me.' Richard pushed her behind him, his arm out to shield her. 'If it is any of your business, sir.'

'It is my business all right. She is mine.'

'She was mine first. And she dances with whoever she likes, not some brawling lout.' Richard went for Jack, fists flying.

Madelyn knew nothing about fighting, let alone boxing, but she could tell, in the few crowded seconds, that Richard was absolutely no match for Jack. It took two punches and he had joined the groaning, bloody-faced man on the floor.

Before she could tell either of them what she thought—if she had been able to collect together any coherent words—Jack picked her up, slung her unceremoniously over his shoulder and marched off the dance floor.

'Put me down!' It came out as a muffled squawk. She could struggle, but what if her mask came off? Madelyn seethed and clenched her hands into his coat-tails to keep her balance.

There was some pushing and shoving, then the volume of noise dropped and she was aware of another figure, domino swirling about him, beside them.

'I say, Jack, that's a bit drastic. I find they usually come quite willingly if I ask nicely, but then I suppose some females go for the swashbuckling approach. You should have worn a Viking costume.'

'Shut up, Charlie. It was this or drag her kicking and screaming. Go and find the carriage, will you?'

Now they were out of the tent and away from the crowd she could try to get free. But kicking and struggling would be useless and undignified and besides, even if Jack did let her go, how was she going to get home? She could hardly go back to Lady Hitchin and explain that she had just been carried off the dance floor by her betrothed, not without starting a shocking scandal. Madelyn went limp and concentrated on being as heavy and awkward as possible. She heard the sound of carriage wheels and a horse snorted.

'What are you doing up there?' Jack said.

'Thought you'd want a bit of privacy.' The other man's voice came from above them. Presumably he was on the box with the driver.

Madelyn was bundled into a carriage, struggled to sit up as the door closed and succeeded just as it lurched off. 'You—'

'What the blazes did you think you were doing in there?' Jack demanded, throwing himself down on the seat opposite her and dragging off his mask. The carriage had no internal lamp so she could not see his face, but he sounded furious.

'I was enjoying myself.'

Until Richard appeared and then I was startled and happy, and now I am worried.

Was Richard all right? He had never been someone for getting into fights, and Jack had clearly both outweighed him and had the skill he lacked. That blow had been a hard one. He had said he was with friends—someone would look after him, she reassured herself.

'Unchaperoned, unprotected—'

'I was with a party and, no, I am not going to tell you who or you will be unpleasant to them, as well.' She couldn't imagine what Jack would say if he realised just what company she had been in and the fact that he would have every reason to be annoyed was no help at all.

'Unpleasant? It was the Hitchin woman, I assume, I heard her cackling. I find my betrothed at a vulgar masquerade with the raff and scruff of the town, cavorting with some buck who says you were his—what do you expect me to be? Pleased?'

'Well, you cannot talk.' Madelyn made a futile attempt to control her hair. All the pins seemed to have been lost and it was spilling over her face. 'You were brawling like someone in a common alehouse and struck my friend.'

'I was trying to get to you and some drunken buck took exception to letting me past. He hit me first.'

'So that makes it all perfectly all right, of course. Then you hit Richard.'

'I'll tear his bl—his confounded head off if he tries to interfere with you again. Who is he?'

'An old friend who is just returned from India.'

'He's more than that,' Jack said grimly. 'What was Louisa thinking of, allowing you to come here?'

'I employ Lady Fairfield to give me advice. She is not my keeper—unless you are paying her in addition to be my jailer. She is in bed with a bad cold.'

There was a fulminating silence as the carriage turned sharply left and reached a rather better surface than the cart track.

'You asked me to trust you. You told me you were not going to do anything scandalous.'

'And I have not. I am masked, there was no one there who recognised me—'

'Other than your lover.'

'He is not and never has been my lover,' Madelyn retorted.

Oh, but there was a time when I wished he was, so much.

'I am trying to find out about London life, seeing it for myself. Learning. If you had not started a brawl, no one other than Richard would have known who I was—' She broke off. But that was not quite true. 'How did *you* recognise me?'

For a long moment she thought Jack was not going to answer her. 'Your height and the way you moved in that long cloak. You moved like that when I first met you wearing that medieval gown. You walk like a queen.'

'Oh.' The compliment, even if he had said it as though he was furious with her, was still startling. *Like a queen?* Suddenly it was very important that Jack understood the truth. 'Richard being there was a complete coincidence. He recognised my voice when I refused his request to dance. When we were much younger he proposed marriage, but my father refused to allow us to wed and he went away, to London, I think. I haven't seen or heard of him for years, I give you my word. And he is only just returned from India.'

'Do you love him?'

She wished she could see his face. 'I did once. It was a long time ago.'

Love does not last that long without anything to feed upon, does it?

'Is he married now?'

'Apparently not.'

'Do you want to marry him?'

'I… No, of course not,' Madelyn answered without thinking. Was that true? It had to be, she had given her word to Jack that she would wed him and to marry Richard would be to go directly against her father's wishes. But that denial had come without any forethought. It *was* the truth, she realised. 'We are different people now. Goodness,' she added in an attempt to make light of it, 'he positively dragged me onto the dance floor.'

'I dragged you *off* the dance floor,' Jack said in the tone of a man determined to be fair if it killed him.

'You carted me off like a sack of grain, to be accurate,' she retorted. 'Or some Viking warrior intent on pillage.' For some strange reason the anger had drained away for both of them. She could sense Jack's long body relaxing back against the battered old squabs.

'It was a masquerade, after all,' he said mildly, but there was an unsteadiness in his voice as though he was trying not to laugh.

'True. Jack… I am sorry. I knew it was not a respectable affair as soon as we arrived, but I did not know how to get back without waiting for the whole party. It has been a useful lesson,' she added meekly.

Then he did laugh, a snort of amusement. 'Do not overdo the sweet reasonableness, Madelyn.

I believe you. Is this Richard of yours going to be a problem?'

'I should not think he would call you out,' she said. She shivered at the prospect.

'That is not what I meant.'

'I cannot believe he would make any trouble. He is my friend and has no reason to wish me ill. Although he may well resent you hitting him, he wouldn't gossip about me. Besides, I doubt he moves in the circles where it would matter if he did,' she added to reassure him. 'He is with the East India Company.'

Jack stood up, head bent under the roof of the carriage, and shifted across to sit by her. He took her hand in his. 'I find I have a strong desire to kiss you, Madelyn.'

'Why?' she asked, refusing to let her fingers relax into his hold. Her pulse had only just settled down to a steady rhythm after the drama of the last few minutes, now it began fluttering in earnest. 'Because you have been fighting or because you want to stake your claim?' Men were sometimes very *basic* in their reactions, she had observed.

'Because you are looking very desirable to-night.' His thumb stroked up the inside of her bare wrist, a whisper of sensation. 'Because I am going to marry you and I found you in another man's arms and, yes, that makes me feel possessive.'

Her pulse slowed in time to the insidious caress. She could tell herself that she did not want him, because to admit that she did only left her open to rejection and heartbreak. But if he truly did desire her, if what he had said in Green Park and just now was not simply honey to sweeten her so he got what he wanted—his lands—then perhaps there was some hope for this marriage as more than a businesslike exchange.

'If I asked to take you home with me to my rooms tonight, would you come?' His voice was low, muffled because he was kissing her shoulder now, pushing aside the heavy fall of her hair with his mouth until he reached the bare skin.

Yes. 'I do not know.' Would he think less of her if she agreed? Perhaps this was some sort of test. She wished she understood men better in real life, not just from observation and reading. If she had grown up with brothers and their friends, if she had had an ordinary upbringing with her own friends and their families, perhaps she would be more confident.

'You know what I am asking?' Jack lifted his head. 'You do not seem to have any female relatives to talk to about…intimate matters.'

'I know,' she murmured. When she had decided to take the step of marrying she had sought out the information, put what she could glean from books together with observation of nature. She had facts, but facts said nothing about feelings. 'Should we not wait?'

'If that is what you want, of course.'

Jack said it as though it was entirely reasonable that she should choose, not as though he was humouring an irritating female. She knew *that* tone of voice—she had heard it often enough from her father to her mother, and its absence now reassured her.

'Yes, then. I think,' she added, suddenly unsure.

You have to do it some time and you want to. You know you do. You want him.

Somehow, after coming face to face with Richard, who had been her ideal man for so long, her certainties had been shaken. He had changed, or perhaps she had, but he was not Jack and she knew which of them she desired.

'It is not a legally binding contract, agreeing

to sleep with me,' Jack said. 'You may change your mind, you know.' He shifted on the seat and took her in his arms, and Madelyn was suddenly very aware of his breathing and his heat and the strength of him.

'I thought that was very displeasing to a man,' she ventured as his arms tightened.

'Many things are in life. One just has to learn to live with them,' he said and kissed her.

She had thought that she liked Jack's kisses, even when they ended up with the pair of them in an embarrassing and undignified heap on the floor in front of the servants. Madelyn discovered that in a jolting, rather musty carriage in the dark, that she felt far more than liking. This was need and heat and shivery, alarming, sensation and there was no need to think about what to do because all she could do was hold on to Jack, kiss him back and feel.

And she was feeling in the most unexpected places. She knew what his mouth on hers would be like and of course she knew that the secret places between her legs were involved in the matter, but all of her skin tingled, her breasts ached and she realised with horror that she was becoming positively wet *there*. And yet all he was doing was kissing her open-mouthed, his tongue stroking in to tangle with hers, to explore. Then one hand moved down to her right breast and began to caress, and she gasped and pressed into his palm, then gasped again in shame at what she had just done.

Jack made a sound that was almost a laugh. It vibrated against the swell of her breast. 'You like that?'

'I… It… Do it again.'

'So that was *yes*, then.' The simple evening gown she had put on under her domino was cut low, and his fingers were exploring the edge now, then sliding round to the side. 'How does this…? Ah, like that.' There was the sudden release of pressure around her ribcage as the bodice sagged. Somehow, she realised, Jack had found the fastening of her short stays as well as the bodice.

'Jack!' Instead of stiff fabric and slightly scratchy lace her breasts were cupped in warm hands and his tongue was teasing her nipple. *'Jack.'*

It was… It was wonderfully indecent, terrifyingly good and she wanted it to stop and to go on for ever as she felt his hand slide over her garter, onto the warm flesh of her inner thigh and then, gently insistent, higher.

He was kissing her again and one hand was on her breast and the other one *there* and surely it should hurt? Surely she should be fainting with shame? But all she could do was writhe in his arms, arching into that knowing touch, seeking something because this could not go on or she would…

Fall into pieces, Madelyn thought hazily as she came to herself.

She was sprawled across Jack's thighs, her legs apart, her skirts hitched up, her breasts exposed to the cool night air, and she had probably died and gone to heaven.

'Jack,' she murmured, then felt the carriage turn and slow.

He flicked back one corner of the window blind and swore under his breath. 'Damn. We're back in St James's Square already. Charlie must have told the driver to come straight here.'

'We are not going to your rooms?' There was more to lovemaking than that, she knew—there were all the things she had been expecting, in fact.

'I think not. Here, let me help you.' He had her stays in place and fastened and her bodice straight, apparently by touch, then brushed down her skirts as the carriage drew to a halt. She felt it sway: someone was getting down from the box.

Jack moved to sit opposite her as the carriage door opened.

'I'll go and knock, shall I?' said the voice of the man who had been with Jack at the masquerade. 'Oh, no need, they were watching, the door's opening.'

In the light from the torchères by the door, Madelyn tugged her domino around herself, pulled up the hood over her tumbled hair and risked a glance at Jack. He looked very pale in the flickering light and his breathing seemed rather heavy, but from his expression, she thought, no one would have guessed that he had just reduced one virgin to a state of quivering ecstasy in a jolting carriage.

Would he be even better in a bed? she wondered, blushing at her own thoughts, then even more at the recollection of just what had happened, of how she had reacted.

'Will you drop me off, Ransome? Or are you going in?' the other man was saying. He was still masked.

Madelyn fumbled for her own, then gave up

when she could not find it. Anyway, walking into the house masked was as good as announcing to the staff that she had been at a masquerade and word would get back to Louisa as fast as they could whisper it.

'No, I will not be stopping, I will just see the lady to the door, then of course we can detour past Ryder Street.' Jack sounded as casual as if he had been out for a drive in the park.

'Enough for one night, I think,' he murmured as he helped Madelyn descend on shaky legs to the pavement, then gave her his arm up the steps to where her butler was holding the door. 'Evening, Partridge.'

'Good evening, my lord…ma'am.'

'Goodnight, Miss Aylmer,' Jack said. He took her hand, raised it to his lips and kissed her fingers. 'Thank you for a memorable evening.'

'You will call tomorrow?' She tried to make it sound casual, as though he had just escorted her home from a respectable party.

'Yes, of course. We have so much to plan. So much left undone. Sleep well.'

Chapter Thirteen

Sleep well! Jack grimaced as he walked carefully back down the steps to the waiting carriage and climbed in. *I've given myself a sleepless night, but by God, it was worth it.*

He sat down opposite Charlie and saw his friend had let the blinds up. As the coach rumbled off, light from the streets flickered in and out of the interior of the carriage, illuminating Charlie's blandly neutral expression. The other man was doubtless quite well aware of what had just happened—in fact he was probably imagining something rather more than what had actually taken place. There was nothing to be done about that now and Charlie was no gossip. Besides, Jack was marrying the lady.

But she had been no lady when she had come apart in his arms, he thought, somehow managing to control his smile of triumphant discovery.

Madelyn had been sheer, abandoned woman and any doubts he might have had about that aspect of the marriage were well and truly laid to rest. In fact—

'Your face,' his friend said with a grin.

'What about it?' Jack put up one hand and rubbed at his mouth. Madelyn had not been wearing lip stain or powder… 'Ouch.'

'You are going to have a fine bruise on your chin tomorrow and probably a fat lip into the bargain. If I'm not mistaken, it is swelling nicely now.'

That's the kissing, Jack thought. 'The other fellows will look worse,' he said, not troubling to sound modest about it.

'Fellows? I only saw you hit one.'

'There was some buck who'd had a few too many as well as the man dancing with Madelyn.'

'You can't go around hitting every man who dances with your fiancée, Jack. She'd gone to a masquerade, presumably intending to dance, someone asks her—'

'She knew him before.'

'I imagine Miss Aylmer knew many gentlemen before she met you and that it was all perfectly respectable.' Charlie seemed to hesitate, then took the plunge. 'Forgive me, but I was under the impression that your contract with Miss Aylmer was in the nature of a mutually convenient and beneficial one, not the result of a love match.'

Jack grunted.

'So why are you exhibiting all the symptoms of rampant jealousy?'

'Natural possessiveness.' Jack thought he managed that reasonably well. If he didn't understand it himself, he was certainly not going to have Charlie speculating. 'And concern for her reputation. Madelyn should not have been there and she knows it. I was quite reasonably annoyed.'

'Of course you were,' Charlie said with the suspicion of a laugh in his voice. Before Jack could suggest that he get out and walk he added, 'This will do. Set me down here, will you?'

Jack rapped on the coach roof, more than glad to be alone to come to terms with what had just happened. 'Goodnight.'

The door banged closed on Charlie's cheerful farewell and the carriage creaked into motion again.

It wasn't that he had not known that he wanted

Madelyn, even if he had not been able to define exactly what it was that he found attractive about her. At first he had assumed it was the exotic setting of the castle, that magical garden, her strange, composed grace in that sweeping gown. An enchantment, he had told himself. But now he found himself wanting her even when she was gawky and ill at ease in a modern gown, warily negotiating the strange new world she found herself in.

He wanted her even when she put herself and her reputation at risk and ended up in the arms of some old flame into the bargain. What had this Richard meant when he had said that she was his first? Not her lover, not in the full sense of the word: he could recognise innocence when he encountered it. And not her official betrothed, if her father had refused to countenance the match.

So, first love. It was all in the past, a doomed boy-and-girl romance. And he had reacted so strongly out of fear for her. All perfectly normal, in fact, and not the worrying symptom of anything dangerous like…an infatuation.

Jack shook himself like a man waking up from a bad dream. Feeling any deep emotion for one's wife when she had none for you would be a pitiable state of affairs. He was nothing to Madelyn other than a convenience. She had picked him off a list, had him investigated as though he was a business she intended investing in, then cold-bloodedly summoned him to make a thoroughly unmaidenly proposal.

True, she seemed to desire him. Or perhaps she was simply a sensual young woman who was not actually repelled by him. He should be grateful she was not expecting more from him, because he was not at all confident he knew how marriage should work. The only happy one he had ever observed had been his grandparents' and that just in its last years when whatever trials and storms it had gone through were softened by time and familiarity and years of mutual support.

Madelyn had floated upstairs, hampered by her trailing domino and the sensation that her knees were made of sponge. That carriage ride had been a revelation. Embarrassing in retrospect, of course—how would she be able to face Jack again after *that*? But wonderful all the same. Of course she was right to be marrying him. Richard and she had outgrown each other, grown apart. She would not think about him any more.

In the event she need not have worried about embarrassment. When she next saw him Jack seemed briskly practical about arrangements for the wedding, politely involving her in his plans for spending time at Dersington Mote afterwards. On days when he did not call he sent his new secretary, a painfully earnest young man named Douglas Lyminge, who was the younger son of a younger son of a connection of the Duke of Worthing and therefore forced to earn his own living in some socially unexceptional manner.

Madelyn liked him for all his awkwardness and earnest frowns. For his part he seemed so determined to prove his worth that she rather thought he would carry her down the aisle if that was what was necessary to bring the wedding to a successful conclusion, she thought, three days before the date set. Mr Lyminge had just left after delivering the final terrifying list of acceptances, and Partridge came in with his silver salver.

'The morning post, Miss Aylmer.'

Some invitations, an upholsterer's account and a painstakingly written note from the maid who had been left in change of Mist at Beaupierre Castle.

Madelyn read it with a smile and picked up the remaining letter. The handwriting was faintly familiar, but she could not place it. She broke the seal and read the single sheet.

It began abruptly.

Madelyn, my dear,
You do not have to marry Dersington, a total
stranger, just because your father wished it.
He has gone and it is your life now to live
as you please.

I will not try to influence you more, but
should you ever need me you have only to
let me know and I will do everything I can
to help.
Your old friend,
Richard Turner

Madelyn dropped it as though it had become hot in her hand. What was he saying? That he loved her still—or that he truly was her friend and that was all? The address was in the Adelphi buildings, which she understood were respectable apartments close to the river. Richard was clearly staying in London for a while at least.

She sat and stared at the sheet of paper. She had agreed to marry Jack and it would be dishonourable to turn to Richard for anything, whether it was friendship or advice or even something more. She would acknowledge the letter, but tell him she could never see him again.

She sat at her desk and penned a quick note. She thanked him for his concern, hoped that he had not suffered lasting hurt defending her, assured him that she was marrying of her own free will and wished him every happiness for the future.

I think it best if we do not meet again.

She signed it *Your affectionate friend* and sealed it well, then rang for a footman. 'See this goes with the next post, please.'

There, that was done and it was the right thing, she was sure. As the door opened and Louisa came in Madelyn took Richard's note, folded it small and tucked it into her stationery folder. 'Good morning,' she said, smiling. *The past is the past and has gone.*

* * *

She had not allowed herself to think of Richard and everything continued smoothly. But now, on the day of the wedding, all Mr Lyminge's hard work was about to come to disaster because of one major omission—and the fact that the bride's attendant was in a state of near hysteria. Madelyn stood in the lobby leading off the west door of St George's Church while Louisa Fairfield wrung her hands and declared that they would be a laughing stock, that Madelyn would never gain vouchers for Almack's let alone be received at Court and that Lord Dersington would faint dead away at the altar rail.

'Never mind that, Louisa,' Madelyn said, wanting to shake her. 'Who is going to give me away? We never thought of that, any of us.'

Lady Fairfield merely moaned and sank onto a convenient bench.

'I could give myself, I suppose, but I have no wish to cause comment,' she said. Louisa whimpered faintly. 'Any *further* comment,' Madelyn amended. 'Mr Lyminge, you must do it.'

The secretary, who had escorted the bride from St James's Square to ensure there were no last-minute problems, recoiled visibly. 'I could not possibly. I am no relation, I am merely an employee.'

'In that case, either go and find a member of the congregation or some passer-by off the street,' Madelyn said, desperate now. 'Frankly, no one is going to notice, are they? They'll all be staring at me.'

'Very well.' Mr Lyminge, presumably determined to prove himself worthy of the very generous salary his new employer was paying him, or perhaps resigned to instant dismissal, offered his right arm. 'Let us go, Miss Aylmer.'

Madelyn took a deep breath. 'Yes, come along, Louisa. The door, thank you.' A bemused verger flung open the double doors, Louisa blew her nose and fell in behind and the three of them began the slow walk up the aisle.

Jack faced forward, gaze fixed on the brass candlesticks on the altar, on the carved wooden panelling behind. He was not going to turn and look anxiously down the aisle as though worried that his bride might not appear. Nervous bridegrooms were stock figures of fun and he was on his dignity. The church was packed: delicious curiosity and the scent of scandal had brought acceptances from duchesses to deacons. Beside him Charlie muttered under his breath as he checked, once again, that he had the ring safe.

Then the organist stopped the vague twiddling music he had been playing and launched into something purposeful that Jack did not recognise.

'And we're off,' Charlie said. 'And coming down the home straight—'

Jack kicked him unobtrusively on the ankle.

Then behind them the murmuring began, gathering in volume, loud enough to be clearly audible above the organ. Charlie glanced over his shoulder, froze and said something that earned him a furious glare from the Vicar.

Jack turned, stared, found he could not think of the words.

Madelyn was walking up the aisle on the arm of his secretary, who looked as though he was about to be thrown to the lions in the arena. That was enough to cause a stir, but he hardly registered it when he looked at his bride. Madelyn was wearing a gown of heavy leaf-green silk, deeply gathered under her bust and falling to sweep the ground with a hem of some white fur. It was cut in a swooping vee to display her shoulders and décolletage and the deep, dark, primitive glow of the ancient necklace that lay against the curves of white skin. Her hair was loose around her shoulders, straight, unconfined except for the garland of leaves and white flowers that sat like a crown on her head. In her hands, framed by the medieval bell sleeves, she held white lilies and the soft green of ferns.

She might have stepped straight from a tapestry on a castle's walls. There should be a slender greyhound by her side or a lion or, Jack thought wildly, a unicorn.

Madelyn looked magnificent, beautiful, powerful. Magically strange. Jack's body tightened. He felt his pulse kick up, even as he absorbed what a disaster this was. Her gown was scandalous, wildly eccentric and she was defiantly throwing society's expectations back in its face. She was her father's daughter, defying Jack's wishes—his *instructions*, damn it.

Those in the congregation who were not staring at Madelyn were looking at him. He forced his expression into neutrality—a smile was beyond him—inclined his head in greeting, then turned back to face the Vicar.

The rustle of silk dragging over tile, the click

of Lyminge's boot heels, Charlie fidgeting from foot to foot… Then out of the corner of his eye he saw a sweep of green, the sheen of golden hair and caught the scent of lilies over the ecclesiastical odour of damp and dust and prayer books.

'Dearly beloved…' The Vicar's voice trailed off in the face of the whispering from the wedding guests. *'Dearly beloved,'* he repeated with some emphasis.

Finally, the congregation fell silent. Jack wondered fleetingly whether the bridegroom turning on his heel and marching off down the aisle would actually make anything worse. He could always keep going. As far as Bristol, perhaps. Catch a ship, end up in America…

Yes, it *would* make things worse. Much worse. And he had given his word to marry Madelyn. He might be Jack Lackland, but he was still a gentleman. For better or worse. *Worse.* For richer or poorer. *Richer.* With my body… *Yes, that at least. And she looks…wonderful.*

Somehow, they reached the end of the service without disaster, which was a miracle considering that he felt utterly distracted and goodness knew what Madelyn was thinking. Revenge? Was that what this was? he wondered as they turned and she took his arm to walk back down the aisle.

I insisted that she conform and this is her reaction—to make me a laughing stock?

They reached the steps outside the church and stopped, looking down on the crowd in St George's Street. There was the usual scrum of passers-by, idlers, the curious. There were faces he recognised who were runners for the newspapers and who would be scribbling descriptions for the Society columns and, as he had predicted, there were two artists, rapidly sketching. The new Countess of Dersington's wedding gown would feature in *Ackermann's Repository* next month and, in all probability, in *La Belle Assemblée* and *The Lady's Monthly Museum,* as well. Every last, outrageous, medieval detail of it.

Jack took a deep breath, fastened an expression suitable to a bridegroom on his face and led Madelyn closer to the edge of the steps. 'Let the artists have a good look at you, my dear. You want your gown to be accurately depicted, do you not?'

She went, obedient to his direction, and when he glanced at her she was smiling serenely, lovely in the sunlight, a figure out of time magicked there by some mysterious force. 'You do not mind?'

'I mind like hell,' Jack said pleasantly. 'But if you think I am going to make a scene about it in public, you are very much mistaken.' He turned more towards her, the picture of a devoted husband, blinking at the reflected light from the barbaric splendour of the rubies and emeralds on her breast. 'That will do, the carriage is here, we have guests to entertain and, I imagine, gate-crashers to repel once word of this gets around.'

'Jack—'

'Not now.' He helped her mount the step into the open landau, settled her on the cream-leather upholstery and sat beside her. At least that spared him from having to face her directly.

'I wanted to appear my best for you and I know I cannot do that in modern clothes.' Her voice shook, despite the defiance, and he turned to look at her fully for the first time. Her chin was up, the smile was fixed in place, but tears sparkled in the corners of her eyes.

'What flatters you does not matter,' he said harshly. 'And keep your voice down,' he added low-voiced with a jerk of his head towards the coachman and the grooms. 'Conforming matters, fitting in matters, appearing normal matters. I thought you understood that. Or do you think this marriage is all about gaining a legitimate father for this brood of children you want and then retiring to your confounded moated castle to raise them in your fantasy land?'

Meanwhile I am left, the Earl who married this mad woman for my lands... No, she is not mad, just far cleverer than I realised. Cleverer and more ruthless.

'I am now a countess,' Madelyn said in an intense whisper. 'I am a rich countess with my own sense of style. I do not care what they say and neither should you. I thought you were too proud and too independent to care.' The tears had gone, replaced by a look of sparking anger. 'After all, you are the man who had the nerve to reject his own title out of a sense of self-esteem.'

I had years of seeing my father and brother behave with utter self-indulgence, neglecting their lands, ignoring their tenants and every one of their responsibilities. Years of sneers over my lack of land and now the knowing looks and admiring remarks about my skill at catching an heiress. How much worse will it be as word spreads that by marrying you I have restored my inheritance? Do you think I want to continue to be an outsider? Do you think I do not want my children to grow up ordinary, accepted, members of society?

He almost said it all, but he was not pouring out his heart with two pairs of ears flapping on the box and another pair clinging on behind.

'We are nearly there,' Madelyn said as the landau swung out of Old Bond Street into Piccadilly. 'What are you going to do?'

'At the wedding breakfast? Smile, my dear. Smile,' Jack said grimly. And afterwards? How was he going to come to terms with a wife who so utterly failed to understand what was important? Then a cluster of crossing sweepers on the corner of St James's Street set up a cheer at the sight of the carriage and its ribbons. Madelyn smiled at them and waved and he thought, *She looks like a queen and I want her. I have made a devil's bargain.*

Chapter Fourteen

Jack was formidably angry. The very control he was exercising told Madelyn that. His smile was wider, tighter; the beautiful blue of his eyes was cold; the grip of his hand as he helped her from the landau was that of a jailer, not hard enough to hurt, but firm enough to restrain any attempt to bolt.

As though I am going to run away now, Madelyn thought. She felt sick with nerves and with the realisation that her act of defiance had gone so very wrong. She had thought that Jack would see how much better she looked in her own style, she had imagined that the guests would be intrigued, or perhaps charmed, by such a harmless choice. *It is* my *wedding day.*

But at the church the guests had reacted as though she had appeared in wild animal skins, and Jack was livid, even though, when he looked at her, she could sense desire smouldering behind the anger.

He handed her over to Louisa as though delivering a fragile, dangerous object and turned to poor Mr Lyminge, who was lurking in the hallway, not quite wringing his hands.

'It seems I must thank you, Lyminge, for rescuing us from the consequences of a serious oversight.'

'I apologise for my presumption, my lord, but there did not appear to be any alternative.'

'No, do not apologise. After all, if you had not stepped into the breach Lady Dersington would have had to give herself away.' Jack's expression when Lyminge lapsed into confused silence showed that he would not have put that past her, either.

Louisa was tugging at her sleeve. 'Come upstairs, dear. You will want to change.'

Madelyn followed obediently, but she had no intention of removing her gown, of backing down now. She would take off her wreath, have Harper re-dress her hair and go down dressed just as she was. Let the guests have a good look at her clothes and her jewels.

'Now, Harper, where is that pale yellow gown

we bought from Madame de Grange's?' Louisa was flinging open doors in the dressing room without waiting for the maid to reply.

'I am not changing, Louisa. Harper, please braid my hair into a coronet.'

'But you cannot—'

'Harper, please excuse us for five minutes.'

'My lady.' Harper bobbed a curtsy and went out.

'As you just heard, Harper recognises the fact that I am now the Countess of Dersington. I am not going to wear the new gown and, much as I have appreciated your advice and support, Louisa, I am going to make my own decisions from now on.'

'But you do not seem to understand,' Lady Fairfield protested.

'I understand that when I dress as I wish I have the confidence to face those people downstairs and to behave as I should. Please do not try to dissuade me. You have been such a good friend to me and I would hate to part on bad terms with you.'

Louisa sniffed into her handkerchief, then straightened her back. 'I will tell Harper to come back and then I will go downstairs and see what

I can do.' She put her head to one side and peered at Madelyn through narrowed eyes. 'Lady Dorothy Carstairs, who is a cousin of Lord Dersington, is one of the guests. She writes pieces for the *Repository* under the nom de plume "A Lady of Fashion". Perhaps I can persuade her that you are starting a new trend.' She peered distractedly into the mirror on the dressing table, took off her bonnet, patted her hair into place and hurried out.

'Lady Fairfield is going to see if she can bring my style into fashion,' Madelyn told Harper when the maid came in and began to unpin the wreath of flowers. She tried to focus on that and not on the memory of the nerve jumping in Jack's cheek as he had stood beside her on the steps of the church, a smile fixed on his lips.

'I think maybe that might happen when the ladies see the other gowns you've had made. They seem to be much more of a compromise between the old style and modern modes and they are very flattering and romantic.' Harper began to make two plaits of hair from the sides to form into a crown, leaving the mass of Madelyn's hair to fall down her back. 'We will have to work on hairstyles, though, my lady—' She broke off to concentrate on pinning the coronet into place. 'There now. It's a pity you'll not be back in London for some weeks because you could wear your new fashions straight away and let everyone become used to them.'

It did feel like running away now. When Jack had proposed going into Suffolk for several weeks he had intended allowing the talk about the wedding to die down, but now she had caused such a stir, Madelyn wondered if that would work. But now she must go downstairs, greet thirty members of the *ton* as they arrived and deal with their reactions. At least that would stop her wondering what Jack was going to say to her once they were alone.

He was waiting for her just inside the door of the drawing room where they would greet their guests. She could hear the sound of subdued voices from the dining room where the staff were putting the finishing touches to the wedding breakfast and there, just within sight in the hall, was Partridge in his best suit of clothes waiting to direct the footmen and announce each arrival.

'Jack—' He looked at her, frowning as though

she was a cipher he could not read, then there was a sudden breeze and the front door was opened.

'His Grace the Duke of Ospringe, Her Grace the Duchess of Ospringe, Viscount de la Salle, Lord James Howlett.'

'As Charlie Truscott would say,' Jack muttered, 'we're off.'

It was not as bad as it might have been, Madelyn concluded when the front door closed behind the last guest. Everyone had been polite, Jack had acted as though he entirely approved of her gown and only three people—all young men somewhat high flown on champagne—had asked him if he was practising jousting or had taken up falconry or had been measured for a suit of armour yet.

The ladies had been polite and curious and Lady Carstairs—'Call me Dotty, dear, after all we're cousins of some sort now'—had been the most friendly. *Probably hoping to extract juicy titbits for her column,* Madelyn thought warily. But she smiled and chatted and hoped she had managed to convey the impression that she dressed as she did because it suited her and not because she was some eccentric obsessed with the Middle Ages.

Then the Duke had asked Jack where they were going to spend their honeymoon and he had replied, 'Dersington Mote.'

'You bought it back as well as this place? Well done, Dersington, I like your attitude,' the older man said. 'Damn shame when old family properties are lost like that. Who had it, can I ask? They kept very quiet about it. My man had a look at it a while back, but heard the owners couldn't get tenants, which made him wary.' All the guests within earshot were unabashedly listening by then. Jack had expected the rumours about the estates to have spread far and wide, he had told her. Apparently not.

'It came with my wife,' Jack replied coolly. 'That and all the Dersington estates.'

If someone had said out loud, 'So *that's* why he married her!' Madelyn would not have been surprised. In a way the heavily tactful silence was worse. Jack had been right to want to leave London, she realised. They would be out of town while that was talked about and digested and he would not have to lose his temper and hit anyone, or even call them out. By the time they got back, surely a viscount's wife would have run off with her footman or the Prince Regent would have done something outstandingly stupid and extravagant and she and Jack would no longer be of much interest.

When they were finally alone she left her husband in the drawing room while she sought out Partridge and the staff to thank them for their efforts and then went upstairs to her bedchamber. It was not running away, she told herself, resisting the temptation to lock the door.

With the reinstatement of the ground-floor rooms the upper floors had been cleared of surplus furniture and had been renovated. Only the servants' rooms and the kitchen remained, but Partridge assured her that he had those in hand and that everyone was comfortably accommodated.

Now she sat at her dressing table and stared at the connecting door through into Jack's room. Behind was a room of pale cream walls above oak panelling with dark blue curtains and fine old furniture that now gleamed with polish— *lemon* polish, she had instructed the staff. There were Chinese bowls full of dried lavender on the table tops, the scent of Jack's childhood memories as best as she could recreate them. And against the wall facing the window was the bed.

Madelyn had skirted around it, not looking at it directly, on all the occasions she had been in the room ever since she had realised that this house was where she would be spending her wedding night. Dersington Mote was over eighty miles away, deep in the Suffolk countryside, a full day's drive with an early start. They would leave tomorrow morning and arrive in the evening, but tonight there was an entire evening to get through, alone with her husband. Her very angry husband.

Now she wondered whether perhaps she was supposed to wait for her bridegroom in her own bed. The only wedding customs she knew about were hundreds of years out of date, from a time where the bride and groom were led to the bridal bed by their cheering guests, some of whom stayed to witness the consummation if the couple were of high rank. Madelyn shivered. It was going to be bad enough without a bishop to observe proceedings.

Who could she ask? Louisa had left, returned to her own home. Harper was unmarried and therefore, even if she did know, it was inappropriate to ask her. She supposed she would have to ask Jack.

But even with the worry about which bed to choose, she felt more apprehensive about the evening than the night. Once they were together, surely the desire that had gripped them in the carriage returning from the masquerade would sweep them up, take them past recrimination and mistrust. But now she was faced with hours alone with a man whose pride had taken some hard knocks that day and who had been confronted with a bride who must have seemed to be flaunting every desire he had ever expressed about her behaviour.

'I will bathe and change, Harper. The half-dress evening gown, I think. And my hair in some simple style, perhaps just in one long plait.' She had worn the gown she had always dreamed of for her wedding, she had made her point that *this* was her style, who she was. She could afford to be less provocative now.

When she emerged from her bath somewhat less tense, Harper was laying out her fresh clothes. The new gown was less dramatic, although the fabric, as befitted an evening dress, was a damask silk in deep emerald green. The sleeves were tight to the wrist, the pleating far simpler than on the wedding gown, but it still brushed the floor when she walked and was cut so that it supported her breasts without the severity of the stays.

She fastened the sixteenth-century gold and freshwater pearl necklace around her neck and added pearl ear drops. 'What time is it?'

'Six, my lady.'

I am 'my lady'. Lord Dersington is my husband.

How long was it going to take to become used to that? Madelyn descended the stairs and could not help smiling at how much better she felt in the heavy, sweeping skirts and with the familiar weight of braided hair. No silly little curls to tickle her cheeks, no flimsy fabrics to flutter around her ankles and no corset to make breathing an effort.

The smile stayed on her lips when she found she had the drawing room to herself. Lord Dersington was bathing, Partridge informed her. The light supper she had ordered would be served at eight. Might he pour Her Ladyship a glass of sherry?

Madelyn had never drunk sherry and she had already learned to be wary of the bubbles and dry, deceptively light taste of champagne, but if sherry was what countesses drank in the evenings, then she would learn to like it. 'Thank you, Partridge.'

It was sweeter than she had expected and the taste was almost nutty, with fruity overtones that made her think of plum pudding. It tasted quite innocuous, in fact, and it slipped down with no difficulty at all, warm and soothing. She felt herself relaxing with the first sip. 'You may leave the decanter there, Partridge.'

Should she ring for the footman to fetch her embroidery frame? Perhaps that was rather too prosaic for a wedding night and, besides, Jack might see the designs as medieval, a provocation. On the other hand, she would never be able to concentrate on a book and Louisa had said that embroidery was a perfectly acceptable occupation for a lady. Charles, the junior footman, came when she tugged the bell and set the frame in its stand beside her, fetched the basket of wools and refilled her sherry glass. Perhaps the rhythm of setting the stitches would calm her enough to cope with Jack's reproaches with, at least, some dignity. She took another reviving sip of sherry.

How the devil was one supposed to fill the hours before bedtime under these circumstances? Tanfield, relieved of all the other duties he used to perform for Jack and now solely his valet, had produced a freshly sharpened razor, clearly expecting his master to go to his marital bed with a perfectly smooth chin, so Jack had submitted to the second shave of the day. Then he had lingered over dressing again, finally changing shirt and neckcloth and resuming the elegant suit he had worn for the wedding.

Scooping up one's bride and carrying her off to bed at seven o'clock was hardly civilised behaviour. It might be excusable for a couple wildly in love, but not as a tactic to avoid making conversation. Nor, however angry he was, could he spend their first evening as man and wife haranguing Madelyn on the subject of inappropriate wedding gowns. The wedding breakfast had not been quite the nightmare he had been braced for. Madelyn seemed to be the subject of more curiosity than outright condemnation and a marriage to reclaim his family estates had found approval from the Duke. Had he overreacted in the church? He found himself walking slowly downstairs rehearsing topics of conversation in his head as though for a difficult dinner party.

Ridiculous. Jack stopped on the half landing and absently stirred his fingers through the bowl of dried lavender on the small chest that stood there. *Lavender and lemon and beeswax polish.* Madelyn had listened when he was reminiscing in that maudlin way in the study. Listened and acted. His bedchamber and the dressing room had been comfortable and elegant, masculine yet light. Those rooms had been his grandfather's and his memory of them was of gloom and clutter and faded textiles. Madelyn's hand had transformed them without, he realised, losing their essential nature.

He felt the simmering anger that had heated his blood ever since he had turned to look down the aisle begin to fade, to turn to something uncomfortably like shame when he recalled the harsh words he had flung at her over her first attempts to decorate the house. *No taste* had been the least of it. Left to follow her own instincts she had great discrimination—he should have remembered her garden.

'My lord?' Partridge was standing at the foot of the stairs looking up, far too well trained to express surprise at his employer's odd behaviour, standing stock-still with dried lavender trickling between his fingers. 'Her Ladyship is in the drawing room.'

'Thank you, Partridge.' Jack walked down the final flight of stairs. *His* stairs, he realised. He owned this house now, owned all the estates his family had accumulated over the centuries. Lyminge would be joining them at the Mote in a day or so, accompanied by the accountant he had employed to help organise all the management across the various properties.

The thought carried him across the hall and into the drawing room with all his carefully prepared topics of conversation quite forgotten.

'Good evening, my lord.' Madelyn sat on a high-backed armless chair, an embroidery frame in front of her. As she spoke she pulled the needle through the canvas, trailing a strand of vivid red wool behind it.

Jack became aware that his mouth was open, closed it so sharply he caught the end of his tongue and stared at his wife through the haze of tears that the sharp pain produced. Madelyn looked as though she had stepped down from an antique tapestry and settled herself with her embroidery at his hearth. The deep green gown pooled around her feet, the heavy weight of her plait lay down her back like a golden rope and she swayed gracefully as she reached to set another stitch.

She is beautiful and she looks so right, sitting there. How had I not realised how lovely she is? How wrong I was to try to force her into being something she is not.

Madelyn glanced at him, apparently too polite to demand that he come in and close the door and stop creating a draught. 'I am embroidering a new set of seat covers for the dining-room chairs. They were so worn that it is impossible to see what the original design was.' She moved the stand so he could see the canvas stretched on it. 'I am using the beasts from your family coats of arms—this is the griffin from your mother's family crest.'

Jack closed the door and went to stand beside her. 'That is exceedingly clever. Did you design it yourself?' The red griffin reared up against a background scattered with tiny flowers that made it seem to be prancing in a grassy meadow. Somehow Madelyn had given the fearsome beast an amiable expression, despite its claws and the curling black tongue.

'Mmm,' she said, bending to set a stitch in one pointed wing-tip. 'I am giving all the beasts a flowery meadow as background.' She finished the stitch, stuck the needle in the margin of the canvas and pushed the frame away a little. 'I wanted to finish that wing, the shading is quite complex.'

'Don't stop, unless you really want to,' Jack said as he took the chair on the other side of the fireplace. 'It is soothing, watching you.'

Madelyn coloured up as she drew the frame back. 'I imagine you need soothing.' She stooped to rummage in the basket of wools at her feet, effectively hiding her face from him.

'That was not what I meant. I had no intention of reading you some lecture, if that is what you thought.'

Damn, now I am snapping. And lying. I had been brooding on that lecture all through the breakfast.

'This is our wedding night.'

Chapter Fifteen

From Madelyn's expression as she straightened up with a hank of black wool in her hand, a reminder about their wedding night had not been tactful.

'I had hoped for a quiet evening's conversation, a rest after a very crowded day,' Jack said, retrieving his temper. This was like gentling an unbroken mare and he was beginning to find the process of winning his wife's trust even more absorbing than that.

Madelyn was threading the new wool into the needle, peering almost cross-eyed at the little slit, her tongue protruding with the effort of concentration. Jack's body stirred. There was something very sensual and natural about that tiny glimpse of wet pinkness. She ran the tip over her lower lip, leaving a glimmer of moisture, and Jack drew an unsteady breath.

'Ah.' The wool went in the eye and she drew it through with a murmur of satisfaction that sent Jack to his feet. He took a couple of rapid strides across the room and stopped with his back to her, turning over the small pile of books on a side table while he got himself under control.

'I do not have any conversation, I am afraid,' Madelyn said. 'I have never had anyone to practise on, you see. It has not been as bad as I thought it would be at parties, because everyone wanted to ask me the same questions about the castle and Father, but I do not know how to make small talk.'

'Surely you held conversations with your father and with visitors?' The more blatant evidence of arousal under control, Jack went back to his chair.

'They discussed things among themselves, but Father never did so with me. He told me what he wanted, or he would tell me about his latest researches or an antique piece he had bought, but we did not *converse*. It was not an exchange.' She adjusted the position of the frame and began to sew again. From the back, Jack could make out that she was giving the griffin his claws.

'Mother and I would talk, of course, when she was not busy, or ill.'

How lonely you must have been.

Jack sensed that it would not be kind to say that out loud. 'No imaginary friends when you were younger?' he asked, his memory jolted as he caught sight of a small portrait of his grandmother. 'Many children have them. My grandmother made up stories with a dashing pirate explorer and he became so real that we would go on voyages around the pond on a raft together, or when I climbed trees they were really the mainmast of his galleon and he was there, too. We would be on the look-out for rival pirates or native war canoes. His name was Randolph the Ruthless.' He found himself smiling at the memory. Lord, how long was it since he had thought of Randolph, let alone gone adventuring with him?

'You were lonely, too?' Madelyn asked betrayingly.

'When I was small, I suppose I missed children of my own age. But later when I went to school I made friends.' Some stayed loyal when his father became more and more of a liability. Who the true friends were became clear when

Roderick died and the full extent of the financial disaster became apparent. Many took the view that a man with no money to throw around was no fun and that an earl who would not use his title and who took commissions for money would somehow pollute their own lofty status. Lackland, they murmured, was showing *bad form* and that was inexcusable in a way that the profligate squandering of a family's assets was not.

It had hurt at the time until he learned to view it as a way of pruning back the dead growth and seeing true character clearly. He had fewer friends now, but, like Charlie, they were true. 'Did you have a governess?'

Madelyn shook her head. 'Mother taught me to read and write and to do my figures. Father ordered my reading and taught me how to carry out research by setting me tasks to do— the right style of hangings for different rooms, or the composition of early glass for windows, that kind of thing. I suppose,' she said thoughtfully, needle poised, 'that did teach me a great deal about history and geography and some science and technology.'

'It must have done,' Jack said. *Window glass?*

It had never occurred to him to wonder how it was made or how he would go about finding out. 'But nothing of the modern world?'

'I found out quite a lot by reading the boteler's—the butler's—newspapers. And sometimes I would go into Maidstone to shop.' She bent over the canvas as though to hide her face. 'I tried not to go very often—I was stared at so much. It was not a very good preparation for actually living in the nineteenth century, I find.'

That was a considerable understatement, Jack realised. And he had thrown her into deep water and expected her to swim with as much care for her fears and feelings as her ghastly father had shown. A number of unutterable swear words came to mind.

'Tell me which other heraldic creatures you are using,' he said, abruptly jerking the subject back from the painfully personal.

Madelyn frowned in concentration, but he was glad to see that she was sitting up straight again and not hiding her face from him. 'There are the golden bats from your maternal grandmother's family—I thought several of those flitting about would be amusing. The blue spotted hound from your maternal grandfather—the one that is the opposing shield supporter to the griffin. Then there are several types of lion.' She carried on listing beasts as Jack felt himself relax back into the cushions, watching her until one particular name caught his attention.

'What in Creation is a pantheon—other than a group of great people or gods or a building?'

'It is an heraldic beast, as well. One of your female Tudor ancestors brought them with her. They look a little like a deer, but with no antlers and a fox's tail, and they are spangled with purple stars. Look.' She picked up the wool basket and pulled out a book from among the skeins. 'Here is a drawing of your full coat of arms with all the quarterings. It is this beast, right down in the corner.'

'You drew this?' He sat back with it in his hands, a delicate, detailed drawing with each tiny section meticulously coloured. 'Do you enjoy art?'

'I wish I was better,' she said. 'It is frustrating not to be able to paint a landscape as I would wish, or to conjure things from my imagination.'

'Take lessons, employ a tutor,' Jack suggested. They could afford it and he found he had no scruples about suggesting luxuries to his wife while he still inwardly recoiled at the reality of his own financial position. He was a rich man now and virtually every penny of that was Aylmer money. His own savings, earned from his commissions, were tiny in comparison with what Aylmer must have commanded.

'You would not mind?'

'Of course not. Why should I?'

'I never know what will displease you.' She jabbed the needle into the embroidery and reached for the glass on the table beside her. It had quarter of an inch of dark liquid remaining.

'Other than dressing in bizarre clothing, attending vulgar masquerades and dancing with your old loves?' Jack asked, the acid escaping into his tone despite his best intentions.

'Yes, other than those things,' she bit back and emptied the glass in one defiant swallow. Suddenly they were looking at each other across a gulf of mutual misunderstanding.

Jack counted to ten in Greek backwards.

Pretend neither of us has just spoken.

'Is that sherry?'

'Yes.' Madelyn sounded wary. 'Would you like some? Shall I ring for another glass?'

'Good G—I mean, no, thank you. Has Partridge brought in all the decanters?' He looked around. 'Yes, I see he has.' He got up to see what was there. What kind of cellar had Aylmer kept? Nothing but mead, ale and Bordeaux, probably from what little he knew of medieval drinking habits. He picked up one decanter filled with a clear amber liquid, sniffed, poured himself a glass and sipped.

'Now this is an excellent dry Madeira. Where did it come from?'

'I sent to Berry Brothers and asked them to restock the cellar here. Lady Fairfield said they were most reliable and they are just around the corner.'

'A good choice,' Jack said. He walked over and refilled her glass. Two glasses of sweet sherry were not going to put her under the table and it might help her relax.

'Thank you.' Madelyn took the glass and raised it to her lips. 'How would I go about finding a drawing tutor?'

'Ask Lyminge, that's the kind of thing he'll know. Or he can find out. That's his job.' He wondered what else might put her at ease. 'Shall I send to the castle to have your dog brought to Dersington?'

'Oh, yes, please.' Jack felt a stab of conscience that he had not thought of it earlier, then her face fell. 'But I wish I could have my mare as well, but it is so far for Shadow, it would take days at an easy pace.'

'I will buy another mare for Dersington and teach you to ride side saddle,' Jack said airily, wondering where the devil he'd have the time to find something suitable in Suffolk. Another task for Lyminge's list, he supposed.

'That is so thoughtful of you, Jack.' Madelyn's smile was eager, unguarded, and it took his breath for a moment.

This could work, he thought, smiling back and lifting his glass in a silent toast. Madelyn lifted hers in return and her eyes continued to smile into his over the rim of the glass as they drank.

'Ehem.'

They both jumped. Partridge was standing there, and Jack realised that he had not even heard the door open.

'What time is it?'

'Eight, my lord. Dinner is served, my lady.'

Somehow they had spent almost two hours together with only one minor spat. Jack realised that he had been neither bored nor irritated. Normally he would spend his evenings with a few close friends, or working on a commission or with his feet up and a good book and a bottle of wine for company. Somehow he had been entertained, moved to pity, enlightened, aroused and annoyed by his new wife in quick succession without feeling the slightest desire to be anywhere else.

He tossed back the remains of his Madeira and stood up. 'Shall we, my dear?'

Madelyn finished her sherry and swallowed rather too fast, he guessed, judging by the colour in her cheeks. He offered his hand for her to rise and she took it with a flattering readiness. Perhaps she, too, had found the time together pleasant or perhaps it was relief that her new husband had managed to control his bad temper for this first evening together.

She was close and warm and sweet-smelling beside him as they walked the short distance to the dining room. Jack found himself wondering what soap she used, what oils in her bath, what rinses for her hair. What would she look like in her bath, her hair wet around her, moulding her shoulders, her breasts, even as it veiled them?

Her knees, pink with the heat, peeping out of the water…

This promising line of speculation took him as far as the table, all its leaves removed to reduce it to a size where they could converse down its length without needing to shout. He led Madelyn to the chair at the foot, then took his own place at the head. His grandfather's place, the Earl's chair. He thought he would have been pleased to see his younger grandson there. Roderick had never troubled himself with his grandparents. 'The old man's mad and the old lady's a bore' was his verdict. Jack doubted that they had set eyes on him since Roderick was seventeen.

'The staff have done excellent work today, Partridge.' he said as the butler proffered the bottle of champagne for his approval. The room was pristine after the wedding breakfast and the only unusual features remaining were the large vases of flowers on the sideboard and stands.

'I will convey that to the Hall, my lord. The staff were most gratified by Her Ladyship's message of appreciation earlier and are most grateful for the guinea apiece that you so kindly instructed Mr Lyminge to distribute to mark the happy occasion.'

'I did? I mean, excellent.' Jack raised an eyebrow in silent signal to Madelyn and she nodded. Thank goodness she had thought of that. He was unused to having a staff of more than two—a valet and a groom—but he should have realised how much work would be involved and how any gesture of thanks would be appreciated. Madelyn had had years of experience with staff and he had not realised how valuable that would be.

'Pour the champagne, Partridge.'

Madelyn had ordered a simple supper, judging well how small an appetite they might have after the wedding breakfast. She certainly seemed to have little, he noticed as he ate an excellent poached plaice with green peas. He indicated her empty glass with a wave of his hand and the footman hurried forward with the wine.

It would help relax her. Eager though he was to make love to his new wife, Jack was conscious of a reluctance to deflower a virgin. He had no experience of inexperience, but he suspected that a bride who was passionately in love and blinded by that passion must be a far easier prospect than one who, however naturally sensual, was marrying as a matter of business.

Alcohol would help, he thought, but not for him. He laid his hand over his glass when the footman next approached with the bottle. He wanted all his wits about him, but Madelyn needed to be slightly in her altitudes, to use the common parlance for *not quite drunk*. Two glasses of sherry and two of champagne were probably one too many of each under normal circumstances, but this, he thought as he watched her taking a small spoonful of syllabub, was not normal.

Charles cleared the dessert plates and Madelyn began to stand. Paul, the other footman, was behind her in a moment, pulling out her chair.

'I think I will retire, my lord.'

She did seem to be clutching the edge of the table rather fiercely. As he stood Jack saw how white her knuckles were. 'An early night? That seems an excellent idea. I will be up shortly.' He sat down, deliberately not staring at her, even when there was the sound of a slight scuffle in the doorway. She was nervous and shy and that was making her clumsy.

Madelyn was not quite certain afterwards how she got upstairs. She reeled into the bedchamber and sat on the edge of the bed with relief. 'Harper, I feel very strange.' She tried to focus on the maid's concerned face.

'Do you feel sick, my lady?'

'Only when I close my eyes. But the room is moving.'

'Excuse me asking, my lady, but what have you had to drink today?'

'Samp... Champagne with the breakfast. Three glasses?' she hazarded. 'P'raps four? And then Partridge gave me some sherry this evening. So did Charles. Oh, and so did Jack. But that's not very alco...alcoholic, is it? It was very sweet and fruity. Nice. And champagne with dinner.'

'My lady, I think you are drunk.'

'Nonsense. Can't be.' Madelyn frowned. Surely the candle flames should not be bending like that? 'I do not get drunk.'

'Perhaps you have never had so much to drink before, my lady. I think you had best get into bed.' She seemed to Madelyn to be worrying quite unnecessarily about something. 'Let me take down your hair, my lady, and help you out of your gown.'

Harper is very clumsy tonight, Madelyn thought

as she sat down with a bump on the dressing-table stool, half-in and half-out of the flimsy bit of nonsense that she had been assured was just the thing for a wedding nightgown. *It seems to be taking her for ever to get me undressed.*

'Which bed do I get into?' she asked as Harper unravelled her plait and tried to brush the hair smoothly over her shoulders.

'Yours, my lady.'

'Are you sheer...sure? Shouldn't I be in Jack's bed?'

'Quite sure, my lady.' Harper almost bundled her in, plumped up the pillows behind her, smoothed down the coverlet. 'I'll be back in just a moment.' She almost ran from the room, through the connecting door into Jack's chamber.

'Strange,' Madelyn murmured to herself. But it was comfortable in bed and she did not feel too bad as long as she did not close her eyes. Perhaps she was ill, but she couldn't seem to care. Where was Jack? She should be nervous, she remembered vaguely, but she wasn't, which was odd. It had been so pleasant, sitting with him...

What was Harper doing? She could hear her talking to Tanfield next door, although not the words. She sounded quite agitated. Then Tan-field said, quite distinctly, 'My lord', and Harper came back in, positively wringing her hands. *Very odd...*

Perhaps she dozed for a moment or so because she could hear Jack now, talking to Harper.

'But, my lord—'

'That will be all, Harper, thank you.'

'But—'

The door closed with a click and Madelyn opened her eyes. Jack looked very large and splendid in a heavy black-silk dressing robe. He smiled and she smiled back.

'Alone at last,' Jack said. 'You look very beautiful, Madelyn.' He moved closer.

'Mmm?' She did wish he was not weaving back and forth, it was worse than the candle flames.

'Are you quite well?' He looked back at the closed door, then came right up to the edge of the bed, leaned over and looked into her face. 'Madelyn, what have you been drinking?'

'Jus' sherry and champagne.'

'How many glasses of sherry before I came into the drawing room?'

'Two?' She frowned with the effort of remembering. 'Three? It's very good. Sweet.'

Jack made a complicated sound somewhere between a laugh and a groan and sat down on the edge of the bed close to her elbow. The mattress dipped and she fell against him. 'You, my lady wife, are drunk. In fact, you are verging on disorderly.' He put one arm around her and sat her back up again.

What he was saying made no sense, so she ignored it. 'That's nice. Don't go.'

'Madelyn, you need to sleep this off.'

'Room goes around if I close my eyes. You come to bed, too.'

'I think I had better.' Jack stood up, untied the sash of his robe and let it fall to the ground.

Madelyn blinked. He had no clothes on, just bare skin everywhere she looked. Naked, bare skin. And dark hair on his chest and lower down. Instinct told her fuddled brain not to look lower, so she focused on those intriguing curls and the glimpses of nipple hiding among them and then he was in bed beside her and the covers were over both of them and the weight of his body tipped her closer to the heat of him.

Jack reached out and must have snuffed the

candles on the night stand because the room grew dim. 'Now you cannot see anything going around. Come here.' She let herself go limp as he pulled her against him and wondered why he groaned when she wriggled to fit her curves around the reassuringly solid muscles.

'G'night, Jack.'

'Goodnight,' he said, his voice oddly strained. But perhaps that was just this feverish cold or whatever it was that was wrong with her.

Chapter Sixteen

Jack was not sure whether he wanted to laugh or beat his head against the bedpost. Perhaps both at once. There he had been, worrying about his virgin bride, trying to get her just a little bit tipsy so everything would be easier for her, and she had been quaffing sherry like lemonade. Lord Dersington could not even keep his wife sober on their wedding night. No wonder his valet and her maid had been so anxious to keep him out of this room.

Madelyn wriggled, pressing those lovely, lush breasts in their thin lawn covering tight against his ribs. He groaned. Then she wriggled some more and flung one long leg over his thigh. Soft, warm, curls caressed him, a faint feminine musk teased his nostrils. Jack gritted his teeth and wished he had a brandy bottle within reach. This was going to be a long, long, night.

* * *

Her head ached, her mouth tasted disgusting and she was much too hot. And very confused.

Madelyn opened one eye, winced at the light coming in through the light summer curtains and recognised the Chinese wallpaper—and something else. She was in her chamber, in her bed, and the heat was coming from the large, naked male body stretched out next to her. Her husband.

Glimmers of the night before came back to her in horribly confused but vivid scenes. The sherry. More sherry. Jack smiling at her down the length of the dining table and feeling he would be hurt if she did not drink the champagne he liked so much. Harper, struggling to get her undressed. Jack looking deeply into her eyes.

'You, my lady wife, are...'

Drunk! Oh, good heavens. She had been intoxicated and this was a hangover that was hammering nails into her temples. Drunk on her wedding night. Was Jack ever going to forgive her? She couldn't imagine why he should, even if it had been an accident.

Madelyn opened both eyes and cautiously

lifted her head, ignoring the pounding headache and the iron band gripping the back of her skull. Asleep, Jack looked younger, but also harder, even ruthless. That must be the piratical dark stubble covering his chin. He was breathing heavily, but not snoring, his lips slightly parted.

Had he… Had they? No, she would have felt different this morning and it would not only have been her head that was sore. She felt herself blush just thinking it.

Madelyn wanted to lean over and kiss him. She ran her tongue over dry lips and grimaced. If she edged to the side of the bed and slid out, she might make it to the dressing room and a toothbrush before he woke. Besides, the amount she had drunk was making itself felt in other ways, as well.

'Where are you going?' Jack muttered the moment she shifted her weight. His eyes were still closed, the long body still relaxed.

'Dressing room. Toothbrush.'

There was a sleepy grunt.

Had Jack gone back to sleep? She eyed him dubiously, then slid out from under the covers and teetered on unsteady legs to the dressing room door.

She found the chamber pot behind the screen and used it, sighing with relief, then poured cold water from the ewer into the basin, pulled off her nightgown and washed all over, shivering. It felt wonderful. Cleaning her teeth was even better. Then she tipped up the ewer and drank the rest of the water, her body feeling like a shrivelled plant that was coming back to life after a shower of rain.

Only then did Madelyn risk looking in the mirror. A pink-nosed, heavy-eyed creature stared back at her from beneath a haystack. Dragging the brush through her hair hurt her aching head, but the result was worth it for the slight improvement. She found another nightgown—all of them seemed to be constructed of a small amount of thin lawn, an excessive amount of lace and a few ribbons to hold everything together—and put it on, vowing never to let Harper out to buy her intimate garments unsupervised again.

Perhaps if Jack kept his eyes closed…

He was sitting up against the pillows when she edged cautiously back into the room, his eyes wide open, the intense blue gaze fixed on her.

'Good morning, Lady Dersington. That is a quite delightful nightgown you are wearing.'

'I am so sorry.'

'For the nightgown?'

Infuriating man.

She was hot with embarrassment. He could probably see her glowing pinkly through every inch of the indecent garment. 'For last night. For drinking too much. I did not realise that the sherry was so strong and I forgot that I had the champagne at the breakfast.'

His lips twitched, then he was serious again. 'I should take the blame. I had thought that a few glasses of wine might make things easier for you. We both miscalculated. Do you have a headache?'

Madelyn nodded, then almost winced. It was not wise to move her head too much, but it certainly was not politic to appear less than eager to join her husband in bed.

'I will have Tanfield give Harper his infallible hangover remedy and you must drink it straight down. I warn you, it tastes ghastly, but it will settle your stomach. Breakfast and then fresh air will do the rest.' He reached for the bell pull beside the bed.

'What are you doing?' Stretching like that had made muscles ripple and drew her attention to that intriguing dark hair on his chest.

Is it rough or silky? Oh, my goodness, I had forgotten he was naked. How could I have forgotten that?

'Ringing for your maid.'

'You do not want to…? I mean—'

'We have rather less than two hours before we need to set off, unless we want to arrive at Dersington long after dark. And besides, you need to give Tanfield's remedy an opportunity to work before you do anything more strenuous than wielding a bath sponge.' He gripped the edge of the covers as though to throw them back, and Madelyn turned tail and fled back into the dressing room.

She was sitting on the edge of a chair trying to will her spinning head into some sort of steadiness when Harper came in carrying a glass of cloudy brown liquid on a small tray. 'Here you are, my lady. Mr Tanfield's remedy for a hang… For a headache.'

'It is a hangover,' Madelyn said grimly, taking the glass. It looked thoroughly nasty. She held her breath and gulped it down, pressed her lips together and waited. Something seemed to be happening. Either she was going to be very ill or cured.

'I think it is working,' she said after a minute.

'Thank goodness. If I'd had to drink that, I'd have cast up my accounts,' Harper said, whisking a napkin over the glass. 'The hot water for your bath is on its way, my lady, and His Lordship has gone back to his own chamber.' She set the screen between the bath and the chair so that Madelyn was hidden when the footmen brought in the water and began to busy herself with soap and towels.

'I do not understand how men can drink so much,' Madelyn said. 'I felt awful. Oh, how could I?' Harper was her maid and she knew she should be maintaining a dignified front before the staff, but she was a woman and Madelyn badly needed a female to confide in. 'On my wedding night!'

'Hush, my lady. Here come Charles and Saul with the hot water.'

Madelyn sat listening to the sound of pouring water and Harper hustling the footmen out again. Her head was slowly clearing and that only made everything worse. Her memory was returning with horrible clarity, presenting her with one disturbing image after another.

'There we are, my lady. Let's get you out of your nightgown and into the bath. That will help.'

'Harper, I fell asleep, almost as soon as he came into the room.' Madelyn climbed in and lay back in the warm water. 'I said a few things—none of them at all coherent, I'm sure—and then I just drifted off. Last night, of all nights.'

'I'm sure His Lordship knew it wasn't deliberate, my lady. Mr Tanfield says he's ever such an understanding gentleman and he has known him for years.'

He is? Madelyn was not at all certain that was how she would describe Jack, although he had certainly been very kind, if teasing, that morning. And he had been considerate the night before. Some men, from what she had heard, would have taken out their frustrations on their wives' unconscious bodies.

'You'll have a nice long journey to rest and talk and everything will be all right tonight—you'll see, my lady. Now, we agreed on the plum-coloured walking dress, didn't we? And the light straw with the satin ribbons. I'll just get everything laid out.'

Madelyn worked up a good lather on the sponge and began to wash. Thinking about her wardrobe was a helpful distraction. Medieval gowns were all very well for evenings, but they looked most strange with modern hats. No lady could go out without a head-covering, of course, but she thought she had managed a workable compromise. She would have to see what Jack thought. If he was in any mood to be civil about her clothes, that is.

What her husband thought of her walking dress was not apparent. He stood up when she arrived at the breakfast table, waited while she asked Saul for scrambled eggs and toast from the sideboard and drank coffee while she sipped gratefully at weak tea.

'The weather appears to be set fine. Provided there are no accidents on the road we should make good time.'

So, he was going to ignore her intoxication the night before, pretend that disaster of a wedding night had not occurred. Perhaps even ignore the stir her wedding gown had caused. On the other hand, it was too delicate a subject to risk the staff overhearing, so he was probably saving a comprehensive scold for the journey.

'The newspapers, my lord.' Partridge removed three folded papers from the salver he was holding and placed them beside Jack's plate. 'Your man asked me to inform you that the chaise will be at the door within the half-hour, as will the carriage for those members of staff accompanying you. He left, riding Your Lordship's horse, over an hour ago.'

'Excellent. Then, if you have finished, Lady Dersington, we will leave.'

When Madelyn came downstairs with the simple jacket like a spencer over the bodice of her gown and a plain bonnet on her head, Jack did raise an eyebrow as he helped her into the chaise. 'I had wondered how you would continue your unique style of dress to accommodate day wear. That is intended as a walking dress, I assume?'

'Yes.' Madelyn took her seat looking forward out of the wide glass-front window of the chaise. The two postilions were mounting, taking control of four horses—Jack clearly intended to make good time. 'The skirt is not as full and it is slightly shorter so it is clear of the ground. The bodice is a very fine silk so that the fitted jacket is not too warm. It is a mixture of the two styles and, I believe, will be practical.'

'But a modern hat.'

'I imagine that a hennin with veil, or even a *bourrelet*, would appear most strange.'

Jack's very silence was comment enough.

Madelyn decided that she was going to have this out, there and then. 'I have no desire to dress as a medieval woman, but I do wish to wear a style of gown that I believe suits me and in which I am comfortable. Surely that is not so unreasonable?'

'From your point of view, I can understand that it is not. That ensemble, and what you wore last night, seem practical and elegant.' Jack unfurled a newspaper. 'The other papers are in the side pocket, should you wish to read.' He cleared his throat from behind the cover of the spread pages. 'You are correct, that style does suit you very well.'

'Thank you,' she said, startled by the concession. 'And thank you, but I will not take a news sheet. I prefer to watch the scenery. This will be unfamiliar countryside for me.'

'No countryside for a quite a while.' Jack lowered his paper and folded it for more convenient reading. 'And you will recognise the streets as far as St Paul's.'

'Very well, I will read until we arrive somewhere new, thank you.' It seemed there would be no lecture. Not yet, at any rate and he thought her gowns *suited her well.*

With a silent sigh of relief, Madelyn opened the *Morning Post*, rather guiltily skipped past the political news and turned to the Court and Society section, which was usually surrounded by various interesting snippets of news from around the country.

The wedding of the Earl and Countess of Dersington took place yesterday at the church of St George's, Hanover Square.

Madelyn almost dropped the paper. Of course she knew society weddings were reported—she had read enough accounts of them since she had been in London, but somehow it had not occurred to her that hers would be among them.

The Earl has only recently taken up the title, which he inherited upon the untimely death of his brother...

She glanced at Jack, but he seemed absorbed by the foreign news section so she read on.

The nuptial service was attended by a large congregation of the most fashionable in society...

Virtually everyone seemed to have been listed. She skipped over the names.

The bride, only child of the scholar and antiquary the late Mr Peregrine Aylmer, created much interest with a gown of medieval cut and design: we have no doubt that images of this innovative form of dress will appear in all the most select journals for the delectation of the Fair Sex.

There was then a long list of the ladies present and their gowns, headed by a description of hers.

In all the most select journals...

Madelyn turned the page hurriedly, then thought again. Jack was certain to work his way through all the newspapers. She could sit here fretting until he found the reports or she could raise the subject now. She cleared her throat. 'The newspaper has an account of our wedding.'

'That was to be expected.' He lowered *The Times.* 'Has it upset you?'

'No, this report is very reasonable, I suppose. They comment that my gown created much interest, but they say nothing unpleasant.'

'But you expect me to be annoyed to see the report?'

Madelyn could tell nothing of his mood from his tone and his expression was no help, either. 'You were angry.'

'I was annoyed that you did not follow my wishes. However, I cannot deny that you looked very well in that gown.' Jack folded up the newspaper crisply, as though snapping it into order somehow relieved his feelings. 'As you do in the other garments which I have seen that you had made to your own design. I was unnecessarily rigid in what I asked of you.' When she simply looked at him, surprised, he said, 'What have I done now?'

'Admitted a fault—no, I apologise, not a fault, an error of judgement, perhaps.' It was Jack's turn to look puzzled. 'I am not used to having a man do such a thing.'

'Your father was not given to reflecting on his own actions?'

Madelyn laughed. 'That is a very tactful way of putting it. I doubt he could conceive of being in error.'

'That must have been trying to live with.'

'Yes,' Madelyn said drily.

'I think I know how to take that! You thought I am as convinced of my own rightness in everything as Mr Aylmer?'

'You seemed very sure that your decisions were correct,' she said with a smile. She found she liked Jack in this ruefully amused mood. 'Perhaps you have been alone for so long, making all the judgements by yourself, and for yourself, that it is hard to adapt to having someone else to consider. Although, to be fair, I doubt many husbands take their wives' wishes into account on matters of major importance.'

'And your gowns are such matters?'

'You thought so,' she retorted. 'What *I* think is important is that we discuss things, even if it means we disagree. Then we will not find ourselves with entrenched positions from which it is difficult to retreat.'

'That seems sound advice, my wise wife.'

Was he laughing at her? Madelyn decided that he was simply teasing a little and found she could smile back.

'Shall we see what all of the newspapers have to say about us?' he asked.

Partridge, it seemed, had sent out the boot boy to buy every journal he could find. The main newspapers were gossipy, but generally approving, and Madelyn began to relax. There were no mentions of 'Castle-Mad' fathers or ruinously rakish ones, either. Beside her, she felt some of the tension leave Jack and, when a bump in the road threw them together, she stayed leaning against his shoulder as they shared out the final two newspapers between them.

Hers was as inoffensive as the others. 'Oh, Jack, do listen! This one says that I may start a fashion for the Gothic in dress, just as Mr Walpole did with architecture.'

Jack did not respond. He was staring, grim-faced, at the paper in his hand. It was one Madelyn had not seen before, much smaller and slightly thicker than *The Times* or the *Morning Post*.

'What is that?'

'The *London Intelligencer*. Full of Grub Street news—lies, insinuation, scurrilous gossip and radical into the bargain. Not fit to wrap rotten fish in.'

'What does it say about us?' The carriage had slowed because of traffic, and Madelyn caught a glimpse of St Paul's Cathedral close beside them.

'That we represent the union of aristocratic debauchery and bizarrely eccentric miserliness. Your father is represented as closing himself up in his castle, clad in armour and cackling over his money chests, and mine—rather more accurately—as running the gamut of expensive depravity. No normal woman would have allied themselves to me for my title, but as you are as peculiar as your father, you will probably be careless of the depths of wickedness that I will plumb with your money.'

'Oh, stupid people! This is what you feared, is it not? I am so sorry if my choice of wedding gown caused this spite. Could you not sue them?'

'It is all Lord D. and Mr A. Besides, it is true enough about my father and I can hardly argue that I have not benefitted materially from our match.' He dropped the window of the chaise and tossed the paper out. It fell into a passing dust cart. 'Best place for it.'

Chapter Seventeen

Madelyn stared ahead at the bobbing backs of the postilions as they guided the team through the heavy City traffic. She felt slightly sick and her headache had returned like a vengeful elf with a hammer. How could people be so unkind? She and Jack were not their parents—they were two quite different people starting married life together. If she had listened to Jack, accepted that modern fashions did not suit her and learned to live with it, would they have still attacked them?

'Stop fretting, Madelyn,' Jack said sharply. 'This is not your fault. You tried hard to adapt to London society, and you were right and I was wrong about your clothes. We are aristocracy, seen as privileged, and they would have attacked us if you had been dressed by the Queen's ladies-in waiting themselves. No one who is of the slightest importance will take any notice of that rag.' When she swallowed, but said nothing, he put an arm around her shoulders and pulled her close. 'It will all have blown over by the time we come back and, when we do, it will be clear that you are a perfectly rational person and that I am not bankrupting us in Pickering Place hells or houses of ill repute.'

His arm around her felt good. More than good, if she was honest. Jack was solid and reassuring to lean against, and she snuggled closer for reassurance. 'I would become exceptionally irrational if you were to do such things,' she said, hoping to lighten the mood.

Jack gave a snort of amusement. 'How is your headache?'

'Ghastly.'

'Close your eyes and try to sleep.'

'No, I will watch where we are going and ask you irritating questions about things I should know perfectly well by now.' It was far too tempting to clutch hold of Jack and that would be dangerous. She was still none too certain of his changing moods and she was conscious of beginning to feel far too attached to him for safety. She had to remember why he had married her, however kind he was being now. 'Where are we?' She sat up straight and, after a moment, he removed his arm.

'Driving out of Whitechapel and into Mile End Old Town. This area keeps growing. Every time I pass through it there are more and more houses and the old market gardens will soon be swallowed up. Mile End will be joined to Stratford-le-Bow in a few years and London will reach to the Essex border, if you can imagine such a thing.'

Jack pulled a road book with maps out of one door pocket of the chaise and traced their route for her. 'Have you travelled much outside Kent before?'

'Never. I had never been beyond Maidstone,' Madelyn admitted. They were out into open countryside now, with neat fields of vegetables and nursery-garden plots. 'These crops all go into London?'

'Every last cabbage. See the carts? I will take you to Covent Garden early one morning and you will see. It is quite a sight. Here is Stratford-le-Bow and we will soon cross the River Lea and be in Essex.'

* * *

Jack turned his head slightly on the cushioned seat back and watched Madelyn absorbing the passing scene. Everything seemed to interest her—a dog pulling a cart, a gaggle of geese being herded by a small girl with a stick bigger than she was or a recruiting sergeant with a drummer and a corporal at his side hammering up posters.

He had expected to be impatient with her ignorance, but her interest in everything was refreshing and it made him look with a fresh eye at things he would have ignored before. Why were so many inn signs of lions—red, black, gold or white? Were donkeys better than mules as beasts of burden for poor people? What was that crop growing in that field?

Then the chaise swerved as a pair of curricles being raced by two young men at high speed dashed past them, making the leaders shy and the postilions shake their fists as they hurtled towards a narrow bridge.

Madelyn gasped and clutched at his sleeve. 'They are going to crash, surely! Oh, no, one has given way. Goodness, what a speed they were travelling at.'

'Fools.' Jack, braced to throw himself over Madelyn if it came to a collision, relaxed. 'One is a bad driver and the other is not much better.'

'Do you drive? I wondered, as you came down to Kent to see me on horseback.'

'If I could have afforded a curricle I would have bought one. I used to drive, before my father died.'

'You can buy one now,' she said cheerfully as the curricles vanished in a cloud of dust. 'We have a carriage at the castle, but that is a ponderous old travelling coach. What else will we need? A town coach and a travelling carriage of our own, of course, as this one is hired. How many horses, I wonder?'

Madelyn talked on, calculating what they needed.

What I can buy now I have her money, Jack thought, his mood darkening even as he told himself to get down off his high horse. Men married every day for financial advantage and he should be grateful that he was not only marrying a rich woman, but one who was bringing his lands with her.

One of the first things he must do when they arrived at Dersington Mote was to go through all the financial records and the details of exactly what he was now master of. His own lawyers had reported that it was all remarkably straightforward and that nothing other than Castle Beaupierre and its small estate was held back in trusts or complicated by inheritance through Madelyn's mother. Essentially, everything that Peregrine Aylmer had died in possession of went to his daughter.'

'Really, there was very little to do, other than to record the marriage,' Mr Torridge, the senior partner, had informed him. 'Miss Aylmer's man tells me that she ordered all outstanding debts to be cleared before the wedding and, by the very act of marriage, all that she owned passes into your control.'

Douglas Lyminge had suggested hiring an accountant to help them get the Dersingham Mote finances straight and then he could decide which of his properties required their own resident steward. He was not even certain how many Dersington family holdings there were, let alone whether there were other properties that Aylmer had acquired in his search for the perfect son-in-law. He hadn't cared to dig too deeply—it made him feel like a fortune hunter, gloating over his new-found wealth.

He told himself not to be so squeamish. Madelyn's assets would have passed to her husband whomever she married. And it was not as though he wanted to be a rich man, he just wanted to restore his family lands to a flourishing state, to live in a manner befitting his rank and to provide well for the next generation.

The thought of creating that next generation made him smile. He was married to an intelligent, if unconventional, woman. She was unusual, certainly, but he was finding Madelyn increasingly attractive now he had learned not to expect the pattern-book simpering little miss that society dictated would be the ideal bride for an earl. She was leaning forward a little now, he saw as he turned to watch her. Her face was alight with interest and curiosity and one lock of that glorious hair was escaping. She laughed as a pig ran across the village street with three people in hot pursuit and that made her lush bosom move enticingly.

'What is it?' She had caught him looking at her. 'Is something wrong?'

'Nothing at all. It simply occurred to me that

there was something I had not done today,' he said, turning completely on the seat to face her. 'Please take off your bonnet, Madelyn.'

'Why?' she asked. But she was untying the ribbons without waiting for his answer.

'Because it will be devilishly in the way when I do this.' He caught her in his arms and, when she gave a startled gasp, kissed her full on her open mouth.

He was laughing against her lips, the wretched man. *And I love it.* Jack could kiss like an angel… No, perhaps there was nothing angelic about the way the movement of his mouth on hers made her feel. Wicked, sinful—and deliciously happy that this was not either of those things, because they were married and he actually wanted her.

His hands slid down, one over her back, the other at the fastenings of her spencer. The simple hook and eye opened with a flick of his fingers and he slid his hand inside, cupping the weight of her breast in his palm.

She heard herself moan against his mouth and his fingers found her nipple through the thin silk and lawn, just as the chaise slowed to a walk.

Jack sat up slowly as though reluctant to let her go, but over his shoulder she could see an inn sign, a busy street, a groom running out to catch the reins.

'Jack, we are stopping and people can see and—'

'This must be Ilford and the first change.' Jack sat back, perfectly at his ease, if one ignored the fact that he was breathing rather deeply. Her gaze strayed downwards. *Oh.* It seemed he had enjoyed that as much as she had.

'Do you want to go in to the inn or shall we press on to the next stage?'

She felt flustered and flushed and she most certainly did not want to face the good people of Ilford in that state. 'Thank you, no.' Jack merely seemed amused by her confusion. 'You know, I do not think that a chaise is the right place for...for that kind of thing,' she added, fanning her flushed cheeks with one hand. 'There is so much glass, anyone might see.'

'You will have to excuse your poor husband who is decidedly frustrated,' Jack said. 'You cannot blame me for my ardour—it was you who were drunk and disorderly on our wedding night, after all,' he said, shaking his head and attempting, not very successfully, to look reproving.

'I was not disorderly! Merely a trifle...um...'

'*In alt* is the phrase you may be looking for. Or *chirping merry.* Or perhaps you would prefer *half-seas over,*' he added with a grin as the postilions swung back into the saddles of the new team.

'I would prefer none of those vulgar phrases. I suppose they are cant,' she said as repressively as she could and then caught his eye and collapsed into giggles. 'Oh, dear, was I so very awful?'

'Not at all.' Jack put one arm around her shoulders and pulled her close. The chaise moved away from the inn and the horses broke into a trot. 'You were very sleepy and rather slurred. Fubsy, perhaps is the word. It was rather endearing.'

'I would wager you did not think so at the time.' Madelyn let herself relax back against his shoulder again.

'Perhaps not. I had been looking forward all day to having you in my arms. How is your headache now?'

'Much better. I think laughing helps.' *And kissing,* but she did not say that out loud.

Madelyn was drowsing, a warm, relaxed weight against his side as they drew out of Castle Hedingham. Almost there now. It had taken eight hours, including a brief stop for a simple meal, and the last of the day had faded into twilight. The postilions, local men picked up at the last change, knew their way and were keeping up a brisk pace, despite the poor light.

Jack tried to remember the house, but the images were vague, like something in a dream, vanishing in the morning with wakefulness. Large, rambling, increasingly ill kempt was all that his memory presented him with. Receiving a beating for drawing pictures in the dust on the windows and on the furniture was one recollection. The smell of musty enclosed spaces was another. He had learned to keep well clear of his father when he had been drinking because his mood was apt to be uncertain, so Jack had found all the places a small boy could hide in.

In the summer there were the ruins of the ancient castle that had given the house its name. There were a few fragments of curtain wall like rotten teeth sticking out of the unmown grass and, because this had been a Norman castle, the motte itself which always made him think of a green pudding, turned out of its mould on to the serving tray.

He'd scramble to the top and peer down between the rusting bars of the grille over the well, dropping pebbles to wait for the distant splash. There was always water in the well, however hot the summer. Men who knew they might have to survive a siege would make certain of their water supply.

He shifted to look out of the right-hand window and Madelyn woke, sat up and rubbed her eyes. 'Almost there,' Jack said. 'Look towards the skyline.' And there, silhouetted against the last pink streaks of the sunset, was the motte.

They had sent staff, in the charge of the new butler, Wystan, on ahead to prepare bedchambers, the staff accommodation, a drawing room, dining room and study. 'We should have sent a gardener, as well,' Jack remarked, peering out at the drive, which was overgrown with grass.

'We will soon have to it set to rights,' Madelyn said, but she looked apprehensive, her lower lip caught between her teeth as she looked out at the looming bulk of the house.

'I do not blame you for it being like this. My father neglected it,' Jack reassured her. *That full lower lip.* 'Are you hungry?' he asked casually.

'No, not really.'

'Tired?'

'I feel quite wide awake. I hope I did not send your shoulder to sleep, leaning on it like that.' He shook his head. 'I am excited about seeing our new home.'

Jack was quite clear in his own mind that if she did not want to sit down to dinner immediately, or fall asleep, then the only thing *he* was excited about was taking his wife to bed and very thoroughly convincing her that they were married.

The chaise drew up in front of the front door, which opened, revealing a tall man who must be Wystan, the butler, and two footmen who ran down to open the doors. Jack jumped down, then stood and held out his hands to Madelyn. 'Let me help you.' She gave a startled gasp when, instead of handing her down, he swept her up in his arms and strode across to the door. Tradition said that brides should be carried across thresholds and, in his opinion, straight upstairs.

'My lord, my lady. Welcome home and on behalf of the staff here, may I offer our congratulations. Dinner—'

'Thank you, Wystan. Please tell Cook to put dinner on hold indefinitely. We will ring when it is required. Bedchamber?'

'Er… Yes, my lord. Second door on the right on the first floor, my lord. When Lady Dersington's maid arrives—'

Jack was already halfway up the stairs. 'Tell everyone to have their own supper,' he said over his shoulder. 'My wife needs to rest.'

'Jack, I don't, really. I am not tired,' Madelyn protested.

'I lied.'

'Jack, I must weigh so much. Do put me down… Oh!'

He shouldered his way through the door, walked to the bed, deposited Madelyn on top and went back to turn the key in the door.

'But, Jack, I should wash.'

'Afterwards.' He shrugged off his coat, glad he had travelled in a comfortable old one that did not require the exertions of a valet to get it off, and began on his neckcloth.

'No, *now.*' Madelyn slid off the bed, revealing a gorgeous flash of long leg, silk stocking and bare thigh, and fled into the dressing room.

Jack found he was grinning. He sat down on the end of the bed and began to pull off his boots, a far more difficult exercise than getting out of his coat. He had them both off, and his stockings, but all that he could hear from the dressing room was frantic splashing. Perhaps he had better stop undressing—virgin brides should not be confronted by stark-naked husbands, even if she had seen him last night. Hopefully she would find him acceptable enough when she was stone-cold sober. He gave the bed an experimental prod. At least there seemed to be a new mattress and clean linen and a pile of soft-looking pillows.

The dressing room door creaked open and Madelyn emerged, swathed in a vast linen bath-sheet.

'Sweetheart.' He got up and went to put his hands on her shoulders. 'You are shivering.'

'Cold water.' She was staring fixedly at the

open neck of his shirt. 'I think… I think I would like you to warm me up please, Jack.'

'There is nothing I would like better.'

'The candles…'

'We could make love in the dark, but I would very much like to see you. Are you shy?'

She nodded, not meeting his gaze.

'Well, so am I. What if you take one good look and say, *Ugh*?'

'Idiot,' she said with a choke of laughter. 'Jack, are you still angry with me?'

'No,' he said and realised that was the absolute truth. 'And I would never hurt you, not intentionally. Although I understand it might not be exactly comfortable the first time.' As he spoke, he let his hands stray slowly over her back, her bare shoulders under the fall of silky hair, gentling and stroking until she began to sway against him, relaxing into his touch.

His fingers explored the edge of the linen sheet to find the corner that had been tucked in to secure it. One tug and it began to unravel, then slid to the floor. Madelyn made a grab for it, missed and pressed closer against him in an effort to hide, which suited Jack very well indeed.

'I am wearing too many clothes,' he remarked.

'But I cannot unfasten my breeches with you so close. Can you reach the buttons?' For a moment he thought she would refuse, then her fingers slid between their bodies and began to search for the fastening of his falls. He was already so erect that the fabric was straining, making it harder to push the buttons through the holes and Madelyn's groping fingers were accidentally wreaking havoc every time they strayed or slipped.

There was a gasp of relief—although which of them made it was difficult to tell—then he pushed at the breeches so they slid down over his hips, taking his small clothes with them, leaving him with just the shirt tails for decency.

'May I look at you?' It was like holding a trapped bird in his hand, the flutter of her pulse where his hand rested close to her neck, the beat of her heart against his.

Jack sensed Madelyn make the decision, felt her shoulders straighten as her head came up and she stepped back, one pace, then another, and stood looking at him with those magical ice-clear eyes wide, her cheeks growing pinker as the silence stretched on and he took in the pale beauty standing in front of him.

Then her hands moved and he thought she was going to cover herself. Instead, Madelyn took a step forward and fisted her hands in the loose fabric of his shirt. 'It is only fair that I look at you, too,' she said, and tugged it upwards.

Chapter Eighteen

She was sober now. Sober and wide awake and there were a lavish number of candles to see by. Jack stood in front of her, brushing back his hair from his forehead as she dropped his shirt to the ground.

He was quite naked, quite shameless, standing there letting her look her fill. He had no need to hide anything, Madelyn thought. No indulgent little belly forming, no pigeon chest or spindle-shanks, just solid, well-muscled, beautifully pro-portioned masculinity in its prime.

Very male...and I do not appear to be repel-ling him. Not if the imposing erection was any guide to Jack's feelings. *Goodness, that must be uncomfortable,* she thought, forgetting for a moment to be shy or apprehensive.

'You are making me blush,' Jack said, and she looked up guiltily to see that the colour was, indeed, up over his cheekbones. Then he moved, scooped her up in his arms so that her breasts were tickled by the dark hair on his chest and, before she could focus on that sensation, she was on the bed and Jack was beside her.

Instinct made her turn, burrow into his arms, as though he would protect her from what was about to happen. Which was ridiculous, she thought a little wildly. *He will make it happen and I want it. I want him.* That wonderful dark hair was tickling again. Madelyn leaned back a little so that she could see and ran her fingers through it. Soft, springy and yet coarse, it fascinated her and she petted it while Jack lay quite still until her nails scratched over one nipple and he gasped.

'Oh, I'm sorry. Did that hurt?'

He moved so fast that she had no time to react. One moment she was on her side focused on his chest, the next she was flat on her back and Jack was straddling her, leaning forward and caressing her breasts. 'No, it doesn't hurt,' he said, his voice low and husky. 'It feels…good.' His short nails scratched lightly across her own nipples and she saw them harden, then he caught the nubs between thumbs and forefingers and began to roll them, gently at first, then with an insistent pressure that sent waves of sensation down to her belly, to the part between her thighs where his weight pressed them together so intimately.

She wanted to push him away, make him stop because it was so shaming to feel this wanton, mindless need and yet that was the very last thing she wanted. Madelyn closed her eyes and bit her lip to somehow stop the soft moans.

'Open your eyes, Madelyn.' Jack shifted, came down so that they were lying chest to breast, his weight on his elbows.

Somehow her legs had parted so that he was lodged between her thighs, cradled there. Instinctively, she closed her legs to hold him there. Reluctantly she opened her eyes.

'You are lovely,' he said simply. 'Don't be frightened, don't be ashamed. We are made for this. Let me pleasure you.' His weight shifted again so he could free his right hand. It slid between their bodies, down to where she could already feel him pressing against her. His fingers stroked and probed as they had in the carriage and she felt the cresting pleasure that he had given her then, tightening, straining, and she arched up to meet it and let it break her into shards of light.

'Open for me, sweeting.' He was nudging against her, but she was still dizzy, still riding the waves of sensation and she did not resist, even when he pushed and she realised he was inside her, pushed again, filling her.

It was too much, too tight, too...

'Ah.' Jack was still, tight against her. She looked up into his face, strained and dark-eyed and taut with pain or pleasure, she no longer could tell which was which. 'Madelyn?'

'Yes,' she said. 'Yes.' Although quite what she was agreeing to she was not certain, all she knew was that she needed him, all of him. Now.

He began to move, gently at first, and her body tried to resist until, quite suddenly, she felt herself soften, open to him, accept him as though they were one being struggling up towards the light. That spiralling tension was back, different somehow, more involved with Jack and the feel of him all around her. Then it broke and she cried out and heard his shout and felt the hot wash of his release inside her and fell into the star-dusted darkness.

* * *

Jack woke to the sound of carriage wheels on the drive below and voices. One glance at the candles told him he had only drowsed for a few minutes, but Madelyn was deep asleep in his arms.

He smiled and eased her gently away to one side so that he could slide off the bed. He picked up his clothes and went quietly into the dressing room, emerging washed and redressed ten minutes later. Madelyn stirred as he moved on stockinged feet to the doorway and a board creaked loudly under his weight.

'Jack?'

'I'm here. Our people have arrived. I'll have Harper come up and order water for a bath for you. We can eat up here, then all you need put on is your robe.' It was not cold—the new staff had clearly aired the room properly. He went to the bed and touched her cheek with the back of his hand. 'Are you well, sweeting?'

She blushed and pulled up the coverlet over her naked body, but she nodded without hesitating. 'Yes.' She appeared quite convinced of the fact, he saw with some relief. 'Are you?'

'Oh, yes.' He found that he was very well indeed. Madelyn was not the wife he would ever have chosen, but he realised that now all his doubts about her had evaporated. It might not be easy adjusting to each other, they had so little in common, but at least they were unlikely to have any problems in bed, he thought.

He was still feeling buoyant by the time their delayed supper was served. Tomorrow he was going to have to go and make his peace with Cook, but she had managed to produce an excellent meal despite the delays and despite what he suspected must be a thoroughly antiquated kitchen. The staff that Lyminge had found for the Mote appeared, so far, to be excellent.

Madelyn had bathed, changed into a magnificent heavy silk robe and was looking composed and happy as she sat across the small table from him, toying with a plate of sweetmeats.

They had spoken very little during the meal. Footmen had come in and out, Wystan had hovered, carafe in hand. They had smiled, exchanged commonplaces about the food; Madelyn had firmly rejected a second glass of wine, but under the table their feet met and touched.

Madelyn had eased off her shoes, he realised as a bare foot teased down his calf.

'Stop it, you wicked woman,' he murmured, leaning forward. 'Thank you, that will be all,' he added to Wystan. 'We will ring when we want you to clear.'

The door closed silently, leaving them alone. 'You, my lady, should retire to your chamber and sleep now.'

Madelyn looked at him, blushed, then dropped her gaze. 'We do not make love again tonight?'

'Tonight you are tired and you will be sore and I want you to rest,' Jack told her, very conscious that every instinct was telling him to be selfish, to take her back to bed and revel in her all night long.

'This is not my bedchamber?'

'No, it is mine. Yours is through there. As I remember it, it is a much more intimate room with a view of the gardens and a larger dressing room.'

'It was your mother's?' She was playing with the end of her braid, twisting the hair around her fingers as though conscious that this was likely to be a sensitive subject for him.

'No, my grandparents were still living here

when she died and this was their suite.' He glanced around the room they were in. 'This would have been my father's after they moved permanently to London.'

'Is that difficult for you?' she asked, reaching across the table to touch his hand.

Jack tried to think of the last time that anyone had touched him like that, reached out to give comfort.

I am here with you now, that touch seemed to say. *You are not alone any longer.*

He told himself that Madelyn was feeling sentimental after their lovemaking, that he should not start feeling the same way about their relationship, but he turned his hand over so that he could curl his fingers into hers.

'No, I thought that it might be, but there is nothing of him here. He probably spent his nights in the beds of other men's wives or drunk on the sofa.' And they had laid any ghosts to rest in that bed just now.

She nodded, her eyelids drooping, and he got up to ring for her maid. The feeling of those long, cool fingers in his seemed to linger.

'You are half-asleep already. Come, let me show you your chamber and Harper can put you to bed.' He paused as he opened the door between the two rooms. 'I am glad you chose me, Madelyn. Do you think you can come to feel the same way?'

'I already do,' she said, standing on tiptoe to brush her lips over his.

Jack closed the door before the temptation to follow her into the room proved too great.

'Tell me what you are thinking about to make you smile,' Jack asked three days later as they picked their way through the remains of the formal garden towards the motte of the old castle. The house had been built in what had been the outer bailey of the castle where all the old walls had long since crumbled away. The inner bailey with its jagged sections of battlemented wall had become the gardens and the motte stood alone at its far end.

'It would make you blush,' Madelyn said demurely and laughed when his hand closed tightly around hers and he swung her round to face him. 'I was thinking about last night. And the night before. Oh, and this morning, of course.'

'Stop it,' Jack growled. 'or I'll pick you up and go straight back to the bedchamber.' But he kissed her instead and after a moment they began to walk again, Mist, her little Italian greyhound, cavorting at their heels.

I have fallen in love with him, Madelyn thought as she had, with a sense of wonder, ever since the day before when Mist had arrived, scrambling down from Jenny the maid's lap in an ecstasy of happy wriggling and almost choking on the soft little barks she so rarely produced.

She had watched Jack running his hands over the little dog, checking that she had not suffered from the journey, talking softly to her to reassure Mist, who was inclined to be protective of her mistress and wary of large, strange men. Jack was gentle and empathetic with animals, just as he was with her, she realised. This could not be easy for him, coming to this house where he had been unhappy as a child, dealing with the memories, learning to live with a new wife who had not been his choice.

She loved him now and, perhaps, he was coming to be fond of her, she thought. His lovemaking told her he was rather more than fond, but she cautioned herself against setting too much store by that. Men, she understood, wanted physical relations on a far more basic level than women and set less emotional value on the experience. But even so...

'Can you make a garden here?' Jack asked, pulling her out of her thoughts. 'It is bigger and less sheltered than your plot at Beaupierre.'

'Yes.' Madelyn looked around. 'It will be very different. And a modern garden, I think.' She stopped to look at the motte. 'This castle is much older. Did it ever have a keep on top of the mound?'

'A wooden one, we think. There are no remnants of stonework. Do you want to climb to the top?'

'Yes, please. I will get a much better idea of the whole estate from up there, I think.'

It was a steep climb. The original staircase had long since vanished, leaving only a winding path through the turf. Madelyn was panting by the time they reached the top and thinking that she must design some gowns with rather shorter skirts for daywear.

'There is the well. Be very careful of the grille over the top—it must be almost rusted through and it is a long way down.' He dropped a pebble in, and she gasped at the length of time before the faint splash.

'I feel unsteady just thinking about it. Shall we sit here?' There was a low bank, and Madelyn perched on that, looking out. 'I do not know much about agriculture,' she said after a few minutes. 'But there do not seem to be many fields with crops in them, or animals, either.'

'No,' Jack said. 'This estate is going to need a lot of work and investment to make it productive again.'

There did not seem to be much to say to that. His father and brother had stripped it of its assets and neglected it and her own father had paid it no heed at all. Jack had already told her that the tenant at the Home Farm seemed to be lazy and old-fashioned in his methods and on the other holdings drainage and fertilising was needed and the farm buildings repairing before there was any hope of decent yields and better rents.

'There's that row of cottages by Cherry Brook,' Jack said, pointing. 'I told you about them—you can see from here how bad the roofs are.'

'Look, a carriage is turning in off the road.' Madelyn pointed, glad of an excuse to change the subject.

'That will be Lyminge and the new accountant,' Jack said, getting to his feet. 'I had best go down and greet them. Are you coming?'

'I will stay here and enjoy the sunshine,' Madelyn said. 'And plan the garden.'

She watched, a warm feeling of happiness behind her breastbone, as Jack jogged down the slope, then strode, long-legged, to the house.

We can do this together, she thought. *We will bring this house and the estate back, make it a home.* She found an empty snail shell and tossed it into the well.

Lucky children, they are going to have two castles to grow up in. And, if I am very lucky, two parents who love each other.

It felt intrusive having more people in the house, she decided after breakfast next morning. Both Mr Lyminge and Mr Paulson, the accountant, were gentlemen and professionals, and as such, took their meals in the dining room with Jack and Madelyn. They were perfectly pleasant and would give her an opportunity to practise her skills as a hostess and to practise small talk, she told herself briskly. She and Jack could not hope to spend every day for weeks dining intimately alone and Jack clearly enjoyed the masculine company.

Mr Paulson was a cheerful, bouncing redhead, which surprised Madelyn, who had expected accountants to be earnest characters with spectacles, stooped shoulders and a jaundiced view of life. Paulson was clearly an enthusiast. 'There is music in numbers, Lady Dersington,' he had explained over dinner. 'Music and magic and mystery and it is my task to unravel the mystery and to make the music play in tune.' But he would, he confessed, be delighted to take up Jack's offer to borrow a rod and fish in the lake.

Mr Lyminge, with a nervous glance at Madelyn, confessed that he did not enjoy fishing, but that if it did not become cooler soon, he would very much like to swim.

'I will join you,' Jack had said, prompting Madelyn's imagination to produce any number of highly provocative images of her husband rising from the water and striding towards her as she stood on the shore. Or perhaps he would teach her to swim. When they were alone, of course.

Now, as the last of the bacon and eggs were consumed and the men began to spread preserves on toast, Mr Paulson asked where the best place for him to work would be.

'The estate office,' Jack said. 'Wystan will show you the way. The older books are all there as far as I can see, but Mr Aylmer held the recent ones, dating from when he acquired the estate.'

'Mr Lansing at Castle Beaupierre has sent them all, retaining only the ones relating to that castle,' Mr Lyminge told him. 'We will make a start this morning and hope to give you a preliminary report by tomorrow evening.'

'In that case,' Jack said, directing a heavy-lidded look at Madelyn, which made her toes curl, 'perhaps I will investigate the lake with Lady Dersington.'

Chapter Nineteen

'It is an exaggeration to call this a lake,' Jack said when they stood on the bank and looked out across the water to the trees on the other side. 'There were all kinds of cuts and ponds made to divert water from the river into the moat and to provide fish ponds when the castle was built. My grandfather, when he first inherited, wanted to have the grounds landscaped by one of the leading designers, like Brown or Repton, but there were never the funds so he had the fishponds joined up, raised the height of the dam on the lower one and we have this.'

'But the fishing is good and it is deep enough to swim in?' At his side Madelyn was already easing off her shoes, one hand on his shoulder for balance. He had noticed that she had got into the way of touching him. It was quite unconscious, he was certain, but he was com-

ing to enjoy her fingers on his arm to emphasise a point, the way she would brush a piece of
lint from his lapels or run her fingers along his
shoulder when she passed behind him when he
was sitting in a chair. He was all too aware that
when he touched her he wanted far more than
that momentary caress.

'I always wanted to learn to swim,' she was
saying now when he pulled his attention back to
the present. 'But there was only the moat and it
is very deep with sides that go straight down.'

Jack grimaced. 'Definitely not good. The sides
shelve quite gently here and the river is clean. I
have no idea how good the fishing is because I
expect that every poacher in the area has been
emptying it along with any game in the coverts.'

'Will you hire a keeper?' Madelyn sat down
on the grass and began to untie her garters, as
unconcerned as though she was in her own bedchamber.

He found the way that she had shed her inhi-
bitions with him both erotic and humbling. He
had tried to make their lovemaking good for her,
but he had not expected the trust she showed in
him nor her sensual delight, not just in what he

did to her, but in the ways she was discovering to pleasure him.

Madelyn stood up, tipping her head to one side to study him as he looked at her. 'What is it, Jack?'

He shook his head. 'Nothing.' He was not ready to tell his wife that he thought he was falling in love with her. He was not even sure himself that was what this feeling was: desire, excitement and, under it, a deep, calm warmth. It was novel and precious and he was not risking losing it by speaking too soon.

'Unhook my gown, please.'

The cut of the gown with its support under the breasts did away with the need for stays and Madelyn wore only a long under-shift. 'You are very easy to undress,' Jack remarked, taking the gown from her as she stepped out of it and laying it across a bush.

'I suspect you have had practice,' she said over her shoulder, teasing.

'Enough,' he admitted. 'Are you going to practise some more with my clothes?'

'Of course.' She walked towards him through the soft grass, the summer flowers, and he thought of the flowery meadow she was embroidering behind the heraldic beasts.

'Do I have a unicorn among all those creatures you are copying for the chair seats?' he asked as she pushed back his coat and caught it before it fell to the ground.

'No, neither of us has a unicorn. It is a pity. Perhaps I can lure one out of hiding for you. This is a magical place, so wild and peaceful.' She tossed his neckcloth onto the handy bush and began to unfasten his cuffs.

'I'm afraid not,' Jack said, feigning regret. 'They will only come to virgins, don't you remember? You no longer qualify.'

She pulled the shirt over his head. 'Oh. Well, never mind, I would rather have you than a unicorn.'

Jack sat down and took off shoes and stockings as an excuse to hide his face. There had been something in Madelyn's voice, a tenderness, a possessiveness, that touched something inside him and took his breath. Was he hearing what he wanted to hear or did she have feelings for him that she was not yet ready to put into words, just as he had for her?

He stood up, took off his breeches and advanced on the lake. 'Come on, off with that shift.'

'Shouldn't I keep it on?' Madelyn stood hesitating on the bank. 'I've seen pictures of ladies using bathing machines at the seaside and they are wearing shifts.'

'It will cling and feel uncomfortable and there is only me here to see.' He waded in knee-deep. 'It is surprisingly warm.'

'But it is broad daylight.' Her fingers were tugging at the shift, though.

'Off with it!'

Madelyn dragged it over her head, blushed and ran down the bank, splashing past him until she tripped and fell into the water.

Jack hauled her up, coughing and spluttering. 'You see? Lovely and warm. We need to go deeper, though.' This was going to be fun.

She wouldn't exactly describe the water as *warm*, but it was lovely, slipping over her skin. And Jack was patient and funny, tickling her ribs when she wouldn't relax lying across his arms, so she flailed and flapped and suddenly his arms had gone and she was floating. It only lasted a few seconds until she sank and stood up, rubbing the water out of her eyes, but when she tried it again she managed to float for longer and then watched as Jack swam up and down, showing her how to move her arms and legs.

'It feels so gorgeous and it is such *fun*. I can't remember enjoying myself so much doing something physical, except for riding. And making love, of course,' she said, laughing and splashing him when he threatened her with water weed. 'How long will it be before I can swim properly?'

'Not long. But no more today or you will get chilled. Come and sit on the grass and let the sun dry you.'

They had brought towels and a flask of lemonade and a napkin with buttered rolls stuffed with ham and Jack spread one towel in lieu of a rug. They sat, side by side, wet and bare and covered in goose bumps, and demolished the food.

'This is so wicked,' Madelyn said with a happy sigh.

'And you are covered in crumbs,' Jack said, brushing at a trail of them down over her breasts.

'Behave!' Madelyn snatched up a towel and wrapped herself in it. 'Tell me why you left here as a child.'

'Do you want to spoil the mood?' Jack said.

'I want to understand.'

'My grandmother insisted. It took her a little while, I think, to realise and accept just what a wastrel her son had become or I think she would have sent for me earlier. My grandfather was the same—Father was the only child, they kept telling themselves at first he would grow out of it, or that it was simply high spirits and that marriage would steady him.

'Then it only got worse. There was a terrible argument, a falling-out, and by that time my grandfather was beginning to be unwell. Grandmother insisted they live in London because being near my father agitated him so.'

'But they left you and your brother here with him. I do not understand that,' she confessed, watching not his face, but his restless movement as he got up and tied a towel around his waist, threw another around his shoulders and sat down again.

'My mother was alive then and my father was always a good father towards my brother. At least, where you call teaching him to gamble and fight and whore is concerned. But he saw that he had a suitable education, he showed him some affection, he never punished him, whatever he did.'

'But you—'

'I was an expense and, I suppose, an awkward little devil. He did not like me and the feeling was mutual. He'd make promises and then forget and then lie about it. That was almost worse than everything else. Somehow I could cope with him being drunk or angry if only he was consistent, but every so often there would be hope that he had forgiven me for whatever it was he thought was so bad. Hope that perhaps he loved me after all. But I learned eventually not to trust because broken trust is worse than broken bones. He was a lout to my mother and sometimes I think she simply wasted away out of misery.'

'What happened in the end? You got free eventually.'

'I had the awkward habit of reminding him about things he wanted to forget, so he'd knock me around when I annoyed him. One day he broke my arm.' Jack held out his left hand and flexed the fingers as though to reassure himself that the old wound had healed.

'I wrote to my grandparents asking if I could

live with them, stole money from my father's desk, bribed one of the grooms to deliver the letter.' He shrugged. 'I never thought they would send for me and they didn't. My grandmother arrived instead, took one look at me and had me in the carriage within the hour. I never came back.'

'I hate raised voices, shouting, people losing their temper,' Madelyn said, huddling close. 'You can never relax, never forget that something might make them angry, never quite be unconditionally happy in a moment.'

'Your father struck you?' Jack sat back, his expression appalled.

'Rarely. But he would go white with anger if he was displeased and his voice would become quieter and quieter until you were straining to hear, to understand what it was that you had done that was so dreadful. And then he would shout.'

'You are trembling. Are the memories so bad—or do you think that I might be like my father? I used to worry about that, work at controlling myself.'

'No, I am not afraid of you. That was one reason why I spoke to you as I did when we first met. I wanted to see how easily you became angry, what happened when you did.'

'Have I reassured you?'

'Oh, yes.' The sun was directly on him, making the water droplets in his spiky wet hair glint, making him seem younger, less hard and experienced.

I love you. Dare I tell you?

'Make love to me, Jack. Here, now.'

She lay back, and he parted the damp folds of cloth until she was bare to him again and, without speaking, he began to kiss her, everywhere except her mouth. His lips moved over her from temple to toes. His tongue laved trails of heat then his teeth nipped, tiny sparks of desire laved immediately by the pressure of his mouth. Madelyn closed her eyes and the sunlight was red through her lids as Jack's mouth and hands spun magic out of the lightest touches, the heat of his breath.

Pleas and gasps did not divert him until, at last, he parted her thighs and kissed into the water-wet folds.

Jack had never done that before, kissed her there, his hands firm on her hips, holding her when she would have hidden from him, shielded herself from the intimate onslaught. He was ruthless until she came apart, crying his name, and he came up over her and entered her in one smooth stroke.

'Did you call? I am here,' he said. 'I will always be here.' He took her up again, aching and desperate and waited, waited, until it was all too much and his shout mingled with her sobbing, whispered, ecstasy.

'I love you, I love you.'

When Madelyn was conscious again Jack was still sprawled across her, relaxed into sleep. Had he heard her? Surely he would have said something, would have reacted, whether he was pleased or appalled. No, she must have whispered and he was too caught up in his own climax to hear her words. Perhaps it was for the best. They would make love again tonight and if she had the courage she would say it then when he was calm and she could watch his face for his reaction. That was best—they had all the time in the world to get this right.

They walked back to the house hand in hand, still slightly damp, very tousled, sleepy with heat and exercise and passion, and halted at the edge of the outer bailey, looking at the house, sullen in the sunlight.

'That is never going to be handsome,' Jack said.

'The first thing is to have all the windows cleaned, inside and out. They are the eyes of the house and that will make them sparkle. Cut those creepers back on the west side, too, and let the light in. Have the grass scythed.' Madelyn tipped her head to one side and squinted her eyes to blur the imperfections. 'It may not be handsome, but it will be characterful.'

'Like me?' Jack said, chuckling as he led the way around to the front door.

'Stop fishing for compliments. You know perfectly well that you are very handsome.'

'Just for that I am going to take you upstairs and make love to you all over again.' He picked her up and strode over the threshold as she laughed and pretended to struggle.

The study door opened as they were halfway to the foot of the stairs. Jack stopped and set her on her feet, for which she was grateful. It was embarrassing enough to be caught looking as though she had been tumbled on the lake shore without actually being in Jack's arms.

'Excuse me, my lord.' Mr Lyminge saw her and blushed. 'My lady.'

She could see Mr Paulson behind him looking uncharacteristically serious.

'Did you want to speak to me?' Jack asked. He was smiling, but she could hear the impatience he was trying to conceal and his hand still held hers.

'If it is not inconvenient. There is something… You might be aware of it, of course—' Douglas Lyminge was clearly uncomfortable.

'But I very much doubt it,' Paulson said. 'I do feel that you should look at what we have found, my lord.'

'I will probably drip pond weed on you,' Jack said. 'But very well, if it is urgent, we will come now.'

'It is nothing we need concern her ladyship about,' Paulson said hastily.

She should insist, of course, but the magic of the afternoon lingered and accounts were like a black cloud on the horizon. Jack would tell her about it later and they could decide how to deal with whatever the problem was. 'In that case,

I will leave you to the ledgers,' she said with a smile.

'I will see you at dinner, my dear,' Jack said quietly and squeezed her hand.

Madelyn rang for Harper and bathed, washed her hair, sat on the window seat in the sunshine brushing it dry and studied the garden. She listened for Jack coming up to his room to bathe and change, but the two men must be keeping him over the accounts. She did hope they had not found bad news about the state of the other estates. It was beginning to dawn on her that her father had neglected all of them, not taking trouble to find the best tenants, not investing as he should.

It would mean a great deal of work, worry for Jack, considerable investment. But they could do it—she would discover how she could best help. It might take several years, but they would restore all the Dersington lands, repair the damage their fathers had wrought.

And there, at last, was the sound of his footsteps in the room next door. She knew his tread, knew it was not Tanfield. The connecting door opened, banged back against the wall.

Madelyn turned, swung her feet down off the

window seat. *Goodness, but he is in haste!* It was rather flattering. Then she saw his face.

'Get out,' he said to Harper, who had put down her mending and stood up to bob a curtsy.

The maid looked to Madelyn and she nodded. Harper went to the connecting door and closed it behind her, leaving them alone.

'I am not sure what I ever did to deserve this of Aylmer—perhaps my father caused him harm in the past,' Jack said, as though carrying on an ordinary conversation over the teacups. 'I would not be surprised. But I am at a loss to understand why you should dislike me quite so much.'

'I do not... I... Jack what are you talking about?' There was ice in the pit of her stomach. 'What is wrong?'

'I had thought that what you proposed to me, what your father had so carefully constructed, was a fair exchange. After all, he was a gentleman, you are a lady. One would think one could trust your word. A wife and my lands back for me and, for you, a husband of his choosing and the family and status you wanted.'

'Yes,' Madelyn agreed. 'Exactly that.'

'How long did you think you could keep me distracted with your kisses and your smiles and your imitation of an affectionate wife? It was very good, I have to tell you. I was quite taken in, quite sure that you were becoming fond of me. Fool that I am.'

'But I *am*. Jack, I love you.'

'Very good.' He applauded, three slow handclaps. 'If you had said that a few hours ago on the lake shore, I think I would have believed you.'

'But it is true.' The ice was chilling her entire body now.

'Don't, Madelyn. Don't make it worse with more lies. I thought I was agreeing to an exchange, but what I was doing was walking into a trap, one baited with rotten meat.'

'I don't understand.' She sat down, unable to stand, let alone go to him. 'I know the estates are not in as good a condition as they should be. My father was careless, did not pay them the attention they needed. But we can make the neglect good.'

'Really? What with, might I ask? Not with that damn castle of yours and its land and its treasury of valuables because that is all in trust, is it not? And not with any ready cash or investments either, because you spent all that on settling debts and paying off mortgages before their time and meeting loans that had years to run. I have my estates, thank you, Madam Wife. I have my estates in tatters and not a penny piece to restore them with.'

Chapter Twenty

'I did it for the best,' Madelyn said, fighting for composure as the truth sank in. Jack only cared about the land and the money. He had not grown fond of her, let alone come to feel anything stronger. 'My father never settled accounts until he had to and I did not want to leave tradespeople and shopkeepers out of pocket. I believed he was a rich man, that the loans and mortgages were just his way of making money go further.'

'I imagine he was a rich man until he started to restore that confounded castle,' Jack said, pacing. 'When I first saw it I wondered at the cost of repairing the walls and that great expanse of roof to such a high standard. It should have made me suspicious, but I trusted you. There is a saying that if something is too good to be true then it probably is. I should have thought of that.'

'You are very angry,' she said, but he silenced her with a wave of his hand.

'There is no need to worry, Madelyn. I will not shout at you because I remember that you fear that and I am not my father. I will not take out my anger on my family.' He smiled thinly. 'Such as it is.'

He turned on his heel, went through into his own chamber, and Madelyn heard him speaking to someone. Then the key turned in the lock.

Jack is shutting me out of his room, she thought, dazed. *Closing the door between us.*

She felt like weeping, but her eyes were dry and tears had never done any good before. She wanted to run to him, plead with him to understand that it was her ignorance and desire to do the right thing that had caused this, not spite or some kind of ploy to take what she wanted at his expense. But Jack thought she had lied and deceived him, that he could not trust her, and that must have struck at every one of the half-healed wounds left by his upbringing and his situation.

Dinner was an ordeal. Jack behaved as though nothing was wrong between them. Madelyn wondered whether Mr Lyminge and Mr Paulson noticed anything, but Jack had always been formal and reserved in his manner towards her in their presence, so she thought not. She did her best to appear normal but it was clear that the two men were worried about what they had found, were aware that there must be a strain between husband and wife.

She rose after the dessert course, leaving a dish of almond custard and fruit untouched. 'Goodnight, gentlemen. I will not join you for tea later—I have a slight headache.'

As the footman closed the door behind her she turned and walked along to the study, waited until she heard the man close the door to the staff area behind him, then slipped out and tiptoed into the small breakfast room that adjoined the dining room. There was a connecting door and she put her ear to the panel. She could hear almost everything.

'...could see the books relating to Castle Beaupierre...have a better idea...course,' Mr Paulson was saying.

'The agreements...separate.' Jack sounded weary, as though they had chewed over this before, again and again.

'There is no reason...that anything is amiss,

other than Lansing taking Lady Dersington's instructions...vigorously.' That was Douglas Lyminge.

'Bloody fool, should have consulted.' That was clear enough. So were the grunts of agreement from the other two men.

Madelyn tiptoed away and went to her bedchamber, surprising Harper who was tidying up. 'I will undress, take down my hair and put on my robe. I have a headache.'

'Yes, my lady.' Harper, who had the tact to keep silent, moved soft-footed around the room, putting away Madelyn's clothes, finding her nightgown and wrapper and then, as she sat at the dressing table, unpinning her hair and brushing it out.

Madelyn took off her earrings and her bracelet, caught the necklace as Harper unfastened it and sat with the glittering gems in her cupped hands. She had worn the diamonds that evening, some instinct making her choose the most modern, least controversial of her jewellery as though that might somehow please Jack.

I could sell these, she thought.

They were a bequest from her mother, not something that her father had bought. She sat up straighter, seized with an idea. Surely she must own other things of value that were not covered by the trust. Certainly there were odds and ends of jewellery, some silver that had come from her mother's family that her father had locked away because it was eighteenth century in date and he disliked the Baroque style.

What else had been squirreled away in the attic and store rooms deemed unworthy of her father's vision for the castle?

The diamonds pooled on the dressing table and Madelyn almost rose to run downstairs and tell Jack that they had a source of ready money. Then she sank back. He would not react well, she realised. It would hurt his pride to think she had been scratching around trying to find things to sell. It would need some thought about how to manage it in a way he would accept.

'Lock these away, please, Harper, and then I will not need you again this evening.'

Depressed again, Madelyn paced restlessly about the room. Perhaps Jack would forgive her. He was a civilised man, a gentleman. He would not hold a grudge, she thought. Possibly he would not even mention it to her again, but simply withdraw into himself and deal with all the business of the estate without talking to her about it.

That was the kind of marriage she had been expecting, but now, now that she knew that she loved him, suspected that he had been growing to love her, it felt like a tragedy. Eventually, she climbed into bed, blew out the candle and tried to sleep.

She must have dropped off eventually. Madelyn lay in the dark, eyes open, and wondered what had woken her. She felt puzzled, she realised, as though she had been dreaming about some complexity, some riddle. Wide awake now, she sat up against the pillows and tried to recall. Mr Lansing…that had been it. Mr Lansing in her dream had been in his room surrounded by teetering piles of ledgers, his hair stuck full of quills.

'It is very complex, you understand…very complex…'

But it wasn't. Or it should not have been. Madelyn reached for the striker and lit the candle. Lansing was hiding something. He had been uneasy, shifty almost. There was something wrong—and he had held on to the books, not sent them to Paulson and Mr Lyminge because he had said they related only to the lands and property in trust.

She swung her feet out of bed and reached for her wrapper. She would go and wake Jack, tell him that in the morning they must go down to Kent and confront Lansing. The bare boards were cold on her warm feet and the shock jerked her fully awake. What if Jack thought this was an excuse, that she was trying to blame Lansing for her own decision to cheat him?

Lansing must be confronted, made to give up the books, but he would hide behind the trust— she knew that. He'd argue that Jack had no right of audit and by the time they had fought that to a standstill he would probably have been able to cover his tracks. But he could not refuse her and he knew she would not have the knowledge to discover what was wrong.

But she did know an expert and one who would help her.

'Rooting out the discrepancies in the books, dealing with incompetence and corruption. Fascinating...' Richard's voice at the masquerade, telling her about his new life.

Her desk was in the corner of her chamber and

she wrote swiftly, outlining the problem, but not telling Richard of Jack's anger and accusations, only that she needed to gain access to the books before Lansing could change anything.

If you can help me, do not come to the house openly. Send me a note on your arrival at the Dersington Arms.

She could only hope Richard did not refuse on the very reasonable grounds that her husband could provide transport and an accountant, even if he could not demand to see the books himself.

With the letter addressed she went back to bed and lay awake, wondering if Jack was ever going to forgive her for her actions, even if she gave him proof that they had been meant for the best.

Madelyn looked drained and he knew that he probably appeared just as bad. Jack managed not to look at his reflection in the glass. He had tossed and turned for most of the night, listening for sounds from the bedchamber next door, but there was nothing. No loud sobs, at least. He felt enough of a brute without that on his conscience.

At about three in the morning, when he had

been jerked fully awake by the sound of her moving about, he wondered if he should simply accept what she had said, make the effort to believe her, to trust blindly. Would he be a fool, a man blinded by feelings he was half-afraid to acknowledge and gulled by his wife?

At five, standing at the window and watching the morning sun bring the neglected grounds to life, he admitted to himself that he had fallen in love with Madelyn. And she either hated him now for his lack of trust and anger or she was smiling behind a mask of indignation at his discomfiture. But he had to learn to trust somehow and if it was not with the woman he loved, then with whom?

Now he watched his wife over the breakfast table as she made polite, stilted, conversation with Lyminge, who looked acutely uncomfortable at being in the middle of domestic tension and was probably itching to escape back to the company of Paulson, who was apparently taking his breakfast in his room.

Madelyn finished reducing a bread roll to crumbs, pushed away her coffee cup and stood up.

Jack reached the door before her. 'I would like

to speak with you. We will not be disturbed in the study.'

'Very well, my lord,' she said, her voice colourless.

She stood in front of the desk as though expecting him to take his seat on the other side and deliver a lecture and looked up, colour flooding her face, when he took her hand and turned her to face him.

'I should not have lost my temper with you yesterday. I apologise. I accept that you had no idea what effect paying off the debts and loans would have.'

He had expected her to smile, to look relieved, happy even. Instead, she bit her lip, then said, 'On what grounds have you come to believe that?'

'On no grounds. I have none. But it seems to me that I should be able to take my wife's word on any matter.'

'I see.' She nodded slowly, then raised her head to look into his eyes, her own darker than he had ever seen them. 'It is a matter of principle, then?'

'Yes.' Jack smiled, although it was difficult under that steady gaze. This was not what he expected and he did not understand.

'That is very trusting of you.'

'I thought I should make the effort.' That had not come out quite as he meant it. 'We are married now.'

'And there is no going back,' she said carefully, as though each word was eggshell thin and might break. 'So we must make the best of it.'

'Exactly. I do not expect this is the last…misunderstanding we will have.'

Madelyn sighed. 'No, I am quite sure it is not. Is that all?'

She'd caught him off balance, trying to decide whether it would be wise to kiss her now and tell her he loved her. With that cool question it was clear that a kiss would not be wise, let alone a declaration. There had been no hope he could detect that perhaps he *would* kiss her, not the faintest glimmer of that joy he had seen in her face only yesterday.

Had he been wrong and she felt nothing for him, had intended to cheat him and was even now despising him for apologising weakly for assuming the worst? Or had he hurt her so badly that he had crushed that spark and would never be able to fan it back into life again?

'Yes,' he said. 'Yes, that is all.'

He sat down at the desk after she had gone and stared blankly at the portrait of his grandfather that he had found banished to the attic and had rehung so he was working under that honest, kindly gaze. The old Earl had loved his son, refused to see what manner of man he was, even as the evidence piled up before him. Was he as blindly trusting as his grandfather had been?

Jack made himself relax, let his mind wander, collecting random memories as they floated past. Madelyn, pale with nerves, yet determined to make her proposal. Madelyn in her garden surrounded by fragrance and an exquisite world she had created with care and love. Madelyn, trembling as she came apart in his arms and then the look in those clear eyes as she came back to herself and saw him watching her.

He would trust her. He would put faith and love before cold reason and caution and, if it broke his heart, then he would have to live with the pain.

Madelyn had the grace of courage, Jack thought, watching her at dinner that night. She did not sulk, she did not show him a sullen or resentful face, nor give any hint of triumph that he had apologised. If the smile she wore did not reach her eyes and if she was focusing all her attention on Lyminge and Paulson, then he was certain he was the only one who noticed.

She was working on her embroidery when they joined her in the drawing room and she presided over the tea tray and kept a conversation going in a way that made him realise how hard she had studied with Louisa Fairfield. He had never complimented her on that, he realised. In fact, had he done anything to make her feel warmly towards him other than pleasure her in bed? he wondered.

He gave her half an hour after she retired before he followed her upstairs and listened after he dismissed Tanfield and sat in his robe, paring his nails. Madelyn was talking to Harper—he could hear the low murmur of voices through the connecting door, then the sound of the door onto the landing closing. Bed had been the one place where they had always been in harmony—he would see if that would work its magic again.

Madelyn was sitting at her dressing table when he unlocked the connecting door. She looked up, her thoughtful expression becoming blank.

'I am sorry,' she said. 'Tonight is not… Not a good time in the month.'

It took him a moment to realise what she meant. 'Of course,' Jack said meaninglessly. 'Goodnight.'

'Goodnight,' Madelyn said as he closed the door again. This time he did not lock it.

'Anything of any interest in the post?' Jack asked the table at large over breakfast the next morning.

Correspondence was beginning to come in quantity for his two employees as they sent for reports from the home farms and stewards at the various estates and wrestled with leases and other legal documents.

'The usual things,' Lyminge said, flicking over his pile, and Paulson nodded agreement.

There were two letters beside Madelyn's place. Jack had told himself from the beginning that he was not the kind of husband who insisted on reading his wife's correspondence and he was not going to begin now, but as though in answer to an unspoken request she slit both seals.

She glanced at one. 'An old friend who missed the wedding.' Then she opened the other and peered at the closely crossed lines. 'Lady Fairfield. She has bought a… Oh, a pug. And is calling it Albert. It has bitten one footman and the butcher's delivery boy, but she says it is adorable. I find that hard to believe.'

Jack's correspondence appeared to consist entirely of bills. 'It is a matter of discipline,' he said. 'She needs to train the creature to be civilised in the house.'

Madelyn glanced down to her side, her lips tight, and Jack guessed that Mist was pressed close against her leg. She must have thought he was annoyed because the little dog had come with her into the breakfast room.

'As Mist is,' he added and was rewarded by a faint smile.

'Will you be going out today?' Madelyn asked and Jack realised it was probably the first topic of conversation that she had initiated since they had made love on the lake shore. 'You said something yesterday about the woods to the north.'

'Yes. I shall probably be out well past luncheon. I will ask Cook to pack me some bread and cold meat. It may be possible to fell several acres for timber, so I am meeting the owner of a sawmill to discuss the suitability of the trees.'

'Felling large areas of woodland? That would be quite drastic, would it not?'

'Drastic and necessary now,' Jack said, then wished he had said something more tactful like *prudent* or *they need thinning.* Unless Madelyn was a superb actress that look of dismay was surely genuine. He would try to talk to her again tonight, see if they could begin to find that short-lived trust and happiness again.

'How do you intend to spend the day?'

'I thought I would take the pony and trap into the village, look at the church, see what shops there are.'

The little two-wheeled trap was the only carriage they owned and now probably would be for some time. 'Will you take a groom?'

'There is hardly room and I am very used to driving one horse. That fat little pony will not be a problem. I hope you have a profitable day.' She gathered together her post, got up with a nod to the other two men and went out, leaving Jack feeling uneasy for some reason he could not quite put his finger on.

Chapter Twenty-One

Jack returned at four o'clock to a quiet house. He had thought long and hard about the past few days, had kicked himself mentally from every direction for not having told Madelyn straight out that he loved her and rehearsed just how he was going to set things right. All he had to do now was find his wife and keep his head.

He discovered Paulson with his head down in the account books and Lyminge checking leases against vast estate maps unrolled on the library table. Neither had seen Madelyn since breakfast, they explained when he looked in on them. They had eaten at their work, interrupted only by an occasional stroll up and down the weed-grown terrace outside to stretch their legs.

Jack rang for Wystan, expecting to hear that Madelyn was resting in her room or perhaps exploring the garden, notebook in hand, but the

butler shook his head. 'No, my lord. Her Ladyship has not returned from the village.'

'What time did she go out?'

'Just after you left, my lord. Certainly before
ten. She drove herself.'

Madelyn had said she was going to explore
the village but even allowing for a lengthy
period of prayer or reflection in the church, that
could not have kept her away for more than two
hours.

'Did she say anything about going into the
town?' The nearest was Castle Hedingham, but
it was hardly more than a large village itself.
Surely she would not have driven as far as Hal-
stead by herself?

She would probably come up the drive at any
moment, coolly dismissive of his worries, Jack
thought, trying to reassure himself.

'I fear Lady Dersington may have suffered
an accident to the trap or the pony has gone
lame,' he said. 'I will ride into the village and
see if I can find her.' A simple mishap was the
most likely cause of a delay, the roads, although
not busy, had plenty of traffic and respectable
local people to help someone with a lame horse

or a broken shaft. There was nothing to worry about—nothing except the deep-down fear that Madelyn had left him.

The village boasted one disreputable ale house and one decent inn. They faced each other across the green, with the church halfway between them and the Squire's brick Queen Anne house opposite that, with the vicarage beside it. Jack rode into the Dersington Arms to enquire if they had seen his wife and found the fat grey pony tied to a ring in the stable yard lipping at a pile of hay and the trap resting on its shafts in a corner.

A stable lad came running as Jack rode into the yard. 'Take your horse, sir?'

'The lady who came in the trap there. Is she inside?'

'No, sir. She went off in the carriage with the gent. She left a letter, sir. Gave me a crown to take it up to the big house with the pony and trap, but not until six o'clock, she said.'

'Give me the letter now,' Jack said, hearing his own voice coming from a long way away.

'Aye, sir.' The lad ran for the back door of the inn and Jack sat quite still, feeling the cold, sick feeling in his gut build into actual pain. He should have listened to his instincts—Madelyn had left him. But with whom? Altair fidgeted, aware of his rider's emotions, and Jack stilled him with a curt word.

'Here you are, sir.' The boy handed up the letter and waited while Jack broke the seal.

I never meant to do harm, only the right thing. You say you are sorry for doubting me, but I know you only believe you should say that because now you are burdened with me.

I can think of only one thing to do to try to make this right.
Madelyn

'Do you know who the man was?' he asked abruptly, making the boy jump and Altair snort.

'He was a stranger, sir, but he stayed last night. I can go and look in the book, sir.'

He was off and running before Jack could agree and he came back with a piece of paper in his grubby hand. 'Guv'nor wrote it down, sir.'

Richard Turner Esq
Long Meadow Grange

Maidstone
Kent

3 Adelphi Apartments
East India House
Leadenhall Street
London

That was the masked highwayman at the masquerade, the *old friend who did not come to the wedding* of that morning's post. Madelyn was running off with him—why? So that Jack had grounds for a divorce?

The cold in his gut was turning into hot anger with himself now.

I never meant to do harm...

His instinct to believe her had been right, but he had been too clumsy in telling her, reassuring her. He was not normally tactless or maladroit, but it seemed that love had tied his tongue into knots and turned his brain to porridge.

'When did they leave?'

That provoked much head-scratching and thought. 'Must have been just after eleven, sir, 'cos Vicar came in to see Jem Slater, the ostler, who's in bed powerful sick and he came hurrying down when the clock struck, saying he'd be late for seeing someone about a christening. And the lady and gent came out just after that.'

'Well done.' Jack managed to find a smile and a crown piece. 'What was the carriage and did you see which way they went?'

'Chaise and four. Lunnon road, sir.' The boy shrugged. 'Most everyone goes that way.' He caught the coin one-handed. 'Thank you kindly. Do I take the trap back?'

'You do, soon as you are able.' Jack was already heading out of the yard and he set Altair on the road back to the Mote at a canter. He needed ready money and his pistols. He was gambling on Madelyn heading back to Kent and the castle. If he was wrong he might lose her in London, but instinct told him that she wanted the high walls and the moat around her. She was wounded and she was going to where she felt safe. Was she trying to give him the appearance of grounds for a divorce, or was she with Turner as his lover? Jack told himself to have faith in her.

And if she wants nothing more to do with you? the nagging voice in the back of his mind asked.

Then I swallow my pride, tell her how much

I love her, give her a reason to come back. Try to remember all the right words I have been rehearsing all morning.

'We are not going fast enough,' Madelyn fretted when she asked Richard for the time yet again and he replied patiently that it was seven o'clock.

'If we order more speed, firstly the postilions will assume we are eloping, and secondly, now it is dark, we could have an accident,' Richard said with an aggravating calm that made her want to scream. The fact that he was perfectly correct was no consolation at all. 'We will be in London in another hour and a half, I would estimate.'

How long would it take for Jack to realise that she had gone? He would be out all day. She had told Harper that she expected to take luncheon at the inn so the staff would not be anxious and she had tossed a small portmanteau with a few changes of linen, toiletries and her hairbrush out of the window, so there was no reason anyone would suspect that she had gone anywhere except the local villages. With good fortune it would not occur to the staff to wonder where she was until late afternoon and then the assumption would be that the trap had a broken wheel or the pony had gone lame.

'It might be morning before Jack sets out after me,' she said out loud, for comfort.

'Even if not, we are hours ahead,' Richard said. 'But I would wager he knows where you are going and will drive straight to Castle Beaupierre. He could be there by late tomorrow, perhaps earlier. What will you do if we have not got to the bottom of this by then?'

'Raise the drawbridge,' Madelyn said grimly. 'It cost enough to repair the mechanism, it might as well be used at least once for the purpose for which it was originally intended.'

It was a journey of over ninety miles and took them twelve hours with regular changes and fleeting stops for refreshment. At just past nine in the morning the chaise clattered over the drawbridge and into Castle Beaupierre and a puzzled groom and stable boys ran out to meet them.

'Mistress! My lady, I should say. We were not expecting you—welcome home.' Roger, the head groom, was beaming at her.

'It is good to be here. See the postilions have refreshment, Roger. I will send Carlton down to pay them. Is Mr Lansing in the castle?'

'Yes, my lady.'

'Close the gates, if you please. No one is to leave except these men with the chaise when they are ready. Once they have gone, raise the drawbridge and secure the mechanism. No one is to enter or leave without my permission.'

'Yes, my lady. A siege, is it?' Judging by his grin the idea appealed.

'Merely testing out the security,' Madelyn said, trying to look relaxed and amused as Carlton, the butler, hurried down the steps from the main doors. He looked as though she had interrupted him at his breakfast, judging by the way he was tugging his coat straight.

'My lady, welcome home.'

'Thank you, Carlton. This is Mr Turner, my financial adviser. We have just dropped by to bring Mr Lansing up to date with various matters. Please will you pay off the postilions. Once they have gone I have ordered the drawbridge raised. No one is to enter or leave.'

Carlton took that with rather more sangfroid

than Roger. 'Certainly, my lady. Shall I serve breakfast, my lady?'

'In a little while. I will ring. Mr Lansing is in the archives room, I assume?'

'Yes, my lady. I will alert the kitchen. Will Mr Turner be staying?' he asked as he followed them up the stairs. 'The Tapestry bedchamber has been recently aired.'

'That will do admirably, thank you, Carlton. I have no idea of how long we will be here.'

'Let us hope the food supplies will last the siege,' Richard said, following Madelyn across the Great Hall.

She nodded, too tense to find that amusing.

Lansing was at work as usual, surrounded by his ledgers, an abacus at his side. He looked up, startled, when Madelyn entered, then frowned at the sight of her companion as he got to his feet. 'My lady?'

'Good morning. This is Mr Turner, my auditor.' She saw no reason to soothe the flustered accountant.

'But…'

'I believe I am entitled to have access to my own financial records, am I not? Have you had breakfast, Mr Lansing?'

'Yes, my lady, but...'

'Come downstairs with me and have a cup of coffee while Mr Turner and I eat. I am sure you'll need the extra sustenance for explaining everything to him.' She waved him out in front of her, locked the door behind them and handed the key to Richard.

Lansing had gone quite pale.

It seems I was correct. There is something amiss here.

It was a long day. Richard spent the morning with Lansing, then turned the accountant out of the room and worked alone, taking his luncheon on a tray.

Carlton reported that Lansing had been considerably agitated when he found he could not leave the castle. 'I offered him the Red Suite, my lady, I thought he would be better there. Unfortunately, once he was inside the door locked itself. I find I have misplaced the key, but I am sure I will locate it by dinnertime.'

Richard sent a note mid-afternoon. 'What do you know about the estate at Abberley?'

Madelyn frowned at the note. 'Tell Mr Turner

that there is no such estate.' She went back to pacing the battlements, the pennants flapping and cracking above her. She was watching the road for a carriage, wondering whether Jack would hire a chaise or drive himself in a curricle. Or would he come at all?

Then, just as the sun was beginning to dip low over the hills and she was thinking of going for a wrap against the cool breeze, a rider on a black horse breasted the crest and reined in, looking towards the castle.

'Jack.' She would know him anywhere, even at this distance, even though the horse was not Altair. He had come, but there was no word yet from Richard that he had solved the puzzle. She knew she needed to be able to offer her husband facts, an explanation, not wild suspicions, or he was quite likely to dismiss this as simply an excuse to run away from his anger.

'I love you,' she murmured. 'Please forgive me for this.'

As he had months ago when she had first watched from this eyrie, Jack rode down the slope at a walk and reined in a few yards back from the edge of the moat, waiting. That first time she had raised the drawbridge to emphasise who she was, to see his reaction to provocation. Now she chewed at a fingernail as she watched him, relaxed in the saddle, apparently patient.

Then he looked up, as though he could feel her looking down at him. He took off his hat and leaned back, the breeze ruffling his dark hair.

Should she call down? But there was nothing to say yet. Madelyn lifted one hand, then made herself turn and walk away. She would go to the archives room and see how Richard was progressing, because it was breaking her heart to stand there, the deep, cold moat between them.

Diabolo, the stallion that his friend Sir James Clarke who lived just outside Rochester had lent him, fidgeted, apparently determined to live up to his name. He had given Jack a tough ride, but a fast one, and the big horse still had plenty of energy to work off.

'I do not suppose you can fly, you awkward creature.' Jack turned the horse to the left and began to circle the castle. He was feeling grim, but with as tricky a mount as this he could not afford to let his emotions show. That little wave—was it dismissal, farewell—apology? Why would she not let him in?

He could not believe Madelyn had fled with her lover—even at that distance he could tell she was unhappy. *I know her so well now...and yet not at all.* But he was not prepared to wait however long it took for her to lower that drawbridge. The castle surely had some weak point. Aylmer might have been obsessed with accuracy, but he could hardly have been expecting to be besieged. A moat and high walls would be enough to deter any normal housebreaker, but not, he thought, a man in pursuit of his lost love.

On the second circuit he thought he saw it, his way in, but he would wait until after dark to try it. Whistling softly under his breath, he dug his heels into Diabolo and sent the stallion off towards the woods at a gallop.

From the archives room's window, high in a tower, Madelyn saw him go and sighed.

'You really care about him, don't you?' Richard put down his pen and pushed aside a pile of notes.

'I love him,' she said bleakly.

'Does he know?'

'I told him. He did not believe me. I had thought perhaps he was becoming fond of me. He even apologised for his anger, for assuming I knew what a mess I had made with the money by telling Lansing to pay off everything. But it was clear he was making himself do that because, somehow, we have to keep living together. If he loved me, why did he not say so then?'

'Because he's a man,' Richard said with a grimace. 'Why didn't you persist, explain how you feel?'

'And have him think I was saying it to get into his good graces?' Madelyn sat down on the other side of the desk and prodded the stack of ledgers. 'Are you finding anything?'

'I think so. I'm having to dig back through the manorial papers for about twenty years to make doubly certain. Does Lansing assume that all women are without the capacity to understand business matters?'

'Definitely. To be fair, so did my father to some extent, so he encouraged Lansing to be exceedingly...'

'Patronising? Paternalistic?' Richard suggested.

'Yes, both of those,' she said, thinking back.

Lansing's attitude had always been to undermine her confidence in understanding the accounts and she had been too adrift in those months following her father's death to make herself tackle both Lansing and the ledgers.

'I suspect we can add opportunistic and dishonest to those. I'll have the answers in another hour, I think.' He gave her a sideways glance. 'Before your husband turns up with siege engines and scaling ladders, at least.'

'Do not joke,' she said, suddenly even more anxious. She had imagined Jack's anger if she failed to find evidence of Lansing's dubious dealings, but she had not considered how he might view Richard's involvement. 'He might call you out.'

Richard grinned, glancing up from a closely written document. 'He can call all he likes. I am not foolish enough to go up against an enraged husband who has already knocked me down once. Besides,' he added, dipping his pen in the ink to make another note, 'I can just imagine the Company's attitude if I fail to report to the office next week because I have allowed an earl to put holes in me.'

Chapter Twenty-Two

'I thought it was strange to light a fire at this time of year.' Richard stretched out a hand to the blaze on the hearth of the central fireplace in the Great Hall. 'But this place seems to drink up the heat.'

The staff had set up a smaller table in front of the fireplace, one that two people could dine at in comfort.

'Dinner should be ready in a few minutes. Surely now you can tell me what you have found.' Madelyn joined him beside the hearth, although, unless this was very good news indeed, she would need more than the blazing logs to warm her.

'Your father bought an estate called Abberley, twenty miles to the east of here towards London. It has been terribly neglected, but it appears to have good farmland and what could be a very desirable house if it is restored. Mr Aylmer appears to have purchased it as an investment by means of mortgages—it is not linked to this estate in any way. Then he took out loans to carry out the work on it.'

'And it was those I ordered to be paid off? I can sell it?'

'Yes, but—'

He had no chance to finish. Madelyn threw her arms around his neck with a gasp of delight. 'Oh, Richard!'

'Put my wife down.'

Richard dropped her and they both staggered, clutching at each other for balance.

The great double doors stood open and Jack was walking towards them, barefooted, dressed only in shirt and breeches, soaking wet with his hair slicked close to his head. He dragged the back of his hand across his eyes and flicked the water away with an impatient gesture.

'Jack? How did you get in?' It was the wrong thing to say, but his appearance had all the shock of a magic trick.

'I swam the moat at the north-eastern corner. There is an opening about six feet up. I climbed to that. It should have a grille over it.'

'It did, but it got blocked and Father had it removed while it was cleared out. Jack, that is a *drain*.'

'I noticed.'

'A small drain.' There was blood on the shoulders of his shirt, she saw now he was closer. Blood and mud all down the front of him.

'I wriggled.'

'You are hurt,' Madelyn started forward, but Richard caught her arm.

'Not until I know he is not going to be violent.'

'I would not lay a finger on Madelyn. You, on the other hand—' Jack was very close now. Close, large, menacing—and then he turned from Richard and was looking at her as though…

As though he loves me?

She hardly dare hope. 'Richard, ring for Carlton, we are going to need hot water for a bath and dressings for those scrapes. Jack, come nearer the fire or you'll catch pneumonia.'

Jack did not move, did not look at the other man. 'Turner, leave that bell. Go. Now.'

'Yes, please, Richard. It is all right.' She held her breath, it seemed, until the door closed behind him, the sound echoing around the space. 'Jack, I can explain.'

'No. No, I do not want you to explain and it would make no difference.'

She had been wrong. That had not been love in his eyes, not if he did not even want to hear her justification. 'I see.' Madelyn sat down on the nearest bench and felt the hope drain out of her as though it was blood from a severed vein.

She sensed Jack moving, but she did not raise her head when she saw his bare feet right in front of her, water pooling on the flagstones.

'Madelyn, look at me.'

I must tell him how I feel. It doesn't matter if he spurns me or thinks it is only an excuse.

'Jack, I meant it when I said I love you.'

'I love you,' he said at the same moment. Then 'Did you mean it? *Madelyn.*' He was on his knees and she was held against him, the wet soaking through her gown, the thud of his heart against her breast. 'I have been such a fool. I should have told you.'

'I should have, too, but I was afraid,' she confessed, wriggling so she could look into his face. 'I couldn't believe you could really love me for myself and I thought, if I told you how I felt, you would assume I was trying to deflect your anger over the money. And that is what you did think. I was sure that you only cared because of what I brought you in my dowry.'

'And I thought I was simply a duty for you, a potential father for your children.'

'It was good when we…when we made love,' she murmured, rubbing her warm cheek against his cold one.

'Perhaps we should have listened to what our bodies were telling us,' Jack said, his arms tightening around her. 'Why did you leave me? Were you frightened of me?'

'I realised that something was wrong, that I had been naive in trusting Lansing so entirely, even if it was only to tell me the truth about matters, and I thought he was hiding something. I knew he would not let you or your people look at the Castle Beaupierre books. But he could not refuse me.

'I needed an expert of my own, one I could trust, and I remembered Richard telling me about his work with the East India Company. He enjoys tracking down fraud and malpractice, errors and false accounting. I thought that if he could establish the facts then I could show you that my intentions had been good and *then* I could tell you that I loved you. Besides,' she added ruefully, 'I did not think you were in any mood to listen to me stumbling through half-formed hunches and wanting to involve a man you already had suspicions about.'

'You are probably right,' he admitted.

'Jack, you are shivering. Sit by the fire.'

He stood and allowed himself to be pressed down to sit on the fender, but he was tense now under her hands. 'Tell me what was going on when I came in.'

'Richard had found something out. I am not certain what, exactly, because you came in as he was explaining, but enough to prove that Lansing was doing something illegal and that there is money after all.' Madelyn stood up, still only half-believing that this was real, that Jack loved and trusted her. 'I am going to ring for a hot bath for you. Between my father's old wardrobe and what Richard brought with him, we ought to be able to find you dry clothes.'

She tugged the bell pull and the doors opened so quickly that she suspected Carlton had been poised ready.

'Hot water is being taken up to your rooms, my lady. Cook has put dinner back.'

It was hard to let go of him. 'I will come up,

too, my gown is soaked through. And besides, those scrapes must be cleaned and dressed.'

'Very wifely,' Jack murmured as he took her hand.

There was amusement there and deep affection as well as a low vibration of something physical and exciting that resonated down to her toes by way of parts of her that responded eagerly.

Two of the maids were setting out towels and Madelyn sent one of them for salves and bandages, then firmly closed the door on the pair of them.

Jack was prowling around the large tub. 'That is enormous. What is it? A tun cut down?' Water was steaming from the surface and white sheets hung over the edges to protect the bather.

'Yes, cut just below the mid-point to make it easier to get in. There is a stool here and another inside.'

Jack shrugged out of his shirt, wincing as it slid over his abraded shoulders, peeled off the sodden breeches, then climbed into the tub, hissing as the hot water sluiced over his chilled body.

Madelyn picked up another stool, leaned in

and dropped it in beside him before she stripped off her gown and joined him. 'You see, the Middle Ages have some benefits.' She took a sponge. 'Turn around so I can clean your back.'

This was Jack, literally stripped to his essence under her hands, his head bent, exposing the vulnerable nape of his neck. She steadied herself with one hand on his upper right arm, felt the muscle flex as though in welcome to her touch and closed her fingers more tightly.

I am here. I am yours.

The scrapes were nasty, but his shirt had given some protection and only one deeper gouge marked where a piece of metal or rough rock had caught him. She tried to imagine crawling through that tight, stinking tunnel, not knowing if there was a way out at the other end or whether it would be necessary to fight his way back, perhaps trapped like a fish in a net.

When there was no more mud or grit left she rested her forehead against the bump of vertebrae at the base of his neck and wrapped her arms around his body. 'I do love you.'

'Even after I made such a mess of apologising to you for my reaction?' he asked. 'I was trying to tell you that I would trust you whatever the evidence said, but I am not used to apologising or to expressing emotion. Not emotions as important as that.'

'I thought you were simply making the best of things because you had married me and were tied to me. I feared that if I told you that I loved you then you would assume I was trying to deflect your anger.' Against her cheek his skin was smooth, warm now. Madelyn licked a long, slow stroke of her tongue over it, savouring the taste of him and her own happiness.

Jack sat up straight, twisted on the stool and caught her against him. 'I approve of this bath. We will have them in all our homes so I can do this… And this and…'

Movement in the tub, even such a large one, was slow and deliberate and Jack did not seem to be in the mood to be rushed. He kissed and caressed and lifted her and Madelyn settled with a sigh, the length of him sliding home with a delicious deliberation.

'Careful,' he murmured as she gasped and clung to him. 'Gently or there will be tidal waves.'

'I don't care,' Madelyn managed to say before he took her mouth and urged her up to sink and rise, clasped around him, holding her still as she rose so he could lavish kisses on her breasts, keeping her tight as she sank down on him.

'I love you, my lady of the castle,' Jack said against her neck. 'Show me what you want, how you feel.'

'The water is becoming cold,' Madelyn said after what might have been an hour or perhaps just ten tumultuous minutes. 'And the floor is a small lake.'

Jack chuckled and lifted her out of the tub on to the footstool. 'Wade to high ground, my love.'

They dried themselves and each other, breaking off to smile and to touch as though each was a newly discovered treasure, Madelyn thought.

When they made their way downstairs at last they found Richard reading in a chair before the fire, a carafe of wine at his elbow.

'Is dinner quite ruined? I am so sorry,' Madelyn said, trying not to blush.

'Your admirable cook sent up a few minutes ago to say that all is under control and dinner will be served as soon as you ring. The soup course, apparently, will allow time for everything else to be presented in good order.'

Madelyn rang and they took their places at the table. 'Finish the story of what Mr Lansing has been doing,' she said. 'Then we can forget about him.'

'Madelyn's father bought an estate called Abberley, an expensive purchase intended for restoration and a profitable resale,' Richard told Jack. 'When he died I suppose Lansing was going to hand over the papers along with the Dersington estate documents, but then Madelyn told him to pay off all the debts and loans. He must have suddenly realised that, with Aylmer dead, no one else knew anything about that land. Instead of explaining to her about the plans for Abberley he cleared everything on that property using all the liquid assets and kept quiet, protected from your agents' scrutiny by the trust on the Beaupierre lands. He was in the process of creating a duplicate set of ledgers for the period with no references to Abberley at all— and that property had its deeds altered to make him the owner. Between the two separate estates he must have thought that no one would realise where the money had been used.'

'And I suppose he had made the purchase as Aylmer's agent so his name was on many of the records of sale and very little forgery was needed,' Jack said. 'Madelyn, we will have to involve your trustees in this now. There will be a full audit—goodness knows how much he has defrauded the estate out of over the years.'

They waited while the soup was served and the footmen had left them alone again.

'We will have to send for the magistrate in the morning,' she said with a sigh. 'What a horrible mess. It will cause talk, but we cannot let him loose to prey on someone else. But the Abberley estate is mine to do with as I wish and we can raise a new mortgage on it, restore it and sell it on, just as my father intended.'

'Unless Mr Aylmer was very much mistaken you will get a very good return, enough to restore your finances to a healthy state.'

The soup was followed by a fricassee of chicken with peas and a raised pie and the three of them, by unspoken consent, turned the conversation from finance to Richard's tales of India.

When the footmen brought in fruit and dishes of almond custard he excused himself. 'I am for my bed—my head is spinning with figures. I'll make sure Mr Lansing is secure and has been fed—you'll not want to be troubled with him tonight.'

'I like Turner,' Jack said when they were alone. 'But I am glad you did not marry him.'

'So am I. Whatever it was between us is no longer there. I felt it at the masquerade. Liking, yes. Love, no. That faded away over time.'

'Ours will not,' Jack said. He stood up, took a tray from the sideboard and loaded it with grapes and two glasses of sweet wine. 'Shall we have our dessert in your garden under the stars? It should be warm enough in the shelter of the walls.'

The enclosed space had caught and held the heat of the day and the night-scented tobacco plants and the lilies were flooding the garden with their perfume. Jack set the tray down on one of the turf seats by the fountain and glanced around, up at the unlit windows in the high walls. 'Are we overlooked?'

'No. Those two wings are unoccupied, that side has no windows and our own chambers are over the Great Hall. If they are dark, then the staff must have tidied them and left. Why?'

'I have a strong desire to see you naked in the starlight and to make love to you on this seat here.'

'The one you fell asleep on that first day we met? The day I summoned my knight in shining armour and he came to rescue me from my imprisonment?' The gown was easy to unfasten and it slipped from her shoulders, caught at the tight wrists then fell to the ground, a dark pool on the pale stone of the path around the fountain. Under it she was quite naked.

'The day you stole my heart and enchanted me, although I did not realise it then.' Jack dragged his shirt over his head and tossed it onto a lavender bush. 'I was too blinded by pride and anger to see the treasure I had been offered.' He held her gaze as he stripped, an antique statue in the garden, a creature of shadows and strong, beautiful lines.

'All the bad things that happened—my father's refusal to let me marry Richard, his obsession with this castle above his feelings for family, your father's behaviour and the loss of your lands—all of them have come together to give us this, our happiness.'

'I was not a believer in destiny before, my

love, my wise lady of the white towers, but you have made me one.'

Madelyn laid down on the cool turf and held out her arms to him, her lover, her husband, and he came down over her, sheltering her with his body and bent to take her lips.

A while later he raised himself on one elbow and looked up as an owl hooted, drifting above them, then down to see a dark moth settle on the white-blonde spill of Madelyn's hair.

'I did not believe in magic either, but you have spun it here. I was afraid of love, afraid of its power to wound, but you have given me the courage to love.'

'We have both found that,' she whispered, pulling him down to lie against her breast once more. 'It was our destiny.'

* * * * *

LET'S TALK

Romance

For exclusive extracts, competitions
and special offers, find us online:

f facebook.com/millsandboon

⊙ @millsandboonuk

🐦 @millsandboon

Or get in touch on 0844 844 1351*

For all the latest titles coming soon,
visit millsandboon.co.uk/nextmonth

*Calls cost 7p per minute plus your phone company's price per
minute access charge